ATHABASCA

Alistair MacLean

BOOK CLUB ASSOCIATES LONDON

This edition published 1981 by
Book Club Associates
By arrangement with Wm. Collins Sons & Co Ltd

First published 1980

Printed in Great Britain by
Richard Clay (The Chaucer Press) Ltd
Bungay, Suffolk

ATHABASCA

To Sabrina and Tony

PROLOGUE

This book is not primarily *about* oil, but is based on oil and the means whereby oil is recovered from the earth, so it may be of some interest and help to look briefly at these phenomena.

What oil is, and how it is formed in the first place, no one quite seems to know. The technical books and treatises on this subject are legion—I am aware that, personally, I haven't seen a fraction of them—and they are largely, so I am assured, in close agreement—except when they come to what one would have thought was a point of considerable interest: how, precisely, does oil *become* oil? There appear to be as many divergent theories about this as there are about the origins of life. Confronted with complexities, the well-advised layman takes refuge in over-simplification—which is what I now do, as I can do no other.

Only two elements were needed for the formation of oil—rock, and the incredibly abundant plants and primitive living organisms that teemed in rivers, lakes and seas as far back as perhaps a billion years ago. Hence the term fossil fuels.

The Biblical references to the rock of ages gives rise to misconceptions about the nature and permanency of rock. Rock —the material of which the earth's crust is made—is neither eternal nor indestructible. Nor is it even unchanging. On the contrary, it is in a state of constant change, movement and flux, and it is salutary to remind ourselves that there was a time when no rock existed. Even today there is a singular lack of agreement among geologists, geo-physicists and astronomers as to how the earth came into being; but there is a measure of agreement that there was a primary incandescent and gaseous state, followed by a molten state, neither of which was conducive to the formation of anything, rock included. It is erroneous to suppose that rock has been, is and ever shall be.

7

Yet we are not concerned here with the ultimate origins of rock, but rock as we have it today. It is, admittedly, difficult to observe this process of flux, because a minor change may take ten million years, a major change a hundred million.

Rock is constantly being destroyed and rebuilt. In the destructive process weather is the main factor; in the rebuilding, the force of gravity.

Five main weather elements act upon rock. Frost and ice fracture rock. It can be gradually eroded by airborne dust. The action of the seas, whether through the constant movement of waves and tides or the pounding of heavy storm waves, remorselessly wears away the coastlines. Rivers are immensely powerful destructive agencies—one has but to look at the Grand Canyon to appreciate their enormous power; such rocks as escape all these influences are worn away over the aeons by the effect of rain.

Whatever the cause of erosion, the end result is the same: the rock is reduced to its tiniest possible constituents—rock particles or, simply, dust. Rain and melting snow carry this dust down to the tiniest rivulets and the mightiest rivers, which in turn transport it to lakes, inland seas and the coastal regions of the oceans. Dust, however fine and powdery, is still heavier than water, and whenever the water becomes sufficiently still, it will gradually sink to the bottom, not only in lakes and seas but also in the sluggish lower reaches of rivers and, where flood conditions exist, inland in the form of silt.

And so, over unimaginably long reaches of time, whole mountain ranges are carried down to the seas and in the process, through the effects of gravity, new rock is born as layer after layer of dust accumulates on the bottom, building up to a depth of ten, a hundred, perhaps even a thousand feet, the lowermost layers being gradually compacted by the immense and steadily increasing pressures from above, until the particles fuse together and re-form as new rock.

It is in the intermediate and final processes of this new rock formation that oil comes into being. Those lakes and seas of hundreds of millions of years ago were almost choked by water plants and the most primitive forms of aquatic life. On dying, they sank to the bottom of lakes and seas along with the settling

8

dust particles and were gradually buried deep under the endless layers of more dust and more aquatic and plant life that slowly accumulated above them. The passing of millions of years and the steadily increasing pressures from above gradually changed the decayed vegetation and dead aquatic life into oil.

Described thus simply and quickly, the process sounds reasonable enough. But this is where the grey and disputatious area arises. The conditions necessary for the formation of oil are known: the cause of the metamorphosis is not. It seems probable that some form of chemical catalyst is involved, but this catalyst has not been isolated. The first purely synthetic oil, as distinct from secondary synthetic oils such as those derived from coal, has yet to be produced. We just have to accept that oil is oil, that it is there, bound up in rock strata in fairly well-defined areas throughout the world but always on the sites of ancient seas and lakes, some of which are now continental land, some buried deep under the encroachment of new oceans.

Had the oil remained intermingled with those deeply-buried rock strata, and were the earth a stable place, that oil would have been irrecoverable. But our planet is a highly unstable place. There is no such thing as a stable continent securely anchored to the core of the earth. The continents rest on the so-called tectonic plates which, in turn, float on the molten magma below, with neither anchor nor rudder, free to wander in whichever haphazard fashion they will. This they unquestionably do: they are much given to banging into each other, grinding alongside each other, over-riding or dipping under each other in a wholly unpredictable fashion and, in general, resembling rocks in the demonstration of their fundamental instability. As this banging and clashing takes place over periods of tens or hundreds of millions of years, it is not readily apparent to us except in the form of earthquakes, which generally occur where two tectonic plates are in contention.

The collision of two such plates engenders incredible pressures, and two of the effects of such pressures are of particular concern here. In the first place the huge compressive forces involved tend to squeeze the oil from the rock strata in which it is embedded and to disperse it in whichever direction the

9

pressure permits—up, down or sideways. Secondly, a collision buckles or folds the rock strata themselves, the upper strata being forced upwards to form mountain ranges—the northern movement of the Indian tectonic plate created the Himalayas —and the lower strata buckling to create what are virtually subterranean mountains, folding the layered strata into massive domes and arches.

It is at this point, insofar as oil recovery is concerned, that the nature of the rocks themselves becomes of importance. The rock can be porous or non-porous, the porous rock—such as gypsum—permitting liquids, such as oil, to pass through them, while the non-porous—such as granite—does not. In the case of porous rock the oil, influenced by those compressive forces, will seep upwards through the rock until the distributive pressure eases, when it will come to rest at or very close to the surface of the earth. In the case of non-porous rock, the oil will become trapped in a dome or arch, and in spite of the great pressures from below can escape neither sideways nor upwards but must remain where it is.

In this latter case what are regarded as conventional methods are used in the recovery of oil. Geologists locate a dome, and a hole is drilled. With reasonable luck they hit an oil dome and not a solid one, and their problems are over—the powerful subterranean pressures normally drive the oil to the surface.

The recovery of seepage oil which has passed upwards through porous rock presents a quite different and far more formidable problem, the answer to which was not found until as late as 1967. Even then it was only a partial answer. The trouble, of course, is that this surface seepage oil does not collect in pools, but is inextricably intermixed with foreign matter such as sand and clay from which it has to be abstracted and refined.

It is, in fact, a solid and has to be mined as such; and although this solidified oil may go as deep as six thousand feet, only the first two hundred feet, in the limits of present-day knowledge and techniques, are accessible, and that only by surface mining. Conventional mining methods—the sinking of vertical shafts and the driving of horizontal galleries—would be hopelessly inadequate, as they would provide only the tiniest fraction of the raw material required to make the extraction process commerciably viable. The latest oil extraction plant, which went into operation only in the summer of 1978, requires 10,000 tons of raw material every *hour*.

Two excellent examples of the two different methods of oil recovery are to be found in the far north-west of North America. The conventional method of deep drilling is well exemplified by the Prudhoe Bay oilfield on the Arctic shore of northern Alaska; its latter-day counterpart, the surface mining of oil, is to be found—and, indeed, it is the only place in the world where it can be found—in the tar sands of Athabasca.

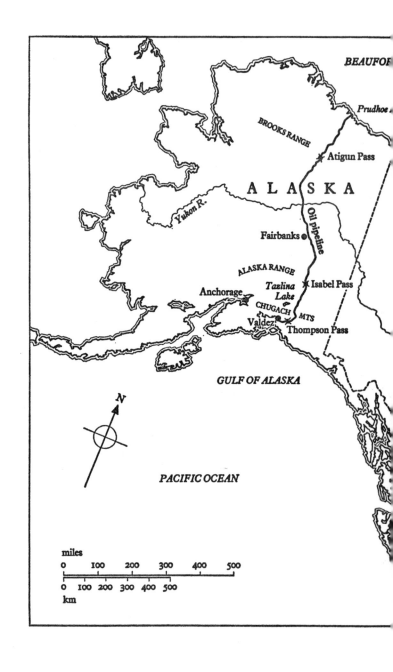

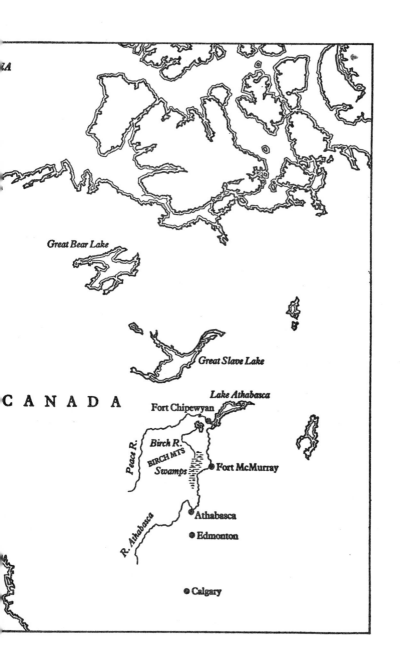

KA

Great Bear Lake

Great Slave Lake

Lake Athabasca

C A N A D A   Fort Chipewyan

Peace R.   *Birch R.*

BIRCH MTS

Swamps   ● Fort McMurray

R. Athabasca   ● Athabasca

● Edmonton

● Calgary

I

'This,' said George Dermott, 'is no place for us.' He eased his considerable bulk from the dining-table and regarded the remains of several enormous lamb chops with disfavour. 'Jim Brady expects his field operatives to be lean, fit and athletic. Are we lean, fit and athletic?'

'There are desserts,' Donald Mackenzie said. Like Dermott he was a large and comfortable man with a rugged, weather-beaten face, a little larger and a little less comfortable. Observers often took him and his partner for a pair of retired heavyweight boxers. 'I can see cakes, cookies and a wide variety of pastries,' he went on. 'You read their food brochure? Says that the average man requires at least five thousand calories a day to cope with Arctic conditions. But we, George, are not average men. Six thousand would do better in a pinch. Nearer seven would be safer, I'd say. Chocolate mousse and double cream?'

'He had a notice about it on the staff bulletin board,' Dermott said wryly. 'Heavy black border, for some reason. Signed, too.'

'Senior operatives don't look at staff boards,' Mackenzie sniffed. He heaved his 200 pounds erect and headed purposefully for the food counter. There was no doubt that B.P./Sohio did extremely well by their staff. Here at Prudhoe Bay, on the bitter rim of the Arctic Ocean in midwinter, the spacious, light and airy dining-room, with multi-coloured pastel walls back-dropping the recurrent five-pointed star motif, was maintained at a pleasantly fresh 72 degrees by the air-conditioned central heating. The temperature difference between the dining-room and the outside world was 105°F. The range of excellently-cooked food was astonishing.

'Don't exactly starve themselves up here,' he said as he returned with a mousse for each of them and a pitcher of heavy cream. 'I wonder what any of the old Alaskan sourdoughs would have made of it.'

The first reaction of a prospector or trapper of yesteryear would have been that he was suffering from hallucinations. All in all, it was hard to say what feature he would have found the most astonishing. Eighty per cent of the items on the menu would have been unknown to him. But he would have been still more amazed by the forty-foot swimming-pool and the glassed-in garden, with its pine-trees, birches, plants and profusion of flowers, that abutted on the dining-room.

'God knows what the old boy would have thought,' said Dermott. 'You might ask *him*, though.' He indicated a man heading in their direction. 'Jack London would have recognised this one right away.'

Mackenzie said: 'More the Robert Service type, I'd say.'

The newcomer certainly wasn't of current vintage. He wore heavy felt boots, moleskin trousers and an incredibly faded mackinaw, which went well enough with the equally faded patches on the sleeves. A pair of sealskin gloves was suspended from his neck, and he carried a coonskin cap in his right hand. His hair was long and white and parted in the middle. He had a slightly hooked nose and clear blue eyes with deeply entrenched crow's feet, which could have been caused by too much sun, too much snow or a too highly developed sense of humour. The rest of his face was obscured by a magnificent grizzled beard and moustache, both of which were at that moment rimed by droplets of ice. The yellow hard hat swinging from his left hand struck a jarring note. He stopped at their table, and from the momentary flash of white teeth it could be assumed that he was smiling.

'Mr Dermott? Mr Mackenzie?' He offered his hand. 'Finlayson. John Finlayson.'

Dermott said: 'Mr Finlayson. Field operations manager's office?'

'I *am* the field operations manager.' He pulled out a chair, sat, sighed and removed some ice particles from his beard. 'Yes, yes, I know. Hard to believe.' He smiled again, gestured at his clothing. 'Most people think I've been riding the rods. You know, hobo on the box-cars. God knows why. Nearest railroad track's a long, long way from Prudhoe Bay. Like Tahiti and grass skirts. You know, gone native. Too many years on the North Slope.' His oddly staccato manner of speech was indeed suggestive of a person whose contact with civilisation was, at best, intermittent. 'Sorry I couldn't make it. Meet you, I mean. Deadhorse.'

Mackenzie said: 'Deadhorse?'

'Airstrip. A little trouble at one of the gathering centres. Happens all the time. Sub-zero temperatures play hell with the molecular structure of steel. Being well taken care of, I hope?'

'No complaints.' Dermott smiled. 'Not that we require much care. There the food counter, here Mackenzie. The watering hole and the camel.' Dermott checked himself: he was beginning to talk like Finlayson. 'Well, one little complaint, perhaps. Too many items on the lunch menu, too large a helping of any item. My colleague's waist-line—'

'Your colleague's waist-line can take care of itself,' Mackenzie said comfortably. 'But I do have a complaint, Mr Finlayson.'

'I can imagine.' Another momentary flash of teeth, and Finlayson was on his feet. 'Let's hear it in my office. Just a few steps.' He walked across the dining-hall, stopped outside a door and indicated another door to the left. 'Master operations control centre. The heart of Prudhoe Bay—or the western half of it, at least. All the computerised process control facilities for the supervision of the field's operations.'

Dermott said: 'An enterprising lad with a satchelful of grenades could have himself quite a time in there.'

'Five seconds, and he could close down the entire oilfield. Come all the way from Houston just to cheer me up? This way.'

He led them through the outer door, then through an inner one to a small office. Desks, chairs and filing cabinets, all in metal, all in battleship grey. He gestured them to sit and smiled at Mackenzie. 'As the French say, a meal without wine is like a day without sunshine.'

'It's this Texas dust,' Mackenzie said. 'Sticks in the gullet like no other dust. Laughs at water.'

Finlayson made a sweeping motion with his hand. 'Some big rigs out there. Damned expensive and damned difficult to handle. It's pitch dark, say, forty below and you're tired—you're always tired up here. Don't forget we work twelve hours a day, seven days a week. A couple of Scotches on top of all that, and you've written off a million dollars' worth of equipment. Or you damage the pipeline. Or you kill yourself. Or, worst of all, you kill some of your mates. Comparatively, they had it easy in the old prohibition days—bulk smuggling from Canada, bath-tub gin, illicit stills by the thousand. Rather different on the North Slope here—get caught smuggling in a teaspoonful of liquor, and that's it. No argument, no court of appeal. Out. But there's no problem—no one is going to risk eight hundred dollars a week for ten cents' worth of bourbon.'

Mackenzie said: 'When's the next flight out to Anchorage?'

Finlayson smiled. 'All is not lost, Mr Mackenzie.' He unlocked a filing cabinet, produced a bottle of Scotch and two glasses and poured with a generous hand. 'Welcome to the North Slope, gentlemen.'

'I was having visions,' said Mackenzie, 'of travellers stranded in an Alpine blizzard and a St Bernard lolloping towards them with the usual restorative. You're not a drinking man?'

'Certainly. One week in five when I rejoin my family in Anchorage. This is strictly for visiting V.I.P.s. One would assume you qualify under that heading?' Thoughtfully, he mopped melting ice from his beard. 'Though frankly, I never heard of your organisation until a couple of days ago.'

'Think of us as desert roses,' Mackenzie said. 'Born to blush and bloom unseen. I think I've got that wrong, but the desert bit is appropriate enough. That's where we seem to spend most of our time.' He nodded towards the window. 'A desert doesn't have to be made of sand. I suppose this qualifies as an Arctic desert.'

'I think of it that way myself. But what do you do in those deserts? Your function, I mean.'

'Our function?' Dermott considered. 'Oddly enough, I'd say our function is to reduce our worthy employer, Jim Brady, to a state of bankruptcy.'

'*Jim* Brady? I thought his initial was A.'

'His mother was English. She christened him Algernon. Wouldn't *you* object? He's always known as Jim. Anyway, there are only three people in the world any good at extinguishing oil-field fires, particularly gusher fires, and all three are Texas-based. Jim Brady's one of the three.

'It used to be commonly accepted that there are just three causes of such oil fires: spontaneous combustion, which should never happen but does; the human factor, i.e. sheer careless-ness; and mechanical failure. After twenty-five years in the business Brady recognised that there was a fourth and more sinister element involved, that would come broadly speaking under the heading of industrial sabotage.'

'Who would engage in sabotage? What would the motivation be?'

'Well we can rule out the most obvious—rivalry among the big oil companies. It doesn't exist. This notion of cut-throat competition exists only in the sensational press and among the more feeble-minded of the public. To be a fly on the wall at a closed meeting of the oil lobby in Washington is to under-stand once and for all the meaning of the expression "two minds with but a single thought, two hearts that beat as one." Multi-plied by twenty, of course. Let Exxon put up the price of gas by a penny today, and Gulf, Shell, B.P., Elf, Agip and all the others will do the same tomorrow. Or even take Prudhoe Bay here. The classic example, surely, of co-operation—umpteen companies working hand-in-glove for the mutual benefit of all concerned: benefit of all the oil companies, that is. The State of Alaska and the general public might adopt a rather different and more jaundiced viewpoint.

'So we rule out business rivalries. This leaves another kind of energy. International power politics. Say Country X could seriously weaken enemy Country Y by slowing down its oil revenues. That's one obvious scenario. Then there's *internal* power politics. Suppose disaffected elements in an oil-rich dictatorship see a means of demonstrating their dissatisfaction against a régime that clasps the ill-gotten gains to its mercenary bosom or, at best, distributes some measure of the largesse to its nearest and dearest, while ensuring that the peasantry re-mains in the properly medieval state of poverty. Starvation does nicely as motivation, this kind of set-up leaves room for personal revenge, the settling of old scores, the working off of old grudges.

'And don't forget the pyromaniac who sees in oil a ludicrously easy target and the source of lovely flames. In short, there's room for practically everything, and the more bizarre and unimaginable, the more likely to happen. A case in point.'

He nodded at Mackenzie. 'Donald and I have just returned from the Gulf. The local security men and the police were baffled by an outbreak of small fires—small, so-called, but with damage totalling two million dollars. Clearly the work of an arsonist. We tracked him down, apprehended him, and punished him. We gave him a bow and arrow.'

Finlayson looked at them as if their Scotch had taken hold too quickly.

'Eleven-year-old son of the British consul. He had a powerful Webley air pistol. Webley make the traditional ammunition for this—hollow, concave lead pellets. They do *not* make pellets of hardened steel, which give off a splendid spark when they strike ferrous metal. This lad had a plentiful supply obtained from a local Arab boy who had a similar pistol and used these illegal pellets for hunting desert vermin. Incidentally, the Arab boy's old man, a prince of the blood royal, owned the oilfield in question. The English boy's arrows have rubber tips.'

'I'm sure there's a moral there somewhere.'

'Sure, there's a lesson: the unpredictable is always with you. Our industrial sabotage division—that's Jim Brady's term for it—was formed six years ago. There are fourteen of us in it. At first it was as a purely investigative agency. We went to a place after the deed had been done and the fire put out—as often as not it was Jim who put it out—and tried to find out who had done it, why, and what his *modus operandi* had been. Frankly, we had very limited success: usually the horse had gone, and all we were doing was locking the empty stable door.

'Now the emphasis has changed—we try to lock the damned door in such a fashion that no-one can open it. In other words, prevention: the maximum tightening of both mechanical and human security. The response to this service has been remarkable—we're now the most profitable side of Jim's operations.

By far. Capping off runaway wells, putting fires out, can't hold a candle, if you'll pardon the expression, to our security work. Such is the demand for our services that we could triple our division and still not cope with all the calls being made upon us.'

'Well, why don't you? Triple the business, I mean.'

'Trained personnel,' Mackenzie said. 'Just not there. More accurately, there are next to no experienced operatives and there's an almost total dearth of people qualified to be trained for the job. The combination of qualifications is difficult to come by. You have to have an investigative mind, and that in turn is based on an inborn instinct for detection—the Sherlock Holmes genes, shall we say. You've either got it or not: it can't be inculcated. You have an eye and a nose for security, an *obsession*, almost—and this can only come from field experience; you have to have a pretty detailed knowledge of the oil industry world-wide: and, above all, you have to be an oilman.'

'And you gentlemen are oilmen.' It was a statement, not a question.

'All our working lives,' Dermott said. 'We've both been field operations managers.'

'If your services are in such demand, how come we should be so lucky as to jump to the head of the queue?'

Dermott said: 'As far as we know this is the first time that any oil company has received notification of *intent* to sabotage. First real chance we've had to try out our preventive medicine. We're just slightly puzzled on one point, Mr Finlayson. You say you never heard of us until a couple of days ago. How come that we're here, then? I mean, we knew of this three days ago when we arrived back from the Mid East. We spent a day resting up, another day studying the layout and security measures of the Alaskan pipeline and—'

'You did that, eh? Isn't it classified information?'

Dermott was patient. 'We could have sent for it immediately on receiving the request for assistance. We didn't have to. The information, Mr Finlayson, is not classified. It's in the public domain. Big companies tend to be incredibly careless about such matters. Whether to reassure the public or burnish their own image by taking thorough-going precautions, they not only release large chunks of information about their activities but positively bombard the public with them. The information, of course, comes in disparate and apparently unrelated lumps: it requires only a moderately intelligent fella to piece them all together.

'Not that those big companies, such as Alyeska, who built your pipeline, have much to reproach themselves about. They don't even begin to operate in the same league of indiscretion as the all-time champs, the U.S. Government. Take the classic example of the de-classification of the secret of the atom bomb. When the Russians got the bomb, the Government thought there was no point in being secretive any more and proceeded to tell all. You want to know how to make an atom bomb? Just send a pittance to the A.E.C. in Washington and you'll have the necessary information by return mail. That this information could be used by Americans against Americans apparent never occurred to the towering intellects of Capitol Hill and the Pentagon, who seem to have been under the impression that the American criminal classes voluntarily retired *en masse* on the day of declassification.'

Finlayson raised a defensive hand. 'Hold. Enough. I accept that you haven't infiltrated Prudhoe Bay with a battalion of spies. Answer's simple. When I received this unpleasant letter —it was sent to *me*, not to our H.Q. in Anchorage—I talked to the general manager, Alaska. We both agreed that it was almost certainly a hoax. Still, I regret to say that many Alaskans aren't all that kindly disposed towards us. We also agreed that if it was *not* a hoax, it could be something very serious indeed. People like us, although we're well enough up the ladder in our own fields, don't take final decisions on the safety and future of a ten-billion-dollar investment. So we notified the grand panjandrums. Your directive came from London. Informing me of their decision must have come as an afterthought.'

'Head offices being what they are,' Dermott said. 'Got this threatening note here?'

Finlayson retrieved a single sheet of notepaper from a drawer and passed it across.

' "My dear Mr Finlayson",' Dermott read. 'Well, that's civil enough. "I have to inform you that you will be incurring a slight spillage of oil in the near future. Not much, I assure you, just sufficient to convince you that we can interrupt oil flow whenever and wherever we please. Please notify ARCO".'

Dermott shoved the letter across to Mackenzie. 'Understandably unsigned. No demands. If this is genuine, it's intended as a softening-up demonstration in preparation for the big threat and big demand that will follow. A morale-sapper, if you will, designed to scare the pants off you.'

Finlayson's gaze was on the middle distance. 'I'm not so sure he hasn't done that already.'

'You notified ARCO?'

'Yup. Oilfield's split more or less half-and-half. We run the western sector. ARCO—Atlantic Richfield, Exxon, some smaller groups—they run the eastern sector.'

'What's their reaction?'

'Like mine. Hope for the best, prepare for the worst.'

'Your security chief. What's his reaction?'

'Downright pessimistic. It's his baby, after all. If I were in his shoes I'd feel the same way. He's convinced of the genuineness of this threat.'

'Me too,' Dermott said. 'This came in an envelope? Ah, thank you.' He read the address. ' "Mr John Finlayson, B.Sc., A.M.I.M.E.". Not only punctilious, but they've done their homework on you. "B.P./Sohio, Prudhoe Bay, Alaska". Postmarked Edmonton, Alberta. That mean anything to you?'

'Nary a thing. I have neither friends nor acquaintances there, and certainly no business contacts.'

'Your security chief's reaction?'

'Same as mine. Zero.'

'What's his name?'

'Bronowski. Sam Bronowski.'

'Let's have him in, shall we?'

'You'll have to wait, I'm afraid. He's down in Fairbanks. Back tonight if the weather holds up. Depends on visibility.'

'Blizzard season?'

'We don't have one. Precipitation on the North Slope is very low, maybe six inches in a winter. High winds are the bugaboo. They blow up the surface snow so that the air can be completely opaque for thirty or forty feet above the ground. Just before Christmas a few years ago a Hercules, normally the safest of aircraft, tried to land in those conditions. Didn't make it. Two of the crew of four killed. Pilots have become a bit leery since —if a Hercules can buy it, any aircraft can. These high winds and the surface snowstorms they generate—that snow can be driving along at 70 miles an hour—are the bane of our existence up here. That's why this operations centre is built on pilings seven feet above ground—let the snow blow right underneath. Otherwise we'd end up the winter season buried under a massive drift. The pilings, of course, also virtually eliminate heat transfer to the permafrost, but that's secondary.'

'What's Bronowski doing in Fairbanks?'

'Stiffening the thin red line. Hiring extra security guards for Fairbanks.'

'How does he set about that?'

'Approach varies, I suppose. Really Bronowski's department, Mr Dermott. He has *carte blanche* in those matters. I suggest you ask him on his return.'

'Oh, come on. You're his boss. He's a subordinate. Bosses keep tabs on their subordinates. Roughly, how does he recruit?'

'Well. He's probably built up a list of people whom he's personally contacted and who might be available in a state of emergency. I'm honestly not sure about this. I may be his boss, but when I delegate responsibility I do just that. I do know that he approaches the chief of police and asks for suitable recommendations. He may or may not have put in an ad. in the *All-Alaska Weekly*—that's published in Fairbanks.' Finlayson thought briefly. 'I wouldn't say he's deliberately close-mouthed about this. I suppose when you've been a security man all your life you naturally don't let your left hand know what the right hand's doing.'

'What kind of men does he recruit?'

'Almost all ex-cops—you know, ex-State troopers.'

'But not trained security men?'

'As such, no, although I'd have thought security would have come as second nature to a State trooper.' Finlayson smiled. 'I

24

imagine Sam's principal criterion is whether the man can shoot straight.'

'Security's a mental thing, not physical. You said "almost all".'

'He's brought in two first-class security agents from outside. One's stationed at Fairbanks, the other at Valdez.'

'Who says they're first class?'

'Sam. He hand-picked them.' Finlayson rubbed his drying beard in what could have been a gesture of irritation. 'You know, Mr Dermott, friendly, even genial you may be, but I have the odd impression that I'm being third-degreed.'

'Rubbish. If that were happening, you'd know all about it, because I'd be asking you questions about yourself. I've no intention of doing so, now or in the future.'

'You wouldn't be having a dossier on me, would you?'

'Tuesday, September 5, 1939, was the day and date you entered your secondary school in Dundee, Scotland.'

'Jesus!'

'What's so sensitive about the Fairbanks area? Why strengthen your defences there particularly?'

Finlayson shifted in his seat. 'No hard and fast reason, really.'

'Never mind whether it's hard and fast. The reason?'

Finlayson drew in his breath as if he were about to sigh, then seemed to change his mind. 'Bit silly, really. You know how whisperings can generate a hoodoo. People on the line are a bit scared of that sector. You'll know that the pipeline has three mountain ranges to traverse on its 8oo-mile run south to the terminal at Valdez. So, pump stations twelve in all. Pump Station No. 8 is close to Fairbanks. It blew up in the summer of '77. Completely destroyed.'

'Fatalities?'

'Yes.'

'Explanations given for this blow-up?'

'Of course.'

'Satisfactory?'

'The pipeline construction company—Alyeska—were satisfied.'

'But not everyone?'

'The public was sceptical. State and Federal agencies withheld comment.'

'What reason did Alyeska give?'

'Mechanical and electrical malfunction.'

'Do *you* believe that?'

'I wasn't there.'

'The explanation was generally accepted?'

'The explanation was widely disbelieved.'

'Sabotage, perhaps?'

'Perhaps. I don't know. I was here at the time. I've never even seen Pump Station No. 8. Been rebuilt, of course.'

Dermott sighed. 'This is where I should be showing some slight traces of exasperation. Don't believe in committing yourself, do you, Mr Finlayson? Still you'd probably make a good security agent. I don't suppose you'd like to venture an opinion as to whether there was a cover-up or not?'

'My opinion hardly matters. What matters, I suppose, is that the Alaskan press was damned certain there was, and said so loud and clear. The fact that the papers appeared unconcerned about the possibility of libel action could be regarded as significant. They would have welcomed a public enquiry: one assumes that Alyeska would not have.'

'Why were the newspapers stirred up—or is that an unnecessary question?'

'What incensed the press was that they were prevented for many hours from reaching the scene of the accident. What doubly incensed them was that they were prevented not by peace officers of the State but by Alyeska's private guards, who, incredibly, took it upon themselves to close State roads. Even their local PR man agreed that this amounted to illegal restraint.'

'Anybody sue?'

'No court action resulted.'

'Why?'

When Finlayson shrugged, Dermott went on: 'Could it have been because Alyeska is the biggest employer in the State, because the lifeblood of so many companies depends on their contracts with Alyeska? In other words, big money talking big?'

'Possibly.'

'Any minute now I'll be signing you up for Jim Brady. What *did* the press say?'

'Because they'd been prevented for a whole day from getting to the scene of the accident, they believed Alyeska employees had been working feverishly during that time to clean up and minimise the effects of the accident, to remove the evidence of a major spillage and to conceal the fact that their fail-safe system had failed dangerously. Alyeska had also—the press said —covered up the worst effects of the fire damage.'

'Might they also have removed or covered up incriminating evidence pointing to sabotage?'

'No guessing games for me.'

'All right. Do you or Bronowski know of any disaffected elements in Fairbanks?'

'Depends what you mean by disaffected. If you mean environmentalists opposed to the construction of the pipeline, yes. Hundreds, and very strongly opposed.'

'But they're open about it, I assume—always give their full names and addresses when writing to the papers.'

'Yes.'

'Besides, environmentalists tend to be sensitive and non-violent people who work within the confines of the law.'

'About any other disaffected types, I wouldn't know. There are fifteen thousand people in Fairbanks, and it would be optimistic to expect they're all as pure as the driven snow.'

'What did Bronowski think of the incident?'

'He wasn't there.'

'That wasn't what I asked ...'

'He was in New York at the time. He hadn't even joined the company then.'

'A relative newcomer, then?'

'Yes. In your book, I suppose that automatically makes him a villain. If you wish to go ahead and waste your time investigating his antecedents, by all means do so, but I could save you time and effort by telling you that we had him checked, double-checked and triple-checked by three separate top-flight agencies. The New York Police Department gave him a clean bill of health. His record and that of his company are—were—impeccable.'

'I don't doubt it. What were his qualifications, and what was his company?'

'One and the same thing, really. He headed up one of the biggest and arguably the best security agencies in New York. Before that he was a cop.'

'What did his company specialise in?'

'Nothing but the best. Guards, mainly. Additional guards for a handful of the biggest banks when their own security forces were under-staffed by holidays or illness. Guarding the homes of the richest people in Manhattan and Long Island to prevent the ungodly making off with the guests' jewellery when large-scale social functions were being held. His third speciality was providing security for exhibitions of precious gems and paintings. If you could ever persuade the Dutch to lend you Rembrandt's "Night Watch" for a couple of months, Bronowski would be the man you'd send for.'

'What would induce a man to leave all that and come to this end of the world?'

'He doesn't say. He doesn't have to. Homesickness. More specifically, his wife's homesickness. She lives in Anchorage. He flies down there every weekend.'

'I thought you were supposed to do a full four weeks up here before you got time off.'

'Doesn't apply to Bronowski—only to those whose permanent job is here. This is his nominal base, but the whole line is his responsibility. For instance, if there's trouble in Valdez, he's a damn sight nearer it in his wife's flat in Anchorage than he would be if he were up here. And he's very mobile, is our Sam. Owns and flies his own Comanche. We pay his fuel, that's all.'

'He's not without the odd penny to his name?'

'I should say not. He doesn't really need this job, but he can't bear to be inactive. Money? He retains the controlling interest in his New York firm.'

'No conflict of interests?'

'How the hell could there be a conflict of interests? He's never even been out of the State since he arrived here over a year ago.'

'A trustworthy lad, it would seem. Damn few of them around these days.' Dermott looked at Mackenzie. 'Donald?'

'Yes?' Mackenzie picked up the unsigned letter from Edmonton. 'F.B.I. seen this?'

'Of course not. What's it got to do with the F.B.I.?'

'It might have an awful lot to do with them, and soon. I know Alaskans think that this is a nation apart, that this is your own special and private fiefdom up here, and that you refer to us unfortunates as the lower 48, but you're still part of the United States. When the oil from here arrives at Valdez, it's shipped to one of the west-coast states. Any interruption in oil transfer between Prudhoe Bay and, say, California, would be regarded as an unlawful interference with inter-state commerce and would automatically bring in the F.B.I.'

'Well, it hasn't happened yet. Besides, what can the F.B.I. do? They know nothing of oil or pipeline security. Look after the pipeline? They couldn't even look after themselves. We'd just spend more of our time trying to thaw out the few of them that didn't freeze to death during their first ten minutes here. They could only survive under cover, so what could they do there? Take over our computer terminals and master communications and alarm detection stations at Prudhoe Bay, Fairbanks and Valdez? We have highly trained specialists to monitor over three thousand sources of alarm information. Asking the F.B.I. to do that would be like asking a blind man to read Sanskrit. Inside or out, they'd only be in the way and a useless burden to all concerned.'

'Alaska State Troopers could survive. I guess they'd survive where even some of your men couldn't. Have you been in touch with them? Have you notified the State authorities in Juneau?'

'No.'

'Why not?'

'They don't love us. Oh, sure, if there was physical trouble, violence, they'd move in immediately. Until then, they'd rather not know. I can't say I blame them. And before you ask me why I'll tell you. For good or bad we've inherited the Alyeska mantle. Alyeska built the pipeline and they run it; but we use it. I'm afraid there's a wide grey area of non-discrimination here. In most people's eyes they *were* pipeline, we *are* pipeline.'

Finlayson reflected on his next words. 'It's hard not to feel a bit sorry for Alyeska. They were pretty cruelly pilloried. Sure, they bore the responsibility for a remarkable amount of waste, and incurred vast cost over-runs, but they did complete an impossible job in impossible conditions and, what's more, brought it in on schedule. Best construction in North America at the time. Brilliant engineering and brilliant engineers—but the brilliance stopped short of their PR people, who might as well have been operating in downtown Manhattan for all they knew about Alaskans. Their job should have been to sell the pipeline to the people: all they succeeded in doing was in turning a large section of the population solidly against the line and the construction company.'

He shook his head. 'You had to be truly gifted to get it as wrong as they did. They sought to protect the good name of Alyeska, but all they did, by blatant cover-ups—it was alleged —and by deliberate lying, was to bring whatever good name there was into total disrepute.'

Finlayson reached into a drawer, took out two sheets of paper and gave them to Dermott and Mackenzie. 'Photostats of a classic example of the way they handle those under contract to them. One would assume they learnt their trade in one of the more repressive police states. Read it. You'll find it instructive. You'll also understand how by simple thought-transference we're not in line for much public sympathy.'

The two men read the Photostats.

Alyeska Pipeline Service Company	Supplement No. 20
Pipeline and Roads	Revision No. 1
Job Specification	April 1, 1974
	Page 2004

C. IN NO EVENT SHALL CONTRACTOR OR ITS PERSONNEL REPORT A LEAK OR AN OIL SPILL TO ANY GOVERNMENTAL AGENCY. Such reporting shall be the sole responsibility of ALYESKA. CONTRACTOR shall emphasise this to all its supervisory personnel and employees.

D. Further IN NO EVENT SHALL CONTRACTOR OR ITS PERSONNEL DISCUSS, REPORT, OR COMMUNICATE IN ANY WAY WITH NEWS MEDIA whether the news media be radio, television, newspapers or periodicals. Any such communication by CONTRACTOR shall be deemed to be a material breach of CONTRACT by CONTRACTOR. All contacts with news media regarding leaks or oil spills shall be made by Alyeska. If news media people contact CONTRACTOR or CONTRACTOR's personnel they shall refer news media to Alyeska without further discussing, reporting or communicating. CONTRACTOR shall emphasise the aforementioned ALYESKA news media requirements to all its supervisory personnel and employees.

Dermott rested the Photostat on his knee. 'An *American* wrote this?'

'An American of foreign extraction,' Mackenzie said, 'who obviously trained under Goebbels.'

'A charming directive,' Dermott said. 'Hush-up, cover-up or lose your contract. Toe the line or you're fired. A shining example of American democracy at its finest. Well, well.' He glanced briefly at the paper, then at Finlayson. 'How did you get hold of this? Classified information, surely?'

'Oddly enough, no. What you would call the public domain. Editorial page, *All-Alaska Weekly*, July 22, 1977. I don't question it was classified. How the paper got hold of it, I don't know.'

'Nice to see a little paper going against the might of a giant company and getting off with it. Restores one's faith in something or other.'

Finlayson picked up another Photostat. 'The same editorial also made a despairing reference to the "horrendous negative impact of the pipeline on us". That's as true now as it was then. We've inherited this horrendous negative impact, and we're still suffering from it. So there it is. I'm not saying we're entirely friendless, or that the authorities wouldn't move in quickly if there were any overt violations of the law. But, because votes are important, those in charge of our destinies rule from behind: they sense the wind of public opinion, then enact acceptable legislation and adopt correspondingly safe attitudes. Whatever happens, they're not going to antagonise those who keep them in power. They are not, with the public's eye on both them and us, going to come and hold our hands because of any anonymous threat by some anonymous crackpot.'

Mackenzie said: 'So it amounts to this: until actual sabotage occurs, you can expect no outside help. So far as preventative measures are concerned, you're dependent solely upon Bronowski and his security teams. In effect, you're on your own.'

'It's an unhappy thought, but there it is.'

Dermott stood up and walked back and forth. 'Accepting this threat as real, who's behind it and what does he want? Not a crackpot, that's sure. If it were, say, some environmentalist running amok, he'd go ahead and do his damnedest without any prior warning. No, could be with a view to extortion or blackmail, which do not have to be the same thing: extortion would be for money, blackmail could have many different purposes in mind. Stopping the flow of oil is unlikely to be the primary purpose: more likely, it'll be a stoppage for another and more important purpose. Money, politics—local or international—power, misguided idealism, genuine idealism or just crackpot irresponsibility. Well, I'm afraid speculation will have to wait on developments. Meantime, Mr Finlayson, I'd like to see Bronowski as soon as possible.'

'I told you, he has business to finish. He'll be flying up in a few hours.'

'Ask him to fly up now, please.'

'Sorry. Bronowski's his own man. Overall, he's answerable to me, but not in field operations. He'd walk out if I tried to usurp his authority. Unless he had the power to act independently, he'd be effectively hamstrung. You don't hire a dog and bark yourself.'

'I don't think you quite understand. Mr Mackenzie and I have not only been promised total co-operation: we've been empowered to direct security measures if, in our judgment, such extreme measures are dictated by circumstances.'

Finlayson's Yukon beard still masked his expression, but there was no mistaking the disbelief in his voice. 'You mean, take over from Bronowski?'

'If, again in our judgment, he's good enough, we just sit by the sidelines and advise. If not, we will exercise the authority invested in us.'

'Invested in whom? This is preposterous. I will not, I cannot permit it. You walk in here and imagine—no, no way. I have received no such directive.'

'Then I suggest you seek a directive, or confirmation of it, immediately.'

'From whom?'

'The grand panjandrums, as you call them.'

'London?' Dermott said nothing. 'That's for Mr Black.'

Dermott remained silent.

'General manager, Alaska.'

Dermott nodded at the three telephones on Finlayson's desk. 'He's as far away as one of those.'

'He's out of State. He's visiting our offices in Seattle, San Francisco and Los Angeles. At what times and in what order I don't know. I do know he'll be back in Anchorage at noon tomorrow.'

'Are you telling me that is the soonest you can—or will—contact him?'

'Yes.'

'You could phone those offices.'

'I've told you, I don't know where he'd be. He could be at some other place altogether. Like as not he's in the air.'

'You could try, couldn't you?' Finlayson remained silent and Dermott spoke again. 'You could call London direct.'

'You don't know much about the hierarchy in oil companies, do you?'

'No. But I know this.' Now Dermott's customary geniality was gone. 'You're a considerable disappointment, Finlayson. You are, or very well may be, in serious trouble. In the circumstances, one does not expect an executive in top management to resort to stiff outrage and wounded pride. You've got your priorities wrong, my friend—the good of the company comes first, not your feelings or protecting your ass.'

Finlayson's eyes showed no expression. Mackenzie was staring at the ceiling as if he had found something of absorbing interest there: Dermott, he had learned over the years, was a past-master of penning an adversary into a corner. The victim either surrendered or placed himself in an impossible situation of which Dermott would take ruthless advantage. If he couldn't get co-operation, he would settle for nothing less than domination.

Dermott went on: 'I have made three requests, all of which

I regard as perfectly reasonable, and you have refused all three. You persist in your refusals?'

'Yes, I do.'

Dermott said: 'Well, Donald, what are my options?'

'There are none.' Mackenzie sounded sad. 'Only the inevitable.'

'Yes.' Dermott looked at Finlayson coldly. 'You have a radio microwave band to Valdez that links up with the continental exchanges.' He pushed a card towards Finlayson. 'Or would you refuse me permission to talk to my head office in Houston?'

Finlayson said nothing. He took the card, lifted the phone and talked to the switchboard. After three minutes' silence, which only Finlayson seemed to find uncomfortable, the phone rang. Finlayson listened briefly then handed over the phone.

Dermott said: 'Brady Enterprises? Mr Brady please, Dermott.' There was a pause, then: 'Good afternoon, Jim.'

'Well, well, George.' Brady's strong carrying voice was clearly audible in the office. 'Prudhoe Bay, is it? Coincidence, coincidence. I was just on the point of phoning you.'

'Well. My report, Jim. News, rather. There's nothing to report.'

'And I have news for you. Mine first, it's more important. Open line?'

'One moment.' Dermott looked at Finlayson. 'What security classification does your switchboard operator have?'

'None. Jesus, she's only a telephone girl.'

'As you rightly observe, Jesus! Heaven help the trans-Alaskan pipeline.' He pulled out a notebook and pencil and addressed the phone. 'Sorry, Jim. Open. Go ahead.'

In a clear, precise voice Brady began to recite a seemingly meaningless jumble of letters and figures which Dermott noted down in neatly printed script. After about two minutes Brady paused and said: 'Repeat?'

'No thanks.'

'You have something to say?'

'Just this. Field manager here uncooperative, unreasonable and obstructive. I don't think we can profitably operate here. Permission to pull out.'

There was only a brief pause before Brady said clearly:

'Permission granted.' There came the click of a replaced receiver and Dermott rose to his feet.

Finlayson was already on his. 'Mr Dermott—'

Dermott looked down at him icily and spoke in a voice as cold as winter: 'Give my love to London, Mr Finlayson. If you're ever there.'

2

Thirteen hundred miles south-east of Prudhoe Bay, at ten p.m., Brady's men met Jay Shore in the bar of the Peter Pond Hotel in Fort McMurray. Among those qualified to pass judgment on such matters, it was readily agreed that as an engineering construction manager Shore had no peer in Canada. His face was dark, saturnine, almost piratical—which was rather an unfair trick of nature to play on him, since that same nature had made him easy-going, companionable, humorous and cheerful.

Not that he felt in the least humorous and cheerful at that moment. Nor did the man who sat beside him, Bill Reynolds, Sanmobil's operations manager, a rubicund and normally smiling man to whom nature had given precisely the kind of diabolical mind that Shore appeared to have but didn't.

Bill Reynolds looked across the table to Dermott and Mackenzie, whom he and Shore had met thirty seconds previously, and said: 'You make fast time, gentlemen. Remarkable service, if one may say so.'

'We try,' Dermott said comfortably. 'We do our best.'

'Scotch?' asked Mackenzie.

'Thanks.' Reynolds nodded. 'Twin jet—is that it?'

'Right.'

'A shade expensive, a man would think.'

'Gets you around.' Dermott smiled.

'Head Office—that's Edmonton—told us you might take up to four days. We didn't expect you in four *hours*.' Reynolds eyed Dermott speculatively over his newly-poured glass. 'I'm afraid we don't know much about you.'

'Fair enough. We probably know even less about you.'

'Not oilmen, then?'

'Of course. But drilling oilmen. We're not familiar with mining the stuff.'

'And your full-time job's security?'

'That's right.'

'So there's no need to ask what you were doing up on the North Slope?'

'Right again.'

'How long were you up there?'

'Two hours.'

'Two hours! You mean you can lick a security—'

'We licked nothing. We left.'

'May one ask why?'

'Operations manager was ... unhelpful, let's say.'

'Me and my big mouth.'

'Meaning?'

'I'm the operations manager here. But I get the message.'

Dermott said pleasantly: 'No message. You asked a question, I answered.'

'And you decided to walk out—'

'We have a backlog of cases all over the world, and no time to waste trying to help those who won't help themselves. Let's not get off on the wrong foot, gentlemen: your company expects Mackenzie and myself to do the questioning while you do the answering. When was this threat received?'

Shore said: 'Ten o'clock this morning.'

'You have it with you?'

'Not exactly. It came by phone.'

'Where from?'

'Anchorage. International call.'

'Who took the message?'

'I did. Bill here was with me, listening in. Caller gave us his message twice. Word for word he said: "I have to inform you that Sanmobil will be incurring a slight interruption in oil production in the near future. Not much, I assure you, just sufficient to convince you that we can interrupt oil flow whenever and wherever we please." That was all.'

'No demands?'

'No—surprisingly.'

'Don't worry. The demands will come when the big threat does. Would you recognise this voice again?'

'Would I recognise the voices of a million other Canadians

who talk exactly as he does? You take this threat seriously?'

'I do. We take most things seriously. How good is security at the plant?'

'Well—fair enough for normal circumstances. I suppose.'

'These promise to be highly abnormal circumstances. How many guards?'

'Twenty-four, under Terry Brinckman. He knows what he's doing.'

'I don't doubt it. Guard dogs?'

'None. The usual police dogs—Alsatians, Dobermans, boxers—can't survive in these extreme conditions. Huskies can, of course, but they make lousy watch-dogs—they're more interested in fighting each other than looking for intruders.'

'Electric fences?'

Shore rolled his eyes upwards and looked sorrowful. 'You want to equip the environmentalists with a gallows right on the site? Why, if even the meanest old wolf were to singe its mangy hide ...'

'Okay, okay. I suppose it's pointless to ask about electronic beams, sensor devices and the like?'

'Pointless is right.'

Mackenzie said: 'How big is this plant site?'

Reynolds looked unhappy. 'About eight thousand acres.'

'Eight thousand acres.' Mackenzie's voice was all doom. 'What kind of perimeter would that make for?'

'Fourteen miles.'

'Yes. We have a problem here,' Mackenzie said. 'I take it your security duties are twofold: the guarding of vital installations in the plant itself and patrolling the perimeter to keep intruders out?'

Reynolds nodded. 'The guards are in three shifts, eight men per shift.'

'Eight men, without any protective aids at all, to guard the plant itself and at the same time patrol fourteen miles of perimeter in the blackness of a winter night.'

Shore was defensive. 'Ours is a 24-hour operation. The plant is brilliantly lit day and night.'

'But the perimeter isn't. A blind man could drive a coach and four—hell, why go on? A couple of army regiments might

38

help, although I doubt even that. As I say, a problem.'

'Not only that,' Dermott said. 'All the brilliant illumination in the world isn't of the slightest help. Not when you've got hundreds of workers on each of the three shifts a day.'

'Meaning?'

'Subversives.'

'Subversives! Less than two per cent of the work-force are non-Canadians.'

'There's been a royal decree abolishing Canadian criminals? When you hire, you investigate backgrounds?'

'Well, not intensive questioning, third degree, lie-detector tests or any of that rubbish. Try that and you'd never hire anyone. We check on previous experience, qualifications, recommendations, and, most important, criminal records.'

'That's the least important. Really clever criminals never *have* criminal records.' Dermott looked like a man who had been about to sigh, explode, curse, or quit, but had changed his mind. 'Well—it's late. Tomorrow, Mr Mackenzie and I would like to talk to your Terry Brinckman and look over the plant.'

'If we have a car here at ten o'clock—'

'How about seven o'clock? Yes, seven will be fine.'

Dermott and Mackenzie watched the two men go, looked at each other, emptied their glasses, signalled the barman, then looked out through the windows of the Peter Pond Hotel, named after the first white man ever to see the Tar Sands.

Pond went down the Athabasca River by canoe almost exactly two hundred years before. He did not take too much interest in the sands, it appears, but ten years later the much more famous explorer Alexander MacKenzie was intrigued by the sticky substance oozing from outcrops high above the river, and wrote: 'The bitumen is in a fluid state, and when mixed with gum, or the resinous substance collected from the spruce fir, serves to gum the Indians' canoes. In its heated state it emits a smell like that of sea-coal.'

Oddly, the significance of the words 'sea-coal' wasn't appreciated for more than a hundred years; nobody realised that the two 18th-century explorers had stumbled across one of the world's largest reservoirs of fossil fuels. But had they not so stumbled, there would have been no Peter Pond Hotel where it is today nor, indeed, the township beyond its windows.

Even in the mid-nineteen-sixties Fort McMurray was little more than a rough, primitive frontier outpost, with a population of only thirteen hundred and streets covered with dust, mud or slush according to season. By now, though still a frontier town, it had become a frontier town with a difference. Treasuring its past, but with an eye to the future, it was the epitome of a boom-town and, in terms of burgeoning population, the fastest-expanding township in Canada. Where there were thirteen hundred citizens fourteen years earlier, there were thirteen thousand. Schools, hotels, banks, hospitals, churches, super-markets and, above all, hundreds of new houses were or were being built. And, wonder of wonders, the streets were paved. This seeming miracle stems from one factor and one factor only: Fort McMurray sits squarely in the heart of the Athabasca Tar Sands, the biggest such known deposits in the world.

It had been snowing heavily earlier in the evening and had still not completely stopped. Everything—houses, streets, cartops, trees—was under a smoothly unbroken cover of white. Hundreds of lights shone hospitably through the gently falling flakes. The scene would have gladdened the eye and heart of a Christmas postcard artist. Some such thought had occurred to Mackenzie.

'Santa Claus should be here tonight.'

'Indeed.' Dermott sounded morose. 'Especially if he brought along some of that peace on earth and goodwill to all men. What did you make of that telephone message to Sanmobil?'

'Same thing you did. Practically identical to the letter Finlayson received up in Prudhoe Bay. Obviously the work of the same man or group of men.'

'And what do you make of the fact that Alaskan oil people got a threatening message from Alberta, while the Albertan oil interests received the same threat from Alaska?'

'Nothing—except that both threats had the same origin. That call from Anchorage. For a certainty, from a public callbox. Untraceable.'

'Probably. Not certainly. I don't know if you can dial direct from Anchorage to here. I don't think so, but we can find out. If not, the telephone operator will have a record. There's a chance that we might locate the phone.'

Mackenzie briefly surveyed Fort McMurray through the base of his glass and said: 'That'll be a big help.'

'It might be a small help. Two ways. That call came in at ten this morning. That's 6 a.m. Anchorage time. Who except a nut—or some night-shift worker—is going to be out in the black and freezing streets of Anchorage at that hour? That sort of odd behaviour, I suggest, isn't likely to go unnoticed.'

'If there's anyone there to notice.'

'State Troopers in a patrol car. Taxi driver. Snow-plough driver. Mailman on the way to work. You'd be surprised the number of people who go about their lawful occasions in the dark watches of the night.'

'I would not be surprised.' Mackenzie spoke with some feeling. 'We've done it often enough in this damned job of ours. Two ways, you said. What's the second way?'

'If we locate this pay-phone, we have the police who have the post office remove the coin box and give it to their fingerprint boys. The chances are good that the person who made the call to Fort McMurray used more high-denomination coins than anyone else who went into the pay-box that day—or night. Get two or three large coins with the same prints, and that's our man.'

'Objection. Coins are handled by many people. You'll get prints, all right, a plethora, shall we say, of fingerprints.'

'Objection. Coins are handled by many people. You'll get the overlay, the last person to touch such a surface, leaves the dominant print. By the same token, we'd print the area round the dial. People don't dial in fur mittens. Then we'd check with criminal records. The prints may be on file. If they are, we'll get the man and ask him all sorts of interesting questions.'

'You do have a devious mind, George. Low cunning, but albeit a mind. First catch your man, though.'

'If we get a description or prints with history, it shouldn't be too difficult. If he's gone to ground, it would be different. But there's no reason why he should think he has to take cover. Might be awkward for him anyway: may well be a pillar of the Anchorage business and social communities.'

'I'll bet the other Anchorage pillars would love to hear you say that. They'd have the same opinion of you as our friend, John Finlayson, has now. What are we going to do about Finlayson, anyway? *Rapprochement* doesn't seem advisable: it's essential. With the tie-up so obvious—'

'Let him stew in his own juice for a while. I don't mean that the way it sounds. But just let him worry a while in Prudhoe Bay until we're ready. He's a good man, intelligent, honest. He reacted precisely the way you or I would have if a couple of interlopers had tried to take over. The longer we stay away, the more certainly we're guaranteed his co-operation when we get back. Jim Brady may have been the bearer of bad news, but that call of his couldn't have come at a more opportune time. Gave us the perfect excuse to make off. Speaking of Jim—'

'I've been thinking that I don't much like any of this. Presentiments. My Scottish forebears, one presumes. You know that Prudhoe Bay and this place here contain well over half the oil reserves of North America. It's an awful lot of oil. A man wouldn't want anything to happen to them.'

'You haven't worried about such things before. An investigator is supposed to be cold, clinical, detached.'

'That's about other people's oil. This is *our* oil. Massive responsibilities. Awesome decisions at the highest levels.'

'We were talking of Jim Brady.'

'I still am.'

'You think we should have him up here?'

'I do.'

'So do I. Must be why I raised the subject. Let's go call him.'

3

Jim Brady, that passionate believer in leanness, keenness, fitness and athleticism for his field operatives, stood five feet eight in his elevator shoes and turned the scales at around 240 lbs. Never a believer in travelling light, he brought with him on the flight from Houston not only his attractive, blonde wife Jean, but also his positively stunning daughter Stella, another natural blonde, who acted as his secretary on these field trips. He left Jean behind at the hotel in Fort McMurray, but kept Stella with him in the minibus that Sanmobil had sent to ferry him out to the plant.

The first impression he made on the hard men of Athabasca was less than favourable. He wore a superbly-cut dark-grey business suit—it had to be well cut, even to approximate to a frame as spherical as his—a white shirt and a conservative tie. On top of these indoor clothes, however, he wore two woollen overcoats and a vast beaver fur coat, the combined effect being to render his vertical and horizontal dimensions approximately equal. He sported a soft felt hat the same colour as his suit, but this too was almost invisible, anchored by a grey woollen scarf that passed twice over the crown and under his chins.

'Well I'll be damned!' he exclaimed. His voice was muffled by the ends of the scarf, tied across his face just below the eyes, which were the only part of him that could be seen. Even so, it was clear to his companions that he was impressed.

'This sure is something. You boys must have a lot of fun digging away here and building these nice little ol' sand-castles.'

'That's one way of putting it, Mr Brady.' Jay Shore spoke with restraint. 'Not much, perhaps, by Texas standards, but it's still the biggest mining operation in the history of mankind.'

'No offence, no offence. You don't expect a Texan to admit

there's something bigger and better outside his own State?' One could almost feel him bracing himself for a handsome admission. 'That beats anything I've ever come across.'

'That' was a dragline, but a dragline such as Brady had never seen before. A dragline is essentially an engine-housing with a control cabin which operates a crane-like boom. The boom is hinged and swivelled at the base of the engine-housing, and so can be both raised and lowered and swung from side to side: control is achieved by cables from the engine-housing which pass over a massive steel superstructure and reach out to the tip of the boom. Another cable, passing over the tip of the boom, supports a bucket which can be lowered to scoop up material, raised again, then swung to one side to dump its load.

'Biggest thing that ever moved on earth,' said Shore.

'*Move?*' Stella said.

'Yes, it can move. Walks, shuffles would be a better word, on those two huge shoes at the base, step by step. You wouldn't want to enter it for the Kentucky Derby—it takes seven hours to travel a mile. Not that it's ever required to travel more than a few yards at a time. Point is, it gets there.'

'And that long nose ...' she said.

'The boom. The comparison most generally used is that it's as long as a football field. Wrong—it's longer. From here the bucket doesn't look all that big, but that's only because everything is dwarfed out of perspective: it scoops up eighty cubic yards at a time or enough to fill a two-car garage. A large two-car garage. The dragline weighs 6,500 tons—about the same as a light-medium cruiser. Cost? About thirty million dollars. Takes fifteen to eighteen months to build—on the site, of course. There are four of them, and between them they can shift up to a quarter of a million tons a day.'

'You win. This is a boom town,' Brady said. 'Let's get inside. I'm cold.' The other four—Dermott, Mackenzie, Shore and Brinckman, the security chief—looked at him in mild astonishment. It seemed impossible that a man so extravagantly upholstered and insulated, both naturally and otherwise, could possibly feel even cool; but if Brady said he was cold, he was cold.

They clambered into the minibus which, if a bit short on

other creature comforts, did at least have heaters in excellent condition. Also in excellent condition was the girl who sat down in the back seat, lowered her parka hood, and beamed at them. Brinckman, who was much the youngest of the men, in his thirties, had not paid much attention to Stella. Now he touched the rim of his fur cap and lit up like a lamp. His enthusiasm was hardly surprising for the white fur parka made her as cuddly-looking as a polar bear cub.

'Wanna dictate anything, Dad?' she asked.

'Not yet,' Brady grunted. Once safely sheltered from the vicious cold, he undid the ends of the scarf that concealed his face. Somewhere in the distant past there must have been signs of the character that had driven him from the back streets of poverty to his present millions, but years of gracious living had eradicated all trace of them: bone structure had vanished under a fatty accumulation which had left him without a crease, line or even the hint of crow's feet. It was a fat, spoiled face like a cherub's. With one exception: there was nothing cherubic about the eyes. They were blue, cool, appraising and shrewd.

He looked through the window at the dragline. 'So that's the end of the line.'

'The beginning of it,' Shore said. 'The tar sands may lie as deep as fifty feet down. The stuff above, the overburden, is useless to us—gravel, clay, muskeg, shale, oil-poor sand—and has to be removed first of all.' He pointed to an approaching vehicle. 'Here's some of that rubbish being carried away now —it's been excavated by another dragline on a new site.

'To impress you further, Mr Brady, those trucks are also the biggest in the world. A hundred and twenty-five tons empty, payload of a hundred and fifty, and all this on just four tyres. But, you will admit, they are some tyres.'

The truck was passing now and they were indeed some tyres; to Brady they looked at least ten feet high and proportionately bulky. The truck itself was monstrous—twenty feet high at the cab and about the same in width, with the driver mounted so high as to be barely visible from the ground.

'You could buy a very acceptable car for the price of one of those tyres,' Shore said. 'As for the truck itself, if you went shopping for one at today's prices, you wouldn't get much change from three quarters of a million.' He spoke to his driver, who started up and moved slowly off.

'When the overburden is gone, the same dragline scoops up the tar sand—as the one we've just looked at is doing now—and dumps it in this huge pile we call a windrow.' A weird machine of phenomenal length was nosing into the pile. Shore pointed and said: 'A bucketwheel reclaimer—there's one paired with every dragline. Four hundred and twenty-eight feet long. You can see the revolving bucketwheel biting into the windrow. With fourteen buckets on a forty-foot diameter wheel, it can remove a fair tonnage every minute. The tar sands are then transported along the spine of the reclaimer—the bridge, we call it—to the separators. From there—'

Brady interrupted: 'Separators?'

'Sometimes the sands come in big, solid lumps as hard as rock which could damage the conveyor belts. The separators are just vibrating screens which sort out the lumps.'

'And without the separators the conveyor belts could be damaged?'

'Certainly.'

'Put out of commission?'

'Probably. We don't know. It's never been allowed to happen yet.'

'And then?'

'The tar sands go into the travelling hoppers you see there. They drop the stuff on to the conveyor belt, and off it goes to the processing plant. After that—'

'One minute.' It was Dermott. 'You have a fair amount of this conveyor belting?'

'A fair bit.'

'How much exactly?'

Shore looked uncomfortable. 'Sixteen miles.' Dermott stared at him and Shore hurried on. 'At the end of the conveyor system radial stackers direct it to what are called surge piles—just really storage dumps.'

'Radial stackers?' said Brady. 'What are they?'

'Elevated extensions of the conveyor belts. They can rotate through a certain arc to direct the tar sands to a suitable surge

46

pile. They can also feed bins that take the sands underground to start the processes of chemical and physical separation of the bitumen. The first of those processes—'

'Jesus!' said Mackenzie incredulously.

'That about sums it up,' Dermott said. 'I have no wish to be rude, Mr Shore, but I don't want to hear about the extraction processes. I've already heard and seen all I want to.'

'Good God Almighty!' exclaimed Mackenzie by way of variation.

Brady said: 'What's the matter, gentlemen?'

Dermott picked his words carefully. 'When Don and I were talking to Mr Shore and Mr Reynolds, the operations manager, last night, we thought we had reason to be concerned. I now realise we were wasting our time on trifles. But, by God, now I'm worried.

'Last night we had to face the fact—the ridiculous ease with which the perimeter can be penetrated and the almost equal ease with which subversives could be introduced on to the plant floor. In retrospect, those are but bagatelles. How many points did you pick up, Don?'

'Six.'

'My count also. First off, the draglines. They look as impregnable as the Rock of Gibraltar: they are, in fact, pathetically vulnerable. A hundred tons of high explosive would hardly dent the Rock of Gibraltar; I could take out a dragline with two five-pound charges of wrap-round explosive placed where the boom is hinged to the machine house.'

Brinckman, an intelligent and clearly competent person in his early thirties, spoke for the first time in fifteen minutes, then immediately wished he hadn't. He said: 'Fine, if you could approach the dragline—but you can't. The area is lit by brilliant floodlamps.'

'Jesus!' Mackenzie's limited repertoire was in use again.

'What do you mean, Mr Mackenzie?'

'What I mean is I would locate the breaker or switch or whatever that supplies the power to the floodlights and immobilise it by smashing it or by the brilliantly innovative device of turning it off. Or, I'd cut the power lines. Simpler still, with a five-second burst from a sub-machine gun I'd shoot them out. Assuming, of course, that they're not made of bullet-proof glass.'

Dermott saved Brinckman the embarrassment of a long silence. 'Five pounds of commercial Amatol would take out the bucketwheel for an indefinite period. A similar amount would take care of the reclaimer's bridge. Two pounds to buckle the separator plate. That's four ways. Getting at the radial stackers would be another excellent device—that would mean Sanmobil couldn't even get the tar sands stockpiled in the surge piles down below for processing. And then, best of all, is this little matter of sixteen unpatrolled miles of conveyor belting.'

There was quiet in the bus until Dermott rumbled on. 'Why bother sabotaging the separation plant when it's so much simpler and more effective to interrupt the flow of raw material? You can't very well carry out a processing operation if you've got nothing to process. It'd be childishly simple. Four draglines. Four bucketwheels. Four reclaimers' bridges. Four separators. Four radial stackers. Sixteen miles of conveyor, four-teen miles of unpatrolled perimeter, and eight men to cover. Situation's ludicrous. I'm afraid, Mr Brady, there's no way in the world we can stop our Anchorage friend from carrying out his threat.'

Brady turned what appeared to be one cold, blue eye on the unfortunate Brinckman. 'And what do you have to say?'

'What can I say except to agree? Even if I had ten times the number of men at my disposal, we still shouldn't be geared to meet a threat like this.' He shrugged. 'I'm sorry, I didn't even dream of anything else like this.'

'Nor did anyone else. Nothing to reproach yourself about. You security people thought you were in the oil business, not a war. What are your normal duties, anyway?'

'We're here to prevent three things—physical trouble among members of the work-force, petty pilfering, and drinking on the plant site. But so far we've had few instances of any of them.'

Visibly, Brinckman's words struck a chord in Brady. 'Ah, yes. Trouble in moments of stress and all that.' He turned in his seat. 'Stella!'

'Yes Dad.' She opened a wicker basket, produced a flask and glass, poured a drink and handed it to her father.

'Daiquiri,' he said. 'We also have Scotch, gin, rum—'

'Sorry, Mr Brady,' Shore said. 'No. The company has very strict regulations—'

Brady gave him some terse suggestions as to what he could do with company regulations and turned to Brinckman again.

'So in effect, you've been pretty superfluous up till now and, if anything, are going to be even more so in the future?'

'I'd agree with half of that. The fact that we've had little to do to now doesn't mean we've been superfluous. Presence is important. You don't heave a half-brick through a jeweller's window if there's an interested cop standing by five feet away. As to the future, yes, I agree. I feel pretty helpless.'

'If you were carrying out an attack somewhere, what would you go for?'

Brinckman was in no two minds. 'The conveyor belting every time.'

Brady looked at Dermott and Mackenzie. Both men nodded. 'Mr Shore?'

'Agreed.' Shore was absentmindedly sipping some Scotch that had found its way into his hand. 'Apart from the fact that there's so damn much of it, it's fragile. Six feet wide, but the steel cord belting is only an inch and a half thick. With a sledge-hammer and chisel I could wreck it myself.' Shore looked and sounded tense. 'Not many people are aware of the vast quantities of material that are processed here. To keep the plant operating at capacity and to make the project commercially viable, we need close on a quarter of a million tons of tar sands a day. As I said, the biggest mining operation ever. Cut off the supplies, and the plant closes down in a few hours. That's a hundred and thirty thousand barrels of oil a day lost. Even Sanmobil couldn't stand this kind of loss indefinitely.'

'How much did it cost to set up this plant?' Brady asked.

'Two billion, near enough.'

'Two billion dollars. And a potential operating loss of a hundred and thirty thousand barrels of oil a day.' Brady shook his head. 'No-one's arguing about the brilliance of the men

49

who dreamed up this idea. Same goes for the engineers who made it work. But there's another thing no-one would question —at least *I* would never question—and that is that those towering intellects had a huge blind spot. Why didn't the bosses foresee this? I know it's easy to be wise after the event, but, goddamn, you don't need much foresight to think of that. Oil is not just another business. Couldn't they have seen the giant potential for hate or crackpots—or blackmail? Couldn't they have foreseen that they'd built the biggest industrial hostage to fortune of all time?'

Shore gazed gloomily at his glass, gloomily drank its contents, and maintained a gloomy silence.

Dermott said: 'Well, not quite.'

'What do you mean "not quite"?'

'Sure, it's an industrial hostage to fortune. But not the biggest of all time. That dubious distinction belongs without any question to the trans-Alaskan pipeline. Their capital outlay wasn't two billion: it was eight billion. They don't transport a hundred and thirty thousand barrels a day: they transport one million two hundred thousand. And they don't just have sixteen miles of conveyor belting to guard: they have eight hundred miles of pipeline.'

Brady handed his glass back for a refill, digested this unpleasant thought, fortified himself and said: 'Don't they have *any* means of protecting the damned thing?'

'To the extent that they can limit damage, certainly. They have magnificent communication and electronic control systems, with every imaginable fail-safe and back-up device, even to the extent of a satellite emergency control station.' Dermott produced a paper from his pocket. 'They have twelve pump stations, locally or remotely controlled. They have sixty-two remote gate valves, all radio-controlled from the pump station immediately to the north. Those gate valves can stop the flow of oil in either direction.

'There are eighty check valves to prevent the oil from flowing backwards and, well, all sorts of other weird valves that would only make sense to an engineer. Altogether they have a remote-control capability at well over a thousand points. In other words, they can isolate any section of the line at any time they want. Because it takes six minutes to shut down a big pump, some oil is bound to escape—up to fifty thousand barrels, it's estimated. That may seem a lot, but it's a drop in the bucket compared to what's in the pipeline. But there's no way the oil can keep on pumping out indefinitely.'

'All very interesting.' Brady sounded cool. 'You can bet they try harder to protect the environment. You can also bet that crooks and extortioners don't give a damn about the environment one way or another. All they want is to interrupt the flow of oil. Can the line be protected?'

'Well, about this huge blind spot you mentioned—'

'What you're trying not to tell me is that the pipeline can be breached any place, any time.'

'That's right.'

Brady looked at Dermott. 'You've thought about this problem?'

'Of course.'

'And you, Donald?'

'Me, too.'

'Well then, what have you come up with?'

'Nothing. That's why we sent for you. We thought *you* might come up with something.'

Brady looked at him maliciously and resumed his pondering. By and by he said: 'What happens if there's a break and the oil is stopped in the pipe? Does it gum up?'

'Eventually. But it takes time. The oil is hot when it comes out of the ground and it's still warm when it reaches Valdez. The pipeline is very heavily insulated, and the oil passing through the pipe generates friction heat. They reckon they might get it flowing again after a 21-day standstill. After that—' He spread his hands.

'No more oil-flow?'

'No.'

'Not ever again?'

'I shouldn't think so. I don't really know. Nobody's talked to me about it. I don't think anyone really wants to talk about it.'

No one did. Until Brady said: 'Do you know what I wish?'

'I know,' Dermott said. 'You wish you were back in Houston.'

The radio-phone rang. The driver listened briefly then turned to Shore.

'Operations manager's office. Will we return immediately. Mr Reynolds says it's urgent.' The bus driver picked up speed.

Reynolds was waiting for them. He indicated a phone lying on his table and spoke to Brady. 'Houston. For you.'

Brady said 'Hello'. Then he made a gesture of irritation and turned to Dermott.

'Horseshit. Damn code. Take it, huh?' This was hardly reasonable of Brady, since it was he who had invented the code and insisted on using it for almost everything except 'Hello' and 'Goodbye'. Dermott reached for a pad and pencil, took the phone and started writing. It took him about a minute to record the message and two more to decode it.

He said into the phone: 'Is that all you have?' A pause. 'When did you get this message, and when did this happen?' Another pause. 'Fifteen minutes and two hours. Thank you.' He turned to Brady, his face bleak. 'The pipeline's been breached. Pump Station No. 4. Near Atigun Pass in the Brook Range. No hard details yet. Damage not severe, it seems, but enough to close down the line.'

'No chance of an accident?'

'Explosives. They took out two gate valves.'

There was a brief silence while Brady surveyed Dermott curiously.

'No need to look so goddamned grim, George. We were expecting something like this. It's not the end of the world.'

'It is for two of the men on Pump Station Four. They've been murdered.'

4

It was half-past two in the afternoon, Alaskan time, almost dark, but with good visibility, a ten-knot wind and a temperature of $-4°F$—36° below—when the twin-jet touched down again on one of the Prudhoe Bay air-strips. Brady, Dermott and Mackenzie had moved quickly after receipt of the message from Houston. They had driven back to Fort McMurray, packed essentials, which in Brady's case consisted primarily of three flasks, said goodbye to Jean and Stella and driven straight to the airport. Brady was asleep when they entered Yukon airspace, and Mackenzie dozed off shortly afterwards. Only Dermott remained awake, trying to puzzle out why the enemy, in carrying out what they said would be—and, in fact proved to be—no more than a token demonstration, should have found it necessary to kill in the process.

As the jet came to a halt, a brightly-lit minibus pulled up alongside and slid open a front door. Brady, third out of the aircraft, was first into the bus. The others followed him in and the door was quickly closed. As the bus moved off the man who had ushered them aboard came and sat down beside them. Aged anywhere between forty and fifty, he was a broad, chunky man with a broad, chunky face. He looked tough but he also looked as if he could be humorous—although he had nothing worth smiling about at that moment.

'Mr Brady, Mr Dermott, Mr Mackenzie,' he said, in the unmistakably, flat accent of one who had been born within commuting distance of Boston. 'Welcome. Mr Finlayson sent me to meet you—as you can imagine he's right now practically a prisoner in the master operations control centre. My name's Sam Bronowski.'

Dermott said: 'Security chief.'

'For my sins.' He smiled. 'You'll be Mr Dermott, the man

who's going to take over from me?'

Dermott looked at him. 'Who the hell said that?'

'Mr Finlayson. Or words to that effect.'

'I'm afraid Mr Finlayson must be slightly overwrought.'

Bronowski smiled again. 'Well, now, that wouldn't surprise me either. He's been talking to London and I think he suffered some damage to his left ear.'

Brady said: 'We're not out to take over from anyone. That's not how we work. But unless we get co-operation—I mean total co-operation—we might as well have stayed home. For instance, Mr Dermott here wanted to talk to you right away. The chairman of your company himself had guaranteed me complete co-operation. Yet Finlayson refused point-blank to co-operate with Dermott and Mackenzie.'

'I'd have come at once if I'd known,' said Bronowski quickly. 'Unlike Mr Finlayson, I've been a security man all my life, and I know who you are and the reputation you have. In a set-up like this I can do with all the expert help I can get. Go easy with him, will you? This isn't his line of country. He treats the pipeline as his favourite daughter. This is a new experience for him and he didn't know what to do. He wasn't stalling—just playing it safe until he'd consulted on the highest level.'

'You don't need lessons in sticking up for your boss, do you?'

'I'm being fair to him. I hope you will be, too. You can imagine how he feels. Says that if he hadn't been so ornery those two men up at Pump Station Four might be alive now.'

'That's plain daft,' Mackenzie said. 'I appreciate his feelings, but this would have happened if there had been fifty Dermotts and fifty Mackenzies here.'

'When,' Brady asked, 'are we going out there?'

'Mr Finlayson asked if you and your colleagues would come first to see him and Mr Black. The helicopter is ready to go any moment after that.'

'Black?'

'General manager, Alaska.'

'You been out at the station?'

'I was the man who found them. Rather, I was the first

man on the scene after the attack. Along with my section chief, Tim Houston.'

'You fly your own plane?'

'Yes. Not this time, though. That section of the Brooks Range is like the mountains on the moon. Helicopter. We've been making a continuous check on the pump stations and the remote gate valves since this damned threat came through, and we'd stayed at Station Five last night. We were just approaching Gate Four, a mile away, I'd reckon, when we saw this damned great explosion.'

'*Saw* it?'

'You know, oil smoke and flames. You mean, did we *hear* anything? You never do in a helicopter. You don't have to—not when you see the roof take off into the air. So we put down and got out, me with a rifle, Tim with two pistols. Wasting our time. The bastards had gone. Being oilmen yourselves, you'll know it requires quite a group of men and a complex of buildings to provide the care and maintenance for a couple of 13,500 horsepower aircraft-type turbines, not to mention all the monitoring and communications they have to handle.

'It was the pump room itself that was on fire, not too badly, but badly enough for Tim and me not to go inside without fire extinguishers. We'd just started looking when we heard shouting coming from a store room. It was locked, naturally, but the key had been left in the lock. Poulson—he's the boss—came running out with his men. They had the extinguishers located and the fire out in three minutes. But it was too late for the two engineers inside—they'd come down the previous day from Prudhoe Bay to do a routine maintenance job on one of the turbines.'

'They were dead?'

'Very.' Bronowski's face registered no emotion. 'They were brothers. Fine boys. Friends of mine; and Tim's.'

'No possibility of accidental death? From the effects of the explosion?'

'Explosions don't shoot you. They were pretty badly charred, but charring doesn't hide a bullet-wound between the eyes.'

'You searched the area?'

'Certainly. Conditions weren't ideal—it was dark, with a

little snow falling. I thought I saw helicopter ski marks on a wind-blown stretch of rock. The others weren't so sure. On the remote off-chance I contacted Anchorage and asked them to alert every public and private airport and strip in the State. Also to have radio and TV stations ask the public to report hearing or sighting a helicopter in an unusual place. I haven't but one hope in ten thousand that the request will bring any results.'

He grimaced. 'Most people never realise how huge this State is. It's bigger than half Western Europe, but it's got a population of just over three hundred thousand, which is to say it's virtually uninhabited. Again, helicopters are an accepted fact of life in Alaska, and people pay no more attention to them than you would to a car in Texas. Third, we've still only got about three good hours of light, and the idea of carrying out an air search is laughable—anyway, we'd require fifty times the number of planes we have, and even then it would be sheer luck to find them.

'But, for the record, we did find out something unpleasant. In case anything should happen to the pump station, there's an emergency pipeline that can be switched in to bypass it. Our friends took care of that also. They blew up the control valve.'

'So there's going to be a massive oil spillage?'

'No chance. The line is loaded with thousands of sensors all the way from Prudhoe Bay to Valdez, and any section of it can be closed down and isolated immediately. Even the repairs would normally present no problem. But neither metal nor men work too well in these abnormally low temperatures.'

'Apparently that doesn't apply to saboteurs,' Dermott said. 'How many were there?'

'Poulson said two. Two others said three. The remainder weren't sure.'

'Not a very observant lot, are they?'

'I wonder if that's fair, Mr Dermott. Poulson's a good man and he doesn't miss much.'

'Did he see their faces?'

'No. That much is for certain.'

'Masked?'

'No. Their fur collars were pulled up and their hats low down so that only their eyes were visible. You can't tell the colour of a man's eyes in the darkness. Besides, our people had just been dragged from bed.'

'But not the two engineers. They were working on the engines. How come at that very early hour?'

Bronowski spoke with restraint. 'Because they had been up all night. Because they were going home to their families in Fairbanks for their week's leave. And because I had arranged to pick them up there shortly after that time.'

'Did Poulson or any of his friends recognise the voices?'

'If they had, I'd have the owners behind bars by this time. Their collars were up to their eyes. Of course their voices would have been muffled. You ask a lot of questions, Mr Dermott.'

'Mr Dermott is a trained interrogator,' Brady said cheerfully. 'Trained him myself, as a matter of fact. What happened after that?'

'They were marched across to the food store and locked in there. We keep it locked because of bears. Unless bears are near starving, they aren't very partial to human beings, but they're partial indeed to all human goodies.'

'Thank you, Mr Bronowski. One last question. Did Poulson or his men hear the fatal shots?'

'No. Both the men Poulson saw were carrying silenced guns. That's the great advantage of those modern educational pictures, Mr Dermott.'

There was a pause in the questioning. Brady said: 'Because I am an acute observer of character, George, I can tell something's eating you. What's on your mind?'

'It's only a thought. I'm wondering if the murderers are employees of the trans-Alaskan pipeline.'

The silence was brief but marked. Then Bronowski said: 'This beats everything. I speak as Dr Watson, you understand. I know that Sherlock Holmes could solve a crime without leaving his armchair, but I never knew of any cop or security man who could come up with the answer without at least visiting the scene of the crime.'

Dermott said mildly: 'I'm not claiming to have solved

anything. I'm just putting forward a possibility.'

Brady said: 'What makes you think that?'

'In the first place, you pipeline people aren't just the biggest employer of labour around here: you're the only one. Where the hell else could the killers have come from? What else could they have been? Lonely trappers or prospectors on the North Slope of the Brooks Range in the depth of winter? They'd freeze to death the first day out. They wouldn't be prospectors, because the tundra is frozen solid, and beneath that there's two thousand feet of solid permafrost. As for trappers, they'd be not only cold and lonely but very hungry indeed, because they wouldn't find any form of food north of Brooks Range until the late spring comes.'

Brady grunted. 'What you're saying in effect is that the pipeline is the sole means of life-support in those parts.'

'It's a fact. Had this happened at Pump Station Seven or Eight, circumstances would have been quite different—those stations are only a hop, skip and jump from Fairbanks by car. But you don't take a car over the Brooks Range in the depth of winter. And you don't back-pack over the Range at this time of year, unless you're bent on quick suicide. So the question remains, how did they get there and away again?'

'Helicopter,' Bronowski said. 'Remember I said I thought I saw ski marks? Tim—Tim Houston—saw the marks too, although he was less sure. The others were frankly sceptical, but admitted the possibility. But I've been flying helicopters for as long as I can remember.' Bronowski shook his head in exasperation. 'God's sake, how else could they have got in and out?'

'I thought,' Mackenzie said, 'that those pump stations had limited range radar-scopes.'

'They do.' Bronowski shrugged. 'But snow plays funny tricks on radar. Also, they may not have been looking, or maybe they had the set switched off, not expecting company in such bad weather.'

Dermott said: 'They were expecting you, surely.'

'Not for another hour or so. We'd had deteriorating weather at No 5, so we left ahead of schedule. Another thing—even if they had picked up an incoming helicopter, they'd automatically have assumed it was one of ours and would have had no reason to be suspicious.'

'Be that as it may,' said Dermott, 'I'm convinced. It was an inside job. The killers are pipeline employees. The note announcing their intention of causing a slight spillage of oil seemed civil and civilised enough, with no hint of violence, but violence there has been. The saboteurs blundered, and so they had to kill.'

'Blundered?' Mackenzie was a lap behind.

'Yes. Bronowski said the key had been left in the store room door. Don't forget, all the engineers locked inside *were* engineers. With the minimum of equipment they could have either turned the key in the lock or slipped a piece of paper, cardboard, linoleum, anything, under the bottom of the door, pushed the key out to fall on it and hauled the key inside. Me, I'd have thrown that key a mile away. But the killers didn't. Their intention was to bring the two pumphouse engineers to the store room and usher them in to join their friends, and lock them in, too. But they didn't do that either. Why? Because one of the saboteurs said or did something that betrayed their identity to the two engineers. They were recognised by the engineers, who evidently knew them well enough to penetrate their disguises. The saboteurs had no option, so they killed them.'

Brady said: 'How's that for a hypothesis, Sam?'

Bronowski was pondering his reply when the minibus pulled up outside the main entrance to the administrative building. Brady, predictably, was the first out and scuttled—as far as a nearly spherical human being could be said to scuttle—to the welcoming shelter that lay behind the main door. The others followed more sedately.

John Finlayson rose as they entered his room. He extended his hand to Brady and said: 'Delighted to meet you, sir.' He nodded curtly towards Dermott, Mackenzie and Bronowski, then turned to a man seated to his right behind a table. 'Mr Hamish Black, general manager. Alaska.'

Mr Black didn't look like the general manager of anything, far less the manager of a tough and ruthless oil operation. The

59

rolled umbrella and bowler hat were missing, but even without them his lean, bony face, immaculately trimmed pencil moustache, thinning black hair parted with millimetric precision over the centre of his scalp and the eyes behind pince-nez made him the eptitome of a top City of London accountant, which he was.

That such a man, who could hardly tell a nut from a bolt, should head up a huge industrial complex was not a new phenomenon. The tea-boy who had painstakingly fought his way up through the ranks to board-room level had become a man of no mean importance: it was Hamish Black, so adept at punching the keyboard of his pocket calculator, who called the industrial tune. It was rumoured that his income ran into six figures—sterling, not dollars. His employers, evidently, thought he was worth every penny of it.

He waited patiently while Finlayson made the introductions.

'I would not go as far as Mr Finlayson and say I'm delighted to meet you.' Black's smile was as thin as his face. His flat, precise, controlled voice belonged to the City, to London's Wall Street, just as surely as did his appearance. 'Under other circumstances, yes: under these, I can only say that I'm glad you, Mr Brady, and your colleagues are here. I assume Mr Bronowski has supplied you with details. How did you propose we proceed?'

'I don't know. Do we have a glass?'

The expression on Finlayson's face could have been interpreted as reluctant disapproval: Black, it seemed, didn't believe in using expressions. Brady poured his daiquiri, waved the flask at the others, who waved it on, and said: 'The F.B.I. have been notified?'

Black nodded. 'Reluctantly.'

'Reluctantly?'

'There's a legal obligation to notify of any interruption of interstate commerce. Quite frankly, I don't see what they can achieve.'

'They're out at the pump station now?'

'They haven't arrived here yet. They're waiting for some specialist Army Ordnance officers to accompany them—experts on bombs, explosives and the like.'

'Waste of time. Among the people who built and run this line are as good—if not better—explosives experts than in any Army Ordnance Corps. The killers wouldn't have left a trace of explosives at Pump Station No. 4.'

If a silence can be said to be cold, the ensuing silence was downright chilly. Finlayson said stonily: 'Does that statement mean what I think it means?'

'I should imagine it does,' said Brady. 'Explain George.'

Dermott explained. When he had finished, Finlayson said: 'Preposterous. Why should any of our pipeline employees want to do a thing like that? It doesn't make sense.'

'It's never a pleasant thing to nurture a viper in your bosom,' Brady said agreeably. 'Mr Black?'

'Makes sense to me, if only because no other immediate explanation occurs. What do *you* think, Mr Brady?'

'Exactly what I was asking Mr Bronowski as we touched down.'

'Yes. Well.' Bronowski didn't seem any too comfortable. 'I don't like it. An inside job is all too damn plausible. Point is, carry this line of thinking a little further, and the finger points at Tim Houston and myself as the prime suspects?' Bronowski paused. 'Tim and I had a helicopter. We were in the right place at approximately the right time. We know of a dozen ways to sabotage the pipeline. It's no secret that we're both pretty experienced in the use of explosives, so taking out Station Four would have presented no problem for us.' He paused. 'But who's going to suspect the security chief and his number two?'

'Me, for one,' said Brady. He sipped his drink and sighed. 'I'd have you clapped behind bars right now were it not for your impeccable record, lack of apparent motive, and the fact that it's incredible that you should have acted in such a clumsy fashion.'

'Not clumsy, Mr Brady. The killers were stupid to the point of insanity, or badly frightened. The job certainly wasn't the work of professional hit men. Why shoot the two engineers? Why leave any evidence that murder had been done? Just knock them unconscious—a dozen ways that can be done without leaving a mark—then blow them to pieces along with the pump station. Act of God, and no hint of foul play.'

'Amateurism is a grievesome thing, is it not?' Brady turned to Finlayson. 'Could we have a line to Anchorage, please? Thank you. Give him the number, then take the call, George.' Dermott did so and within four minutes had hung up, his part of the conversation having been limited mainly to monosyllables.

'Wouldn't you know it,' Dermott said.

'No luck?' said Mackenzie.

'Too much. The Anchorage police have located not one but four hot phone boxes. Suspicious characters either inside them or lurking in the vicinity, and this at a most ungodly hour. All four of them, dammit, with a disproportionate number of high-denomination coins inside them. All four have been dismantled and taken along to the cop shop. But they haven't been fingerprinted yet, and it may be hours before the cops can check the prints against their files.'

Black said with sardonic restraint: 'The relevance of this call escapes me. It has something to do with Pump Station Four?'

'Maybe,' said Brady. 'Maybe not. All we know for certain is that Sanmobil—the people who have the tar sands concession north of Fort McMurray, in Alberta—have also received a threat against their oil production lines. Couched in almost identical forms with the threat you received, the only difference being that while yours arrived by mail, theirs came from a public phone booth in Anchorage. We're trying to trace which booth and, with any fingerprint luck, who the caller may have been.'

Black thought briefly, then said: 'Curious. A threat against Alaskan oil from Alberta, and one against Albertan oil from Alaska. Must tie up with Pump Station Four: the arm of coincidence isn't all that long ... and while you're sitting here, Mr Brady, some ill-intentioned person or persons may be planting an explosive device at some strategic point in Sanmobil's tar sands.'

'The thought had not escaped me. However, surmise and speculation will serve no point until we turn up one or two hard facts. We hope that one may even result from a close inspection of Pump Station Four. Coming out there, Mr Black?'

'Good heavens, no. I'm very much a desk-bound citizen. But I shall await your return with interest.'

'Return? I'm going no place. Those frozen wastes—not for me. My excellent representatives know what to look for. Besides, someone has to stay and run the command post. How far to the pump station, Mr Bronowski?'

'Helicopter miles? Hundred and forty, give or take.'

'Splendid. That will leave us ample time for a belated lunch. Your commissary is still open, Mr Finlayson, I trust, and your wine cellar tolerable?'

'Sorry about that, Mr Brady.' Finlayson made no effort to conceal the satisfaction in his voice. 'Company regulations forbid alcohol.'

'No need to distress yourself,' Brady said urbanely. 'Aboard my jet is the finest cellar north of the Arctic Circle.'

5

Three generator-fed arc-lamps threw the half-demolished pump-house and its shattered contents into harsh relief, glaring white and Stygian blackness, with no intermediate shading between. Snow drifted silently down through the all-but-vanished roof, and a high wind blew a fine white cloud through a gaping hole in the northern wall. Already the combined effects of the two snows had softened and blurred the outlines of the machinery, but not sufficiently to conceal the fact that engines, motors, pumps and switchgear had been either destroyed or severely damaged. Mercifully, the snow had already covered the two mounds that lay side by side before the mangled remains of a switchboard. Dermott looked slowly around with a face again as bleak as the scene that lay before him.

'Damage evenly spread,' he said, 'so it couldn't have come from one central blast. Half-a-dozen charges, more likely.' He turned to Poulson, the charge-hand, a black-bearded man with bitter eyes. 'How many explosions did you hear?'

'Just the one, I think. We really can't be sure. If there were more after the first one, our eardrums were sure in no condition to register them. But we're agreed that one was all we heard.'

'Triggered electrically, by radio or, if they used fulminate of mercury, by sympathetic detonation. Experts, obviously.' He looked at the two shapeless, snow-covered mounds. 'But not so expert in other ways. Why have those two men been left here?'

'Orders.'

'Whose orders?'

'Head Office. Not to be moved until the post-mortems have been carried out.'

'Rubbish! You can't do a post-mortem on a frozen body.'

Dermott stooped, began to clear away the snow from the nearest of the mounds, then looked up in surprise as a heavy hand clamped on his left shoulder.

'You deaf or something, mister?' Poulson didn't sound truculent, just annoyed. 'I'm in charge here.'

'You were. Donald?'

'Sure.' Mackenzie eased Poulson's hand away and said: 'Let's go talk to the head officeman, Black, and hear what he has to say about obstructing murder investigations.'

'That won't be necessary, Mr Mackenzie,' Bronowski said. He nodded to Poulson. 'John's upset. Wouldn't you be?'

Poulson hesitated briefly, turned and left the pump room. Dermott had most of the snow cleared away when he felt a light touch on his shoulder: it was Poulson again, proffering him, of all things, a long-handled clothes brush. Dermott took it, smiled his thanks and delicately brushed away the remaining snow.

The dreadfully charred skull of the dead man was barely recognisable as that of a human being, but the cause of the round hole above the eyeless left socket was unmistakable. With Mackenzie's help—the corpse was frozen solid—he lifted the body and peered at the back of the skull. The skin was unbroken.

'Bullet's lodged in the head,' Dermott said. 'Rifling marks on it should be of interest to the police ballistics department.'

'There's that,' Bronowski said. 'After all, Alaska only covers just over half a million square miles. Optimism is not my long suit.'

'Agreed.' They lowered the body to the ground and Dermott tried to unzip the shredded green parka, but it, too, was frozen. There was a slight crackling of ice as he eased the jacket away from the shirt beneath and peered into the gap between the two layers of clothing. He could see some documents, including a buff-coloured envelope, tucked away in the inside right pocket. By sliding his hand in flat he tried to extract them with his fore and middle fingers, but because he could achieve so little purchase, and because they seemed frozen—not only together but also to the side of the pocket—they proved impossible to move. Dermott straightened to an upright kneeling position, looked at the dead man thoughtfully, then up at Bronowski.

'Could we have the two bodies moved to some place where they can be thawed out a bit? I can't examine them in this state, nor by the same token, can the doctors carry out their post-mortems.'

'John?' Bronowski looked at Poulson, who nodded, albeit with some reluctance.

'Another thing,' Dermott said. 'What's the quickest way of clearing away the snow here from the floor and machinery?'

'Canvas covers and a couple of hot air blowers. No time at all. Want me to fix it now? And the two men?'

'Please. Then there's a question or two I'd like to ask. In your living quarters, perhaps?'

'Straight across. Be with you in a few minutes.'

Outside, on their way, Mackenzie said: 'Your hound-dog instincts have been aroused. What gives?'

'Dead man back there. Index finger on his right hand is broken.'

'That all? Wouldn't be surprised if half the bones in his body are broken.'

'Could be. But this bone appears to have been broken in a rather peculiar fashion. Be able to tell better, later.'

Bronowski and Poulson joined them round the table of the comfortable kitchen living quarters. Poulson said: 'Okay, fixed. Snow in the pump-room should be gone in fifteen minutes. About the two engineers—well, I wouldn't know.'

'Considerably longer,' Dermott said. 'Thanks. Now, then. Bronowski, Mackenzie and myself think it likely that the murderers were employees of the trans-Alaskan pipeline. What would you think of that?'

Poulson glanced enquiringly at Bronowski, found no inspiration there, looked away and pondered. 'It figures,' he said at last. 'The only living souls for ten thousand square miles around here—a hundred thousand as far as I know—are employed by the pipeline. More than that, while any mad bomber could have blown up the pump station, it took an oilman to know where to locate and destroy the bypass control valve.'

'We also theorise that the engineers—what were their names, by the way?'

'Johnson and Johnson. Brothers.'

'We think that the bombers gave themselves away in one fashion or another, that the Johnsons recognised them and had to be silenced for keeps. But you and your men didn't recognise them. That's for sure?'

'For sure.' Poulson smiled without much humour. 'If what you suppose is correct, it's just as well for us that we didn't. But then it's not surprising that we didn't. Don't forget that up here in Number Four we're no better than hermits living on a desert island. The only time we see anybody is when we go on leave every few weeks. Travelling maintenance engineers like the Johnsons—or, come to that, Mr Bronowski here—see ten times as many people as we do, and so are likely to recognise ten times as many people. Which makes your idea that it was an inside job all the more likely.'

'You and your men are certain there wasn't the remotest peculiarity about them, either in speech or dress, that struck a chord?'

'You're flogging a dead horse, Dermott.'

'I suppose. There's a possibility that those saboteurs came by helicopter.'

'Damned if I can see how else they could have come. Mr Bronowski here thought he saw skid marks. I wasn't sure one way or another. It was a bad night for being sure of anything: dark, with a strong wind and drifting snow. Circumstances like that, you can imagine almost anything.'

'You didn't *hear* this helicopter approaching—or imagine you heard it?'

'We heard nothing. Don't forget we were all asleep and—'

'I thought you mounted a radar watch?'

'In a fashion. Any errant bleep triggers off an alarm. But we don't sit with our eyes glued to the screen night and day. Then, because of the extremely heavy insulation, it's difficult for any sound to penetrate from outside. The generator running next door doesn't help much either. Finally, of course, the wind was blowing—as it still is—almost directly from the north and would have carried away the sound of any craft approaching from the opposite direction. I know that a helicopter is one of the most rackety bits of machinery in existence but —even though we were wide awake then, we didn't hear Mr Bronowski's chopper coming in from the south. Sorry, that's all I can tell you.'

'How long will it take to repair the pump-room?'

'A few days, a week. I'm not sure. We'll need new engines, switchgear, pipelines, a mobile crane and a bulldozer. All those we already have at Prudhoe except the engines, and I expect a Herc will fly those in this evening. Then a chopper or two can fly the stuff out here. The repair crews will be on the job in the morning.'

'So a week before the oil starts flowing again?'

'No, no: tomorrow, with luck. The bypass control valve is not a major repair job; parts replacement mainly.'

Dermott said: 'You might look at all this as just a minor disruption?'

'Technically, yes. The ghosts of the Johnson brothers might see it differently. Want to look at the pump-room now? Most of the stuff should have melted by this time.'

The snow in the pump-room had gone, and the atmosphere was warm and humid. Without the protective white covering, the scene was more repellent than before, the extent of the devastation more clearly and dishearteningly evident, and the stench of oil and charring more pungent and penetrating. Each with a powerful hand-torch to lighten the shadows cast by the arc-lamps, Dermott, Mackenzie and Bronowski embarked on a search of every square inch of the floors and walls.

After ten minutes Poulson said curiously: 'What *are* you looking for?'

'I'll let you know when I find it,' Dermott said. 'Meantime I haven't a clue.'

'In that case, can I join in the search?'

'Sure. Don't touch or turn anything over. The F.B.I. wouldn't like it.'

Ten minutes later, Dermott straightened and switched off his torch. 'That's it, then, gentlemen. If you've found no more than I have, among the four of us we've found nothing. Looks as if fire or blasts have wiped the platter clean. Let's have a look at the Johnson brothers. They should be in a fairly examinable state by now.'

They were. Dermott moved first to the man he'd looked at in the pump-room. This time the zip on the green parka unfastened easily. The blast effect that had shredded the parka had not penetrated it, for the plaid shirt beneath bore no signs of damage. Dermott removed some paper, cards and envelopes from the inside right pocket of the jacket, leafed through and replaced them. He then lifted both charred wrists, examined them and the hands in an apparently cursory fashion and lowered them again. He repeated the process with the other victim, then rose to his feet. Poulson bent a quizzical eye on him.

'That's the way a detective examines a murdered man?'

'I don't suppose it is. But then, I'm not a detective.' He turned to Bronowski. 'You all through?'

'If you are.' Sam Bronowski led the way to the helicopter, Dermott and Mackenzie following through the thinly-driving snow that reduced visibility to a few yards. It was intensely cold.

'Clues,' Mackenzie said into Dermott's ear, not from any wish for privacy but simply to make himself heard. 'Man can't move around without tripping over them.'

'None in the pump-room, that's sure. Place had been pretty comprehensively quartered before we ever got there. Almost certainly before the snow had started to cover anything.'

'What do you mean?'

'The old fine tooth-comb is what I mean.'

'Poulson and his men?'

'And/or. Who else?'

'Perhaps there was nothing to find?'

Dermott said—or rather shouted: 'That dead man's forefinger had been deliberately broken. Bent in at forty-five degrees towards the thumb. Never seen anything like it before.'

'Freak accident.'

'"Odd" is better. Something else odd, too. When I searched him first there was a buff envelope in his inner pocket. I was unable to get it out.'

'But you were when you unzipped it later?'

'No. It was gone.'

'"And/or" at work, you think?'

'So it seems.'

'All very curious,' Mackenzie said.

* * *

Jim Brady was of the same opinion. After reporting the results of their investigation, Dermott and Mackenzie had retired with him to the room he'd been allocated for the night.

Brady said: 'Why didn't you mention those things to Black and Finlayson? Those are hard facts—an oddly broken finger, a missing envelope?'

'Hard facts? There's only my word for it. I've no idea what was in the envelope anyway, and although I'd say the forefinger had been deliberately broken, I'm no osteologist.'

'But no harm in mentioning those things, surely?'

'Bronowski and Houston were there too.'

'You really don't trust anyone, do you, George?' Brady's tone was admiring, not reproachful.

'As you never fail to remind people, sir, you taught me yourself.'

'True, true,' Brady said complacently. 'Very well, then, have them up. I'll do my Olympian act while you ply them with questions and strong drink.'

Dermott spoke on the phone and within a minute Bronowski and Houston had knocked, entered and taken seats.

'Kind, gentlemen, kind.' Brady was at his most avuncular. 'Long day, I know, and you must be damnably tired. But we're babes in the wood up here. We're not only *short* of necessary information, we're totally devoid of it, and we believe you two gentlemen are those best equipped to supply us with that information. But I forget myself, gentlemen. I suggest a pre-inquisitional restorative.'

Mackenzie said: 'What Mr Brady means is a drink.'

'That's what I said. You gentlemen like Scotch?'

'Off-duty, yes. But you know the company regulations, sir, and how strictly Mr Finlayson interprets those.'

'Strict? I am iron-clad in the interpretation of my own regulations.' The wave of Brady's arm was, indeed, Olympian. 'You are off-duty. Off regular duty, anyhow. George, refreshments. Mr Dermott will ask the questions, alternating, I do not doubt, with Mr Mackenzie. You gentlemen, if you will be so kind, will fill in the gaps in our knowledge.'

He took his daiquiri from Dermott, savoured it, laid down his glass, relaxed in his chair and steepled his hands under his chin. 'I shall but listen and evaluate.' Nobody was left with any doubt as to which was the most demanding task of the three. 'Health, gentlemen.'

Bronowski lifted his own glass, which he had accepted with no great show of reluctance. 'And confusion to our enemies.'

Dermott said: 'That's precisely the point. The enemy aren't confused, we are. The taking out of Pump Station Four is only the opening skirmish in what promises to be bloody battle. They—the enemy—know where they're going to hit again. We have not the vaguest idea. But you must have—by the very nature of your job you must be more aware of the points most vulnerable to attack than anyone else between Prudhoe Bay and Valdez. Take off your security hats and put on those of the enemy. Where would *you* strike next?'

'Jesus!' Bronowski fortified himself with some of Brady's malt. 'That's more than a sixty-four-dollar question. It's an 800-mile question—and every damned mile is virtually a sitting target.'

'The boss is right,' Tim Houston said. 'If we sit here and drink your whisky while pretending to help, we're only abusing your hospitality. There's nothing we or anyone else can do to help. A combat-ready division of the U.S. Army would be about as useful as a gaggle of girl guides. The task is impossible and the line indefensible.'

Mackenzie said: 'Well, George, at least we're operating on a bigger scale than with the tar-sands boys in Athabasca. There they said a battalion wouldn't be big enough to guard their installation. Now it's a division.' Mackenzie turned to Bronowski. 'Let's switch hats with the enemy. Where *wouldn't* you strike next?'

Bronowski said: 'Well, I wouldn't strike at any of the pump

stations again on the assumption that, until this matter is cleared up, they will be heavily guarded. I'd have been sorely tempted to go for Pump Station Ten at the Isabel Pass in the Alaska Range, or No. 12 at the Thompson Pass in the Chugach Mountains. All pump stations are vital of course, but some are more vital than others, and those are No. 10 and No. 12—along with No. 4 here.' He considered briefly. 'Or maybe I *would* go for them ... I mean, maybe you'd be so damned certain that I wouldn't hit again in the same place that you wouldn't much bother—'

Dermott held up his hand. 'Start in on the double-guessing, and we're up all night. On with the hazards—the low priority ones, I mean.'

'I wouldn't go for the two master operations control centres at Prudhoe Bay. They could be taken out easily enough and, sure, they'd stop all production from the wells immediately, but not for long. It's no secret that contingency plans for by-passing the centres are already in hand. Repairs wouldn't take all that long. In any event, security will be now tightened to the extent that the game wouldn't be worth the candle. So we can be pretty certain that there will be no attempt made to sabotage the oil supply before it enters the pipeline. Same goes for when it leaves the pipe at Valdez. Maximum damage there could be inflicted at the oil movements control centre, where the pipeline controller can monitor and control the flow of oil all the way from Prudhoe to Valdez, and the terminal con-troller—he's in the same room, actually—controls practically everything that moves in the terminal itself. Both of those, in turn, are dependent on what's called the backbone supervisory system computer. Knock out any of those three and you're in dead trouble. But they're pretty secure as they are: from now on, they'll be virtually impregnable. Again, not worth it.'

Dermott said: 'How about the storage tanks?'

'Well, now. If one or two of them were attacked or ruptured —it would be impossible to get them all at once—the contain-ment dykes would take care of the spillage. Fire would be another thing, but even then the snow would have a blanketing effect—we may only have an annual dusting of snow up here, but down there they have over three hundred inches. Anyway, the tank farms are the most open and easily guarded complex on the entire pipeline. There's no way you can really get at them without bombing the area: not very likely, one would think.'

'What about the tanker terminals?'

'Again easily guarded. I hardly think they're likely to run to underwater demolition squads. Even if they did they couldn't do much damage, and that would be easily repaired.'

'The tankers themselves?'

'Sink a dozen and there's always a thirteenth. No way you can interrupt the flow of oil by hitting the tankers.'

'The Valdez Narrows?'

'Block them?' Dermott nodded and Bronowski shook his head. 'The Narrows aren't as narrow as they look on a small-scale chart. Three thousand feet—that's the minimum channel width—between the Middle Rock and the east shore. You'd have to sink an awful lot of vessels to block the channel.'

'So we cross off the unlikely targets. Where does that leave us?'

'It leaves us with eight hundred miles.' Bronowski shifted.

'The air temperature is the over-riding factor,' Houston said. 'No saboteur worth his salt would consider wrecking anything except the pipeline itself. This time of the year any attack has to be in the open air.'

'Why?'

'This is only early February remember, and to all intents we're still in the depth of winter. As often as not the temperature is well on the wrong side of thirty below, and in these parts thirty below is the crucial figure. Rupture the pipeline at, say, thirty-five below, and it stays ruptured. Repair is virtually impossible. Men can work, although well below their norm, but unfortunately the metal they may try to repair or the machine tools they use to make the repairs won't co-operate with them. At extreme temperatures, profound molecular changes occur in metal and it becomes unworkable. Given the right—or wrong—conditions, a tap on an iron rod will shatter it like glass.'

Brady said: 'You mean, all I need is a hammer and a few taps on the pipeline—'

Houston was patient. 'Not quite. What with the heat of the oil inside and the insulation lagging outside, the steel of the pipeline is always warm and malleable. It's the repair tools that would fracture.'

Dermott said: 'But surely it would be possible to erect canvas or tarpaulin covers over the fracture and bring the temperature up to workable levels by using hot-air blowers? You know, the way Poulson did at Station Four?'

'Of course. Which is why I wouldn't attack the pipeline directly. I'd attack the structures that support the pipeline, those that are already frozen solid at air temperature and would require days, perhaps weeks, to bring up to a working temperature.'

'Structures?'

'Indeed. The terrain between Prudhoe and Valdez is desperately uneven and traversed with innumerable water-courses which have to be forded or spanned in one way or another. There are over six hundred streams and rivers along the run. The 650-foot free-span suspension bridge over the Tazlina River would make a dolly of a target. Even better would be the 1,200-foot span—a similar type of construction—over the Tanana River. But one doesn't even have to operate on such a grandiose scale, and I, personally, would prefer not to.' He looked at Bronowski. 'Wouldn't you agree?'

'Completely. Operate on a much more moderate and undramatic scale but one equally effective. I'd go for the V.S.M.s every time.'

Dermott said: 'V.S.M.s?'

'Vertical support members. Roughly half the length of the pipeline is above ground and lies on a horizontal cradle or saddle supported by vertical metal posts. That makes for a fair number of targets—78,000 of them, to be precise. They would be a snip to take out—wrap-round beehive plastic explosives which would need all of a minute to fix in position. Take out twenty of those, and the line would collapse under its own weight and the weight of the oil inside it. Take weeks to repair it.'

'They could still use those hot-air canvas shelters.'

'A hell of a lot of help that would be,' Bronowski said, 'if they couldn't bring up the cranes and crawler equipment to effect the repairs. Anyway, there are places where, at this time of year, it just couldn't be done. There is, for instance, one particularly vulnerable stretch which gave the designers headaches, the builders sleepless nights and security nightmares. This steep and dangerous stretch is between Pump Station Five and the summit of Atigun Pass, which is between four and five thousand feet high.'

Houston said: '4,775 feet.'

'4,775 feet. In a run of a hundred miles from the pass the pipe comes down to 1,200 feet, which is quite a drop.'

'With a corresponding amount of built-up pressure?'

'That's not the problem. In the event of a break in the line a special computer linkage between Four and Five will automatically shut down the pumps in Four and close every remote valve between the stations. The fail-safe procedures are highly sophisticated, and they work. At the very worst the spillage could be restricted to 50,000 barrels. But the point is, in winter the line couldn't be repaired.'

Brady coughed apologetically and descended from his Olympian heights.

'So a break in this particular section, about now, could immobilise the line for weeks on end?'

'No question.'

'Then forget it.'

'Mr Brady?'

'The burdens I have to bear alone,' Brady sighed. 'Let me have men about me who can think. I begin to understand why I am what I am. I find it extraordinary that the construction company never carried out any tests to discover what happens to the viscosity of oil in low temperatures. Why didn't they seal off a couple of hundred feet of experimental pipe with oil inside it and see how long it would take before it gummed up to the extent that it would cease to flow?'

'Never occurred to them, I suppose,' Bronowski said. 'An eventuality that would never arise.'

'It has arisen. An estimate of three weeks has been bandied about. Based on scientific calculations, one assumes?'

Bronowski said: 'I wouldn't know. Not my field. Maybe Mr

75

Black or Mr Finlayson would know.'

'Mr Black knows nothing about oil, and I doubt whether Mr Finlayson or any other professional oilman on the line has anything but the vaguest idea. Could be ten days. Could be thirty. You take my point, George?'

'Yes. Blackmail, threats, extortion, some positive and very material advantages to be gained. Interruption is one thing, cessation another. They require a lever, a bargaining counter. Close down the line completely, and the oil companies would laugh at their threats, for then they would have nothing to lose. The bargaining arm would have gone. The kidnapper can't very well hold a kidnapee for ransom if it's known that the kidnapee is dead.'

'I question if I could have put it better myself,' Brady said. He had about him an air of magnanimous self-satisfaction. 'We are, clearly, not dealing with clowns. Our friends would have taken such imponderables into account and would err on the side of caution. You are with me, Mr Bronowski?'

'I am now. But when I was talking about hazards, I wasn't taking that side of it into account.'

'I know you weren't. Nobody was. Well, I think that will do, gentlemen. We appear to have established two things. It is unlikely that any attack will be carried out on any major installation—that is Prudhoe, Valdez or the intervening twelve major pump stations. It is further unlikely that any attack will be carried out in regions so inaccessible that repairs may be impossible for weeks on end.

'So we're left with the likelihood that any further sabotage will take the form of attacks on accessible stretches of V.S.M.s or the taking out of minor bridges—the possibility of destroying the Tazlina or Tanana bridges is remote, as those could well take weeks to repair. We may not have come up with too much, but at least we have clarified matters and established some sort of system of priorities.'

Not without difficulty Brady heaved himself to his feet to indicate that the interview was over. 'Thank you, gentlemen, both for your time and information. I'll see you in the morning —at, of course, a reasonably Christian hour.'

The door closed behind Bronowski and Houston. Brady

asked: 'Well, what did you make of that?'

Dermott said: 'As you said, just a limitation of possibilities, which, unfortunately, still remain practically limitless. Three things I'd like to do. First, I'd like the F.B.I. or whoever to carry out a rigorous investigation into the pasts of Poulson and his pals at Pump Station Four.'

'You have reason to suspect them?'

'Not really. But I've an odd feeling: something is wrong at Number Four. Don shares my feeling, but there's nothing we can put a finger on except that buff envelope that went missing from the dead engineer's pocket. Even with that I'm beginning to question whether my eyes or imagination were playing tricks on me: the lighting was damned harsh, and I could have got my colours wrong. No matter—as you'd be the first to agree, every pipeline employee is a suspect until his innocence is established.'

'You bet. You said Poulson and Bronowski seemed on pretty cordial terms?'

'Bronowski is the sort of character who seems on pretty cordial terms with everyone. If you're suggesting what I think you are I might mention that according to Finlayson there have been three security checks carried out on Bronowski.'

'And passed with flying colours, no doubt. What does Finlayson know about security checks and how to evaluate them? Has he any guarantee that none of those three professedly unbiased investigators was not, in fact, a bosom friend of Bronowski? Now, *I* have a very good and very discreet friend in New York. As you say yourself, every pipeline operator is as guilty as hell until proved otherwise.'

'I didn't quite say that.'

'Hair-splitting. The second thing?'

'I'd like a medical opinion, preferably that of a doctor with some osteopathic knowledge, on how the dead engineer's finger came to be broken.'

'How can that help?'

'How should I know?' Dermott sounded almost irritable. 'God knows, Jim, you've emphasised often enough never to overlook anything that seems odd.'

77

'True, true,' Brady said pacifically. 'There was a third matter?'

'Let's find out how the fingerprint boys in Anchorage are getting on with that telephone booth affair. Three tiny things, I know, but it's all we have to go on.'

'Four. There's also Bronowski. And now?'

The telephone rang. Brady picked it up, listened briefly, scowled and handed the phone over to Dermott. 'For you.' Dermott lifted an eyebrow. 'It's that damnable code again.'

Dermott gave him an old-fashioned look, put the phone to his ear, reached for a pad and started to make notes. After barely a minute he hung up and said: "And now? That was your last question, wasn't it?'

'What? Yes. So?'

'And now it's back to the old jet and heigh-ho for Canada.'

Dermott gave Brady an encouraging smile. 'Should be all right, sir. Still plenty of daiquiri in your airborne bar.'

'What the devil is that meant to mean?'

'Just this, sir.' Dermott's smile had gone. 'You will recall our three brilliant minds sitting around in Sanmobil's office and coming to the unanimous conclusion that there were six points vulnerable to attack—the draglines, the bucketwheels, the reclaimers' bridges, the separator plates, the radial stackers and, above all, the conveyor belting? Some joker up there obviously didn't see it our way at all. He's taken out the main processing plant.'

6

Four hours later the Brady Enterprises team stood shivering in Sanmobil's sabotaged processing plant at Athabasca. Brady himself was enveloped in his usual cocoon of coats and scarves, his temper not improved by the fact that the flight from Alaska had deprived him of dinner.

'How did it *happen*?' he repeated. 'Here we have an easily-patrolled area, brilliantly lit, as you pointed out yourself, and staffed with 100 per cent—I beg your pardon, 98 per cent—loyal and patriotic Canadians.' He peered through a large hole that had been blown in a cylindrical container. 'How can such things be?'

'I don't think that's quite fair, Mr Brady.' Bill Reynolds, the fair-haired and ruddy-faced operations manager, spoke up for his colleague Terry Brinckman, the security chief at whom Brady's remarks had been directed. 'Terry had only eight men on duty last night—and that was his second shift of the day. In other words, he himself had been continuously on duty for fifteen hours when this incident occurred. You can see how hard he was trying.'

Brady did not nod in assent. Reynolds went on:

'You remember we had all agreed on the priorities, the areas most liable to attack. Those were the places that Terry and his men were doing their best to protect—which didn't leave any men over for patrolling the plant itself. You will recall, Mr Brady, that you were in complete agreement. You also said Terry had nothing to reproach himself with. If we're going to apportion blame, let's not forget ourselves.'

'Nobody's blaming anybody, Mr Reynolds. How extensive is the damage?'

'Enough. Terry and I figure that these guys let off three charges here—that's the gas oil hydrotreater—and the same number next door at the naphtha hydrotreater. In fact we've been extremely lucky—we could have had gas explosions and fuel fires. We had none. As it is, damage is comparatively slight. We should be on stream again in forty-eight hours.'

'Meantime, everything is shut down?'

'Not the draglines. But the rest is. The radial stackers are full.'

'One of the plant operatives, you think?'

Brinckman said: 'I'm afraid we're sure. It's a big plant but it takes surprisingly few people to operate it, and everybody on a shift knows everybody else. A stranger would have been spotted at once. Besides, we *know* it was an inside job—six thirty-ounce explosive charges were taken from the blasting shed last night.'

'Blasting shed?'

Reynolds said: 'We use explosives to break up large chunks of tar sand that have become too tightly bound together. But we've only got small charges.'

'Big enough, it would seem. The blasting shed is normally kept locked?'

'Double-locked.'

'Somebody forced the door?'

'Nobody forced anything. That's why Brinckman told you we're sure it was an inside job. Somebody used keys.'

'Who normally holds the keys?' Dermott asked.

Reynolds said: 'There are three sets. I hold one, Brinckman has two.'

'Why two?'

'One I keep permanently,' Brinckman explained. 'The other goes to the security charge-hand for the night-shift, who passes it on to the person in charge of the morning and afternoon shifts.'

'Who are those other security shift charge-hands?'

Brinckman said: 'My No. 2, Jorgensen—this is his shift, really—and Napier. I don't think that any of the three of us is much given to stealing explosives, Mr Dermott.'

'Not unless you're certifiable. Now, it seems unlikely anyone would risk abstracting keys and having copies made. Not only would they be too likely to be missed, but there's also more than a fair chance that we could trace the key-cutter and so the thief.'

'There could be illegal key-cutters.'

'I still doubt the keys would have been taken. Much more likely someone took an impression: that would need seconds only. And that's where the illegal side would come in—no straight key-cutter would touch an impression. How easy would it be for anyone to get hold of the keys, even briefly?'

Brinckman said: 'About Jorgensen's and Napier's I wouldn't know. I clip mine to my belt.'

Mackenzie said: 'Everybody's got to sleep.'

'So?'

'You take your belt off then, don't you?'

'Sure.' Brinckman shrugged. 'And if you're going to ask me next if I'm a heavy sleeper, well, yes, I am. And if you're going to ask me if it would have been possible for anyone to sneak into my room while I was asleep, borrow my key for a couple of minutes and return it unseen, well, yes that would have been perfectly possible too.'

'This,' Brady said, 'is not going to take us very far. Sticky-fingered characters with an affinity for keys are legion. Would there have been *any* security man in this area tonight?'

'Jorgensen would know,' Brinckman said. 'Shall I get him?'

'Won't he be out patrolling sixteen miles of conveyor belting or something?'

'He's in the canteen.'

'But surely he's in charge, on duty?'

'In charge of what, Mr Brady? There are four men keeping an eye on the four draglines. The rest of the plant is closed down. We think it unlikely that this bomber will strike again tonight.'

'Not much is unlikely.'

'Bring him along to my office,' Reynolds said. Brinckman left. 'I think you'll find it warmer and more comfortable there, Mr Brady.'

They followed Reynolds to the office block, through an external room where a bright-eyed and pretty young woman at the desk gave them a charming smile, and on into Reynolds's office where Brady began divesting himself of several outer layers of clothing even before Reynolds had the door closed. Reynolds took his chair behind the desk while Brady sunk wearily into the only armchair in the room.

Reynolds said: 'Sorry to drag you all over the north-west like this. No sleep, no food, jet lags, all very upsetting. In the circumstances I feel entitled to bend company regulations. Come to think of it, I'm the only person in Sanmobil who can. A refreshment would be in order?'

'Ha!' Brady pondered. 'Early in the morning. Not only no dinner but no breakfast either.' A hopeful look crept into his eye. 'Daiquiri?'

'But I thought you always—'

'We had an unfortunate experience over the Yukon,' Dermott said. 'We ran out.'

Brady scowled. Reynolds smiled. 'No daiquiris here. But a really excellent twelve-year-old malt.' A few seconds later Brady lowered his half-tumbler and nodded appreciatively.

'A close second. Now you two'—this to Dermott and Mackenzie—'I've done all the work so far.'

'Yes, sir.' Not even the shadow of a smile touched Mackenzie's face. 'Three questions, if I may. Who suggested checking up on the amount of explosives in the blasting shed?'

'Nobody. Terry Brinckman did it off his own bat. We have a meticulous checking system and an easy one. The tally sheet's kept up to date twice a day. We just count the numbers of each particular type of explosive, subtract that number from the latest entry on the tally sheet, and that's the number that's been issued that day. Or stolen, as the case may be.'

'Well, that's certainly a mark in favour of your security chief.'

'You have reservations about him?'

'Good heavens no. Why on earth should I? Number two —where do you hang up your keys at night?'

'I don't.' He nodded towards a massive safe in a corner. 'Kept there day and night.'

'Ah! In that case I'll have to rephrase what was going to be my third question. You are the only person with a key to that safe?'

'There's one more key. Corinne has it.'

'Ah. That lovely lassie in the outer office?'

'That, as you say, lovely lassie in the outer office is my secretary.'

'And why does *she* have a key?'

'Various reasons. All big companies, as you must know, have their codes. We're no exception. Code books are kept there. Corinne's my coding expert. Also, I can't be here all the time. Under-managers, accountants, our legal people and the security chief all have access to the safe. I can assure you the safe contains items of vastly more importance than the keys to the blasting shed. Nothing has ever gone missing yet.'

'People just walk in, help themselves and walk out?'

Reynolds lifted his eyebrows and looked hard at Mackenzie. 'Not quite. We are security conscious to a degree. They have to sign in, show Corinne what they've taken and sign out again.'

'A couple of keys in a trouser pocket?'

'Of course she doesn't search them. There has to be a certain amount of trust at executive levels.'

'Yes. Could we have her in, do you think?'

Reynolds spoke into the box on his desk. Corinne entered looking good standing up, in her khaki cord Levi's and nicely disordered plaid shirt, a person with a smile for everyone. Reynolds said: 'You know who those gentlemen are, Corinne?'

'Yes, sir. I think everybody does.'

'I think Mr Mackenzie here would like to ask you some questions.'

'Sir?'

'How long have you been with Mr Reynolds?'

'Just over two years.'

'Before that?'

'I came straight from secretarial school.'

'You have a pretty sensitive and responsible position here?'

She smiled again, but this time a little uncertainly, as if unsure where the questions were leading. 'Mr Reynolds lists me as his confidential secretary.'

'May I ask how old you are?'

'Twenty-two.'

'You must be the youngest confidential secretary of any big corporation I've ever come across.'

This time she caught her lip and glanced at Reynolds, who was leaning back in his chair, hands clasped lazily behind his neck, with the air of a man who was almost enjoying himself. He smiled and said: 'Mr Mackenzie is an industrial sabotage investigator. He has a job to do and asking questions is part of that job. I know he's just made a statement, not asked a question, but it's one of those statements that expects comment.'

She turned back to Mackenzie, with a swing of her long chestnut hair. 'I suppose I've been pretty lucky at that.'

She spoke with marked coolness and Mackenzie felt it. 'None of my questions are directed against you, Corinne, okay? Now, you must know the executive level people pretty well?'

'I can hardly help it. They all come through me to get to Mr Reynolds.'

'Including those who have business with the safe there?'

'Of course. I know them all well.'

'All good friends, I take it?'

'Well.' She smiled, but the smile had an edge to it. 'Lots of them are much too senior to be my friends.'

'But on good terms, shall we say?'

'Oh, yes.' She smiled again. 'I don't think I've made any enemies.'

'Perish the thought!' This came from George Dermott, who took over the questioning on a brisker note. 'Any of the people using the safe ever give you trouble? Like trying to take away what they shouldn't?'

'Not often, and then it's only absentmindedness or because they haven't studied the classified list. And surely, Mr Dermott, if anyone wanted to get something past me they'd hide it in their clothing.'

Dermott nodded. 'That's true, Miss Delorme.' The girl was inspecting his rough-and-ready good looks with a spark of humour in her eyes, as if amused by his blunt approach. He caught the expression and, in his turn, watched her for a reflective moment. 'What do you think now?' he asked her. 'Do you think anyone might have smuggled something past you out of the safe?'

She looked him in the eye. 'They might,' she said, 'but I doubt it.'

'Could I have a list of the people who used the safe in the past four or five days?'

'Certainly.' She left and returned with a sheet which Dermott studied briefly.

'Good Lord! The safe appears to be the Mecca for half of Sanmobil. Twenty entries at least in the last four days.' He looked up at the girl. 'This is a carbon. May I keep it?'

'Of course.'

'Thank you.'

Corinne Delorme smiled at the room in general, but the blue eyes came back to Dermott before she went out.

'Charming indeed,' said Brady.

'Plenty of spunk,' Mackenzie said ruefully. 'She built a whole generation gap between you and me, George.' He frowned. 'What gave you the idea her name was Delorme?'

'There was a plaque on her desk: "Corinne Delorme", it said.' Mackenzie shook his head. 'Hawkeye Dermott,' he said.

The other men laughed. Some of the tension that had grown in the room during the questioning of the girl fell away again.

'Well. Anything more I can do for you?' Reynolds asked.

Dermott said: 'Yes, please. Could we have a list of the names of your security staff?'

Reynolds bent over the voice-box and spoke to Corinne. He had just finished when Brinckman arrived accompanied by a tall, red-haired man whom he introduced as Carl Jorgensen.

Dermott said: 'You were in charge of the night security shift, I understand. Were you around the sabotage area at all tonight?'

'Several times.'

'So often? I thought you would have been concentrating on what we regarded—mistakenly—as the more vulnerable areas.'

'I went round them a couple of times but by jeep only. But I had this funny feeling that we might have been guarding the wrong places. Don't ask me why.'

'Your funny feeling didn't turn out to be so funny after all. Anything off-beat, anything to arouse suspicion?'

'Nothing. I know everybody on the night shift and I know where they work Nobody there that shouldn't have been there, nobody in any place that he hadn't any right to be.'

'You've got a key to the blasting shed. Where do you keep it?'

'Terry Brinckman mentioned this. I have it only during my tour of duty and then I hand it over. I always carry it in the same button-down pocket on my shirt.'

'Could anybody get at it?'

'Nobody except a professional pick-pocket, and even then I'd know.'

The two security men left and Corinne came in with a sheet of paper. Reynolds said: 'That was quick.'

'Not really. They were typed out ages ago.'

Brady said to the girl: You must come and meet my daughter, Stella. I'm sure you'd get on. Both the same age. Stella is very like you, actually.'

'Thank you, Mr Brady. I think I'd like that.'

'I'll have her call you.'

When she had gone, Dermott said: 'What do you mean, like your daughter? I've never seen anyone less like Stella.'

'Dancing eyes, my boy, dancing eyes. One must learn to probe beneath the surface.' Brady heaved himself to his feet. 'The years creep on. Breakfast and bed. I'm through detecting for the day. It's tougher than capping fires.

*   *   *

Dermott drove the rented car back to the hotel, Mackenzie sitting beside him. Brady took his ease across the entire width of the back seat. He said: 'I'm afraid I wasn't quite levelling with Reynolds there. Breakfast, yes. But it'll be some hours before I—we—retire. I have come up with a plan.' He paused.

Dermott said courteously: 'We're listening.'

'I think I'll do some listening first. Why do you think I employ you?'

'That's a fair question,' Mackenzie said. 'Why?'

'To investigate, to detect, to think, to plot, to scheme, to plan.'

'All at once?' Mackenzie said.

Brady ignored him. 'I don't want to come up with a proposal and then, if it goes wrong, have to spend the rest of my days listening to your carping reproaches. I'd like you two to come up with an idea and then if it's a lemon we can all share the blame. Incidentally, Donald, I take it you have your bug-box with you?'

'The electronic eavesdropping locator-detector?'

'That's what I said.'

'Yes.'

'Splendid. Now, George, let's have your reading of the situation.'

'My reading of the situation is that for all the good we're doing we haven't a hope in hell of stopping the bad guys from doing exactly what they want and when they want. There is no way to forestall attacks on Sanmobil or the Alaska pipeline. They're calling the shots and we're the sitting ducks, if you'll pardon the mixing of the metaphors. They call the tune and we dance to it. They're active, we're passive. They're offensive, we're defensive. If we have any tactics, I'd say it's time we changed them.'

'Go on,' his leader urged him from behind.

'If that's meant to sound encouraging,' Dermott said, 'I don't know why. But how's this for a positive thought? Instead of letting them keep us off-balance, why don't we keep them off-balance? Instead of their harassing us, let us harass them.'

'Go on, go on,' the back seat exhorted.

'Let's attack them and put them on the defensive. Let *them* start worrying, instead of us.' He paused. 'I see things as through a glass darkly, but I say plant a light at the end of the tunnel. What we'll do is, we'll provoke them. Provoke a reaction. Provoke the hell out of them. We'll hang it on this one factor: our own pasts, our backgrounds, can be probed until the cows come home, and nothing will be turned up: but you can say *that* about how many people in a hundred?'

Dermott twisted his head briefly to locate a peculiar noise from the back of the car. Brady was actually rubbing his hands together. 'Well, Donald, what's your reading of it?'

'Simple enough when you see it,' Mackenzie said. 'All you have to do is to antagonise anywhere between sixty and eighty people to hell and back again. Investigate them as openly as possible. Deploy maximum indiscretion.'

Brady beamed. 'What sixty to eighty people do we investigate?'

'In Alaska *all* the security agents. Here, the security agents again, plus everybody who'd had access to Reynolds's safe in the past few days. Going to include Reynolds himself?'

'Good heavens, no.'

Mackenzie said inconsequentially: 'She *is* a lovely girl.'

Brady looked aloof. Mackenzie asked him: 'Do you really expect to find your panjandrum among that lot?'

'Panjandrum?'

'The prime mover. Mr Big. Messrs Big.'

'Not for a moment. But if there's a rotten apple in the barrel, he may well find him for us.'

Mackenzie said: 'Right. So we get all their names and past histories. Later on—sooner rather than later—we'll have the lot fingerprinted. Sure, they're going to stand on their civic rights and yell blue murder, and that will please you no end —refusal to co-operate will point the finger of suspicion at the refusee, if that's the word I want. Then you feed the information to your investigators in Houston, Washington and New York: cost no object, urgency desperate. Not that you'll care a damn whether the investigators come up with anything or not. All that matters is that the suspects get to hear such enquiries are under way. That's all the provocation they'll need.'

'What kind of reactions do we expect to provoke?' Dermott asked.

'Unpleasant ones, I should hope. For the villians, I mean.'

'The first thing I'd do,' Dermott told Brady, 'is send your family back to Houston. Jean and Stella could really become a liability. The scheme might rebound on you. Can't you see the word coming through: lay off, Brady, or something unpleasant's going to happen to your family? These people are playing for high stakes. They've killed once, they won't hesitate to kill again. They can't be hung twice.'

'Same thought occurred to me.' Mackenzie turned to face the back seat. 'Either get the girls right back home, or have the R.C.M.P. protect them.'

'Hell—I *need* them!' Brady sat forward with indignation. 'Number one, I have to be looked after. Number two, Stella's handling the Ekofisk business for me.'

'Ekofisk?' Dermott almost turned backwards. 'What's that?'

'Big fire in the North Sea, Norwegian half. Started after you'd come north. We have a team going in there today.'

'Well, okay,' Dermott gave way a little. 'So you have to keep in touch. But why not work through the locals? That red-head of Reynolds's—Corinne. She could field calls for you.'

'What happens when we go back to Alaska?'

'Use somebody up there. Finlayson's got a secretary—must have.'

'No substitute for the personal touch,' said Brady magisterially. He sank back in the seat as though the argument were over.

His two heavyweights turned forward again with an exchange of looks. Having been through all this a hundred times before, they knew that further pressure would be useless for the moment. Wherever he went, Brady maintained the fiction that his wife and daughter were part of his essential life-support system, and he kept them with him regardless of the expense. Or danger.

7

Not that Dermott and Mackenzie in the least minded having Jean and Stella around. Like mother, like daughter: whereas Jean was a strikingly handsome woman in her middle-forties, with that lovely, naturally blonde hair and intelligent grey eyes, Stella looked the spitting image of her mother, only younger, and even livelier, with, as her father was so fond of claiming, dancing eyes.

The men found Jean awaiting their return in the lounge bar of the Peter Pond Hotel. Tall and elegant, she advanced to meet them with her usual expression of tolerant, kindly amusement. This look, Dermott knew from experience, reflected her genuine feelings: an equable temperament was no small advantage for someone who had to spend her life humouring Jim Brady.

'Hi, honey!' He reached up slightly to kiss her on the forehead. 'Where's Stella?'

'In your room. She's got some messages for you—been pretty busy on the phone.'

'Excuse me, then, gentlemen. Maybe one of you would be so kind as to buy my wife a drink.'

He waddled off along the corridor, while Dermott and Mackenzie settled comfortably into the warmth of the bar. In marked contrast to her husband, Jean scarcely drank alcohol at all, and she sipped carefully at a pineapple juice while the two men addressed themselves to the Scotch. Nor did she try to talk shop in Brady's absence: instead, she chatted pleasantly about Fort McMurray and its modest midwinter pleasures until her husband returned.

When he came back, Stella was with him, swinging along with her easy, loose-hipped walk. Dermott—not normally given to flights of fancy—was suddenly struck by the absurd disparity between the two figures. Jesus, he thought to himself: a hippo and a gazelle. What a pair!

Scarcely had Brady subsided into an armchair, with an outsize glass of daiquiri in his podgy hand, than he made a slight sign to Dermott and Mackenzie, who muttered something and slipped off.

Brady seemed in buoyant form, and began to regale his family with an edited account of his movements around the far north. After a while Jean said doubtfully: 'It doesn't seem to me you've *accomplished* very much.'

Brady was unruffled. 'Ninety per cent of our business is cerebral, my dear. When we move into action, what happens is merely the almost mechanical and inevitable culmination of all the invisible hard work that's gone on before.' He tapped his head. 'The wise general doesn't fling his troops into battle without reconnoitring beforehand. We've been reconnoitring.'

Jean smiled. 'Let us know when you've identified the enemy.' Suddenly she became serious. 'It's a nasty business, isn't it?'

'Murder always is, my dear.'

'I don't like it, Jim. I don't like you being in it. Surely this is for the law. You've never come across murder before in your business.'

'So I run away?'

She looked at his ample frame and laughed: 'That's one thing you're not built for.'

'Run?' Stella said, mock-scornfully. 'Dad couldn't jog from here to the john!'

'Please!' Brady beamed. 'I trust no such haste will be necessary.'

'Where did Donald go?' Jean asked.

'Upstairs, doing a little job for me.'

Mackenzie was at that moment moving slowly round Brady's apartment with a calibrated metal box in one hand, a portable antenna in the other, and a pair of earphones on his head. He moved purposefully, a man who knew what he was about. He soon found what he was looking for.

When he came back to the bar he headed straight for Brady's family encampment.

'Two,' he reported.

'Two what, Uncle Donald?' Stella asked sweetly.

Mackenzie appealed to his boss. 'When are you going to start training this incorrigibly nosey daughter of yours?'

'I've stopped. Failed. Mother's job, anyway.' He jerked his head upwards. 'Got them all, did you?'

'Guess so.'

Dermott also reappeared to report.

'Ah, George,' Brady greeted him. 'How did it go?'

'Reynolds seems very co-operative. Unfortunately all records are stored at the head office in Edmonton. He says by the time they've been dug out and flown up here, it may be late this evening or even tomorrow morning.'

'What records?' Stella asked.

'Affairs of state,' Brady told her. 'Well, can't be helped. Anything else?'

'Naturally enough he's got no fingerprinting equipment.'

'Fix it after lunch.'

'He says he'll fix it himself—the police chief's a pal of his, apparently. Thinks the chief might be a bit shirty about the delay in reporting the crime.' He grinned across at Stella. 'And don't ask "what crime?" '

'No, sir, Mr Dermott, sir!' She wrinkled her upper lip in a fetching manner. 'I *never* ask questions! I'm just permitted to fetch and carry, mend and clean.'

Brady went on: 'Reynolds can always claim that at first he thought it was an industrial accident.'

'I understand the chief of police has 20-20 vision and intelligence to match.'

'Well—Reynolds'll have to handle it as best he can. What about Prudhoe Bay?'

'An hour's hold. They'll page me.'

'Fair enough.' Brady shifted his attention to Stella. 'We met an enchanting girl this morning—didn't we, George? Knock spots off you, any day. Wouldn't she, gentlemen?'

'Unquestionably,' said Mackenzie.

Stella looked at Dermott. 'Foul, aren't they?'

'Dead heat,' said Dermott. 'But she's very nice.'

'The manager's secretary,' Brady said. 'Corinne Delorme. I

thought maybe you'd like to meet her. She said she'd like to meet you. She must know all the night-clubs, discos and other iniquitous dens in Fort McMurray.'

Stella said: 'News for you, Dad. You've got to be talking about another town. I don't know what this place is like in summer, but whatever it is, it's a dead city in mid-winter. You might have warned us that this is an *Arctic* town.'

'Lovely choice of phrase. Wonderful sense of geography. That's education for you,' Brady said to no-one in particular. 'Maybe you should have stayed in Houston.'

Stella looked at her mother. 'Did you hear what I just heard, Mummy?' she asked with a scornful shake of the head at her father which brought the pale blonde hair swinging round her face.

Jean smiled. 'I heard. Sooner or later, my dear, you have to face up to the fact that your father is no more and no less than a fearful old hypocrite.'

'But he dragged us up here, kicking and screaming against our will, and now ...' Remarkably, words failed her.

As much as it was possible for so rubicund a face to register an expression, Brady's was registering unhappiness. 'Well, now you've found out you don't like it, maybe you'd rather get back down to Houston.' A note of wistfulness crept into his voice. 'It'll be nearly seventy degrees back there now.'

Silence descended. Brady looked at Dermott and Dermott looked at him. Jean Brady looked at both of them. 'Something goes on that I don't understand,' she said. Brady dropped his eyes, so she switched her attention to Dermott. 'George?'

'Yes, ma'am?'

'George!' He looked at her. 'And don't call me "ma'am".'

'No, Jean.' He sighed and spoke with some feeling. 'The boss of Brady Enterprises is not only a fearful old hypocrite: he's a fearful old coward as well. What he wants, in the good old fashioned Western phrase, is that you should get out of town.'

'Why? What on earth have we done?'

Dermott looked hopefully at Mackenzie, who said: 'You've done nothing. He has—or is about to.' Mackenzie shook his head at Dermott. 'This is difficult,' he said.

Dermott explained: 'We've decided on a course of action to flush the ungodly into the open, make them show their hand. Don and I have this unpleasant feeling that their reaction may be directed against Brady Enterprises in general and its boss in particular. The reaction may be violent—these people don't play by any rules but their own. We don't think they'd go for Jim himself. It's well known that he can't be intimidated. But what's equally well known is what he thinks of his own family. If they got you or Stella, or both of you, they might figure they could force him to pull out.'

Jean reached out to take Stella's hand. 'But this must be nonsense,' she said. 'Drama. Things like that don't happen any more. Don, I appeal to you ...' She looked anxiously at her daughter, gave her hand a little shake and released it.

Mackenzie was dogged. 'Don't appeal to me, Jean. When they snip off your finger with the wedding ring on it, will you still be saying things like that don't happen any more?' She looked hurt. 'Sorry if I sound brutal, but things like that have never stopped happening. It may not come to anything so bad: I'm looking on the blackest possible side. But that's the only sensible way to look. We've got to find a safe place for you and the girl. How can Jim operate at his best if you're on his mind?'

'He's right,' muttered Brady. 'Go pack your bags, please.'

During Mackenzie's speech Stella had sat with her hands clasped together on her lap, like a schoolgirl, listening gravely. Now she said: 'I can't do that, Dad.'

'Why not?'

'Who's going to make your daiquiris for you?'

Her mother cut in sharply. 'There's a little more to this than the damned daiquiris. If we left, who's going to be number one target?'

'Dad,' said Stella flatly. She glowered at Dermott. 'You know that, George.'

'I do,' he answered mildly. 'But Donald and I are pretty good at looking after people.'

'That would be just fine, wouldn't it?' She threw herself back in her chair, hazel eyes blazing. 'All three of you shot or blown up or something.'

'Getting upset isn't going to help,' said Jean soothingly.

94

'Logic will, though.' She transferred her attention to Brady. 'If we went, you'd still be worried stiff about us, and we'd be worried stiff about you. So where would that get us?'

Brady said nothing, and she went on: 'But there's only one point that really matters. Not only will I not run away from my husband. I'll be damned if Jean Brady will run, period.'

Stella said: 'And *I'll* be damned if Stella Brady runs either. Who's gonna maintain communications, for one thing? You know how long I spent on the phone today—to England and all that? *Four hours.*' She stood up decisively. 'Another drink, Dad?' She cocked an ear at him ostentatiously. 'I'm sorry, I didn't hear that.'

'Monstrous regiment of women, was what I said.'

'Ah!' she smiled, collected the empty glasses and headed for the bar. Brady glared at Dermott and Mackenzie. 'Hell of a lot of good you two are. Why didn't you back me up?' He sighed heavily and changed his tack. 'Why don't we all get something to eat? Lunch, and after it I'll catch up on some sleep. What are you girls proposing to do this after-noon?'

Stella came back with full glasses. 'We're going for a sleigh ride. Won't that be nice!'

'Good God! You mean *outside*?' Brady gloomily surveyed the few flakes drifting past the window. 'Very nice for some, I'm sure, but not for the sane.' He struggled to his feet. 'The dining-room in two minutes, then. George, if you will.' He took Dermott aside.

* * *

With a giant Caribou T-bone steak, a quarter of blueberry pie and some excellent California burgundy inside him, Brady watched his befurred wife and daughter go out through the main entrance and sighed with satisfaction at the feeling of physical well-being that enveloped him.

'Well, gentlemen, I really believe I might manage a brief snooze after all. Yourselves too?'

Dermott said: 'Off and on. Donald and I thought we'd chivvy up Prudhoe Bay and Sanmobil and get those names and records through as soon as possible.'

'Well, thank you, gentlemen. Very considerate. Do not wake me up unless Armageddon is nigh. Aha! Here, not unexpectedly, return the ladies.' He waited until his wife had reached the table. 'Something up, then?'

'Something *is* up.' Jean did not sound pleased. 'There are two men on the driving bench of that sleigh. Why two?'

'My dear, I'm not the arbiter of local customs. Are you afraid they're homosexual?'

She lowered her voice. 'They're both carrying guns. You can't see them, but you can, if you know what I mean.'

Brady said: 'Members of the Royal Canadian Mounted Police are entitled to bear arms at all times. Says so in their constitution.'

Jean stared at him, snorted with resignation, turned and left. Jim Brady beamed in satisfaction. Mackenzie said airily: 'They tell me there are some very handsome young constables in the R.C.M.P.'

*   *   *

Apart from chatting with Ferguson, Brady's pilot, Dermott spent the afternoon alone in the lounge, consuming one cup of coffee after the other. About mid-afternoon Jean and Stella returned, rosy-cheeked and in high spirits. Stella, it appeared, had learned from their escorts of a place where the younger people congregated of an evening, and had called Corinne Delorme at work to invite her out. Whether they intended to invite their erstwhile escorts along, Stella did not say nor did Dermott enquire. Brady would have the place comprehensively checked out before he would let them near it. Shortly afterwards Dermott received a call from Alaska. It was Bronowski in Prudhoe Bay: John Finlayson he said, was out at Pump Station Four but was expected back soon; he, Bronowski, would immediately set about obtaining what Dermott wanted and would arrange for the services of a fingerprint expert from Anchorage.

At five o'clock Reynolds came through to say that the fingerprinting was well in hand. The records Dermott required were even then being delivered to Edmonton Airport and would be delivered straight from McMurray Airport to the hotel. At six-thirty Mackenzie appeared, looking refreshed but at the same time reproachful.

'You should have called me. I'd meant to come down a couple of hours ago.'

'I'll sleep tonight,' Dermott said. 'That's four hours you owe me.'

'Three and a half. I put a call through to Houston, explained what we had in mind, told them to alert Washington and New York, and emphasised the urgency.'

'I trust your unofficial listener got it all down.'

'He could hardly fail to,' Mackenzie said. 'There was a bug installed inside the base plate of the telephone.'

'Well, that should be the final stirring-up of the hornets' nest. Let's hope the wrong people don't get stung. How's Jim?'

'Peered round his door on the way down. Looked like he'd died in his sleep.'

At seven o'clock a call came through from Sanmobil. Dermott indicated to Mackenzie that he should listen in to the extension earphone slotted onto the back of the receiver.

'Mr Reynolds? Not more bad news, I hope.'

'For me it is. I've been told to shut down the plant for a week.'

'When?'

'Now. Well, a few minutes ago. And I'm to be contacted in forty-eight hours to see if I've complied.'

'Was the message from Anchorage?'

'Where else?'

'Phone?'

'No. Telex.'

'They sent an open message?'

'No. Code. Our own company code.'

Dermott looked at Mackenzie. 'Pretty sure of themselves, aren't they?'

Reynolds said: 'What was that?'

'Talking to Donald Mackenzie. He's listening in. So they know that we know it's an inside job. They must be pretty sure of themselves. Who's got access to the code books?'

'Anybody who's got access to my safe.'

'How many people does that make?'

'Twenty. Give or take.'

'What do you intend to do?'

'Consult Edmonton. With their approval I intend to be on stream again inside forty-eight hours.'

'I wish you luck.' Dermott replaced the receiver and looked at Mackenzie. 'Now what?'

'Do you think Armageddon is nigh enough to justify waking up the Boss?'

'Not yet. Nothing he, we or anybody can do. Infuriating. Let's try Anchorage. What's the betting they've had a similar threat to close down the pipeline?' He lifted the phone, asked for the number, listened briefly then hung up. 'Hold, they say. One hour, two hours. They're not sure.'

The telephone rang. Dermott picked it up. 'Anchorage? No it can't be. I've just been told—ah, I see.' He looked at Mackenzie. 'Police.' Mackenzie picked up the extension receiver. They both listened in silence, Dermott said: 'Thank you. Thank you very much,' and both hung up.

Mackenzie said: 'Well, they seem pretty confident.'

'They're certain. Perfect copies of the prints from the Anchorage phone boxes. But they can't match them up with any on their lists.'

'It all helps,' Mackenzie said gloomily.

'It's not all that bad. The Photostat is promised for tomorrow. Might just match up with some of the prints we hope to collect. The Alaskan ones, I mean.'

'Of course?'

'Yes. It would be too easy to check up on anyone here who made a brief stopover in Anchorage.'

Stella came into the lounge, all set for dancing in black sequined silk and coloured tights, and carrying her coat. Dermott said: 'And where do you think you're going?'

Stella said: 'I'm going out with Corinne. First a snack and then the bright lights and the light fantastic.'

'You'll confine your dancing activities strictly to this hotel. You're not going any place.'

When she had got through a diatribe, calling him a stuffed shirt and a spoil-sport, she added: 'Mr Reynolds said it's all right.'

'When did he say this?'

'We phoned about an hour ago.'

'It's not up to Mr Reynolds to give you permission.'

'But he knows Corinne is coming with me. She lives near here. You don't think he'd let his secretary walk into danger, do you?'

'*She* wouldn't be walking into danger. Nobody would be interested in her. But in you, yes.'

Stella said: 'You sound as if you're convinced something is going to happen to me.'

'That's the way to make sure that nothing will happen to you—by taking precautions. See what your father says anyway.'

'But how would *he* know what's safe and what isn't? How would he check up?'

'He'd go to the top: the chief of police, I'm certain.'

Stella smiled brilliantly and said: 'But we've talked already to him. Over the phone. He was with Mr Reynolds. He says it's perfectly okay.' She smiled again, impishly. 'Besides, we won't lack protection.'

'Your friends of this afternoon?'

'John Carmody and Bill Jones.'

'Well, I suppose that does make a difference. Ah, here comes Corinne.' He beckoned her across, made the introductions and watched as they moved off. 'Well, I suppose we worry too much'. He glanced at the doorway. 'When I look at that lot coming in, I hardly think we need worry at all.'

'That lot' were a pretty formidable looking pair—big men in their late twenties or early thirties who looked eminently capable of taking care not only of themselves but of anyone who might be along with them. Dermott and Mackenzie rose and crossed to meet them.

Dermott said: 'I could be wrong, but you wouldn't be two policemen disguised as civilians?'

'There we go,' said the fair-haired man. 'Can't be very good at undercover work if it's as obvious as that. I'm John Carmody.

This is Bill Jones. You must be Mr Dermott and Mr Mackenzie. Miss Brady described you to us.'

Mackenzie asked: 'You gentlemen on overtime tonight?'

Carmody grinned. 'Tonight? Two gallant volunteers. Labour of love. Doesn't look like being any great hardship.'

'Watch them. Beautiful she may be, but Stella's a conniving young minx. One other thing: you know we have a feeling some bad actors might try to hurt her. Or take her out of circulation. Just a suspicion, but you never know.'

'I think we might be able to take care of that.'

'I'm sure you can. Most kind of you gentlemen. Very much appreciated, I can tell you. I know Mr Brady would like to thank you himself, but as he's in the land of dreams I'll do it on his behalf. The girls are through there. I hope you have a pleasant evening.'

Dermott and Mackenzie returned to their table, where they talked in desultory fashion. Then the phone rang again. This time it was Alaska: Prudhoe Bay.

'Tim Houston here. Bad news, I'm afraid. Sam Bronowski is in the hospital. I found him lying unconscious on the floor of Finlayson's office. Appears to have been struck over the head with a heavy object. He was hit over the temple where the skull is thinnest. Doctor says there may be a fracture— he's just finishing some X-rays. He's certainly concussed.'

'When did this happen?'

'Half hour ago. No more. But that's not all. John Finlayson is missing: he vanished soon after coming back from Pump Station Four. Searched everywhere. No trace of him. Not in any of the buildings. If he's outside on a night like this—well ...' There was a grim pause. '... he won't be around for long. We've got a high wind and heavy drifting, and the temperature's between thirty and forty below. Every man in the place is out looking for him. Maybe he was attacked by the same person who attacked Bronowski. Maybe he wandered out dazed. Maybe he was forcibly removed—although I don't see how that could be possible with so many people around. Are you coming up?'

'Are the F.B.I. and the State police there?'

'Yes. But there's been another development.'

'A message from Edmonton?'

'Yes.'

'Telling you to close down the line?'

'How did you know?'

'They make similar demands, we've got one here. I'll talk to Mr Brady. If you don't hear, you'll know we're on our way.' He replaced the receiver and said to Mackenzie: 'Armageddon? Enough to wake Jim?'

'More than enough.'

8

Ferguson, the pilot, was unhappy and with good reason. Throughout the flight he was in more or less continuous touch with the operations centre in Prudhoe Bay, and knew that the weather ahead was dangerous. The wind was gusting at 40 miles per hour: flying snow had cut ground visibility to a few feet, and the thickness of the drifting snow-blanket was estimated at sixty feet or even more—less than ideal circumstances for landing a fast jet in darkness.

Ferguson had every modern navigational and landing aid, but although he could make a hands-off touch-down if he had to, he preferred to see *terra firma* before he put his wheels down on it. One factor in Ferguson's favour was that he was a profound pessimist: his three passengers well knew that he was not given to endangering his own life, let alone those of other people on board, and would have turned back had the risks been too great.

Brady, who had been wakened from a deep sleep and was in a sour mood, spoke scarcely a word on the way north. Mackenzie and Dermott, aware that the flight might be their last opportunity for some time, spent most of the trip asleep.

The landing, with much advancing and retarding of the throttles, was a heavy, bouncing one, but nonetheless safely accomplished. Visibility was down to twenty feet, and Ferguson crept cautiously forward until he picked up the lights of a vehicle. When the cabin door was opened, freezing snow whirled in, and Brady lost no time in making his customary elephantine dash for the shelter of the waiting minibus. At the wheel was Tim Houston, lieutenant to the invalided Bronowski.

'Evening, Mr Brady.' Houston wore no welcoming smile. 'Filthy night. I won't ask if you had a good flight because I'm sure you didn't. Afraid you haven't had too much sleep since you came to the north-west.'

'I'm exhausted.' Brady didn't mention that he'd had six hours' sleep before leaving Fort McMurray. 'What's the word about John Finlayson?'

'None. We've examined every building, every pump-house, every last shack within a mile of the operations centre. We thought there was a remote chance that he'd gone across to the ARCO centre, but they searched and found nothing.'

'What's your feeling?'

'He's dead. He must be.' Houston shook his head. 'If he isn't—or wasn't—under cover, he couldn't have lasted a quarter of the time he's been missing. What makes that even more certain is that he didn't take his outdoor furs with him. Without furs? Ten minutes, if that.'

'The F.B.I. or police come up with anything?'

'Zero. Conditions are bad, Mr Brady.'

'I can see that.' Brady spoke with feeling and shivered. 'I suppose you'll have to wait for daylight before you can carry out a proper search?'

'Tomorrow will be too late. Even now it's too late. Anyway, even if he is around, the chances are we won't find him. We might not find him until warmer weather comes and the snow goes.'

'Drifting, you mean?' This was Mackenzie.

'Yes. He could be in a gully or by the roadside—our roads are built five feet high on gravel—and he could be lying at the bottom of a ditch with not even a mound to show where he is.' Houston gave a shrug.

'What a way to die,' Mackenzie said.

'I'm accepting the fact that he is gone,' Houston said, 'and though it sounds callous, maybe, it's not such a bad way to go. Perhaps the easiest way to go. No suffering: you just go to sleep and never wake up again.'

Dermott said: 'You make it sound almost pleasant. How's Bronowski?'

'No fracture. Heavy contusions. Dr Blake reckons the concussion is only slight. He was stirring and seeming to make an effort to surface when I left the camp.'

'No further progress in that direction?'

'Nothing. Very much doubt whether there will be either. Sam was the only person who could have told us anything or identified his assailant. It's a thousand to one that he was attacked from behind and never caught a glimpse of his attacker. If he had, the attacker would probably have silenced him for keeps. After you've killed two people, what's a third?'

'The same people, you reckon?'

Houston stared. 'It's too much of a coincidence to be different people, Mr Brady!'

'I suppose. This telex from Edmonton?'

Houston scratched his head. 'Told us to close down the line for a week. Says they're going to check in forty-eight hours.'

'And in your own company code, you said?' Dermott asked him.

'They didn't give a damn about letting us see it was an inside job. Damned arrogance. And the telex was addressed to Mr Black. Only someone working on the pipeline would know that he was up here. He spends nearly all his time in Anchorage.'

Dermott said: 'How's Black taking this?'

'Difficult to say. Bit of a cold fish; not much given to showing his feelings. I know how I'd feel in his shoes. He's the general manager, Alaska, and the buck stops with him.'

Houston was doing Black a degree less than justice. When they arrived at his office in the operations centre, he had a distinctly unhappy and *distrait* air about him. He said: 'Good of you to come, Mr Brady. Must have been a highly unpleasant trip—and in the depths of a winter's night.' He turned to a tall tanned man with iron-grey hair. 'This is Mr Morrison. F.B.I.'

Morrison shook hands with all three. 'Know of you, of course, Mr Brady. I'll bet you don't get too much of this sort of thing out in the Gulf States.'

'Never. Don't get any of this damnable snow and cold either. Mr Houston here tells me that you're all up against a blank wall. Finlayson's just vanished.'

Morrison said: 'We were hoping that a fresh mind might be of use.'

'I'm afraid your hopes are misplaced. I leave detection to the professionals. I'm merely, as are my colleagues here, a sabotage investigator, although in this case it's clear that sabotage and crimes of violence have a common ground. You've had Mr Finlayson's office fingerprinted, of course.'

'From top to bottom. Hundreds of prints, and not one seems to be any use. No prints there that shouldn't have been there.'

'You mean that the owners of those prints all had regular and legitimate access to the office?'

Morrison nodded. 'Just that.'

Brady scowled. 'And since we're convinced that this character is someone working on the pipeline, any one of those fingerprints might be his.'

Mackenzie asked the FBI man: 'Any sign of the weapon used on Bronowski?'

'Nothing. Dr Blake believes the blow was administered by the butt of a gun.'

Dermott asked: 'Where's the doctor?'

'In the sick bay, with Bronowski, who's just recovered consciousness. He's still dazed and incoherent, but it seems he'll be okay.'

'Can we see the two of them?'

'I don't know,' Black said. 'The doctor, certainly. I don't know whether he'll allow you to talk to Bronowski.'

'He can't be all that bad if he's conscious,' said Dermott. 'It's a matter of urgency. He's the only person who *might* be able to give us a clue about what happened to Finlayson.'

When they arrived in the sick bay, Bronowski was speaking coherently enough to Dr Blake. He was very pale; the right-hand side of his head had been shaved, and a huge plaster, stretching from the top of his skull to the lobe of the ear, covered the right temple. Dermott looked at the doctor, a tall, swarthy man with an almost cadaverous face and a hooked nose.

'How's the patient?'

'Coming on. The wound's not too bad. He's just been soundly stunned, which is apt to addle anyone's brains a bit. Headache for a couple of days.'

'A couple of brief questions for Bronowski.'

'Well, brief.' Dr Blake nodded at Dermott's companions.

Dermott asked: 'Did you see the guy who knocked you down?'

'See him?' Bronowski exclaimed. 'Didn't even hear him. First thing I knew of anything was when I woke up in this bed here.'

'Did you know Finlayson was missing?'

'No. How long's he been gone?'

'Some hours. Must have gone missing before you were clobbered. Did you see him at all? Speak to him?'

'I did. I was working on those reports you asked me to get for you. He asked about the conversation I had with you, then left.' Bronowski thought about it. 'That was the last I saw of him.' He looked at Black. 'Those papers I was working on. Are they still on the table?'

'I saw them.'

'Can you have them put back in the safe, please? They're confidential.'

'I'll do that,' Black said.

Dermott asked: 'May I see you a minute, doctor?'

'You're seeing me now.' The doctor looked quizzically at Dermott down his long nose.'

Dermott smiled heavily: 'Do you want me to discuss my chilblains and gout in public?'

In the consulting room Dr Blake said: 'You look in pretty good shape to me.'

'Advancing years, is all. Have you been up to Pump Station Four?'

'Ah, so it's that business! What stopped you discussing it out there?'

'Because I'm naturally cagey, distrustful and suspicious.'

'I went up with Finlayson.' Blake made a grimace at the memory. 'Place was a ghastly mess. So were the two murdered men.'

'They were all that,' Dermott agreed. 'Did you carry out an autopsy on them?'

There was a pause. 'Have you the right to be asking me these questions?'

Dermott nodded. 'I think so, Doctor. We're all interested in justice. I'm trying to find out who killed those two men. May be three, by now, if Finlayson stays missing.'

'Very well,' Blake said. 'I carried out an autopsy. It was fairly perfunctory, I admit. When men have been shot through the forehead, it's pointless to try to establish the possibility that they died of heart failure instead. Although, mind you, from the mangled state of their bodies, it's clear that the blast effect of the explosion would in itself have been enough to kill them.'

'The bullets were still lodged in the head?'

'They were and are. A low-velocity pistol. I know they'll have to be recovered, but that's a job for the police surgeon, not for me.'

'Did you search them?'

Blake lifted a saturnine eyebrow. 'My dear fellow, I'm a doctor, not a detective. Why should I search them? I did see that one had some papers in an inside coat pocket, but I didn't examine them. That was all.'

'No gun? No holster?'

'I can testify to that. I had to remove coat and shirt. Nothing of that nature.'

'One last question,' Dermott said. 'Did you notice the index finger on the same man's right hand?'

'Fractured just below the knuckle bone? Odd sort of break in a way, but it could have resulted from a variety of causes. Don't forget the blast flung both of them heavily against some machinery.'

'Thank you for your patience.' Dermott made for the door, then turned. 'The dead men are still at Pump Station Four?'

'No. We brought them back here. I understand their families want them buried in Anchorage, and that they'll be flown down there tomorrow.'

*   *   *

Dermott looked round Finlayson's office and said to Black: 'Anything been altered since Bronowski was discovered here?'

'You'd have to ask Mr Finlayson. At the time, I was across seeing my opposite number in ARCO and didn't get here for twenty minutes.'

The F.B.I. man asked: 'Some things have been touched, naturally. My men had to when they were carrying out their fingerprinting.'

Mackenzie nodded to the buff folders on Finlayson's desk. 'Are those the reports on the security men? The ones that Bronowski said he was studying when he was clobbered?'

Black looked at Houston, and the security man said: 'Yes.'

'There were fingerprints, too.' Mackenzie raised an eyebrow.

'Those will be in the safe,' Houston said.

'We'd like to see those and the records,' Dermott said. 'In fact, we'd like to see everything in that safe.'

Black intervened. 'But that's where all our company confidential information is kept.'

'That's precisely why we'd like to examine it.'

Black compressed his lips. 'That's a very large order, Mr Dermott.'

'If our hands are to be tied, we might as well go back to Houston. Or have you something to hide?'

'I consider that remark offensive.'

'I don't.' Brady had spoken from the depths of the only armchair in the room. 'If you have something to hide, we'd like to know what it is. If you haven't, open up your safe. You may be the senior man in Alaska, but the people in London are the ones that matter, and they've promised me we would be afforded every co-operation. You are showing distinct signs of lack of co-operation. I must say that gives me food for thought.'

Black's lips were very pale now. 'That could be construed as a veiled threat, Mr Brady.'

'Construe it any damned way you like. We've been through this up here once before, earlier. And John Finlayson has gone walk-about or somewhere even less attractive. Co-operate or we leave—and leave you with the task of explaining to London the reason for your secretiveness.'

'I am not being secretive. In the best interests of the company—'

'The best interest of your company is to keep that oil flowing and head off these killers. If you don't let us examine that safe, we can only conclude that for some reason you choose to obstruct the best interest of your company.' Brady poured himself a daiquiri as if to indicate that his part of the discussion was over.

Black surrendered: 'Very well.' The lips had now thinned almost to nothing. 'Under protest and under, I may say, duress, I agree to what I regard as an outrageous request. The keys are in Mr Finlayson's desk. I will bid you goodnight.'

'One moment.' Dermott didn't sound any more friendly than Black. 'Do you have records of *all* your employees on the pipeline?'

It was clear that Black was considering some further opposition, and then decided against it. 'We do. But very concise. Couldn't call them reports, just brief notes of, mainly, previous jobs held.'

'Where are they? Here?'

'No. Only reports on security personnel are kept here, and that's because Bronowski regards this as his base. The rest are kept in Anchorage.'

'We'd like to see them. Perhaps you can arrange for them to be made available?'

'I can arrange it.'

'I understand from Dr Blake that you have a flight to Anchorage tomorrow. Is it a big plane?'

'Too big,' said Black the accountant. 'A 737. Only one available tomorrow. Why?'

'One or more of us might want to hitch a lift,' Dermott answered. 'We could, among other things, pick up those reports. Seats would be available?'

Black said: 'Yes. No more questions, I trust?'

'One. You received this threatening telex message from Edmonton today, telling you to close down the line or else. What do you propose to do?'

'Carry on production, of course.' Black tried to smile sardonically, but the moment was wrong. 'Assuming, of course, that the criminals have been apprehended?'

'Where's the telex?'

'Bronowski had it. It may be on his person. Or in his desk.'

'I'll find it,' Dermott said.

'I don't think Bronowski would like you rummaging about his desk.'

'He's not here, is he? Besides, he's a security man. He would understand.' Dermott shook his head. 'I don't think you ever will.'

'No,' Black said. 'Goodnight.' He turned on his heel and left. No-one said 'goodnight' to him.

'Well, well,' Brady exclaimed. 'A friend for life in three minutes flat. Don't know how you do it, George. Pity he acts so suspiciously—otherwise he'd have made a splendid suspect.'

'Badly ruffled feathers,' Morrison said. 'To put it in a restrained fashion, ruffling other people's feathers is his speciality. A martinet of the first order, they say, but an extraordinarily able man.'

Dermott said: 'Not, I gather, universally popular. Does he have friends?'

'Professional business contacts, that's all. Socially, nothing. If he has any friends, he hides them well.' He tried to conceal a yawn. 'My normal bedtime lies well behind me. In the F.B.I., we try to get to bed by ten p.m. Can I be of any assistance before I go?'

'Two things,' Dermott said. 'The maintenance crew at Pump Station Four. Fellow called Poulson in charge. Could you have their backgrounds investigated as rigorously as possible?'

'You have a reason for asking?' The F.B.I. man sounded hopeful.

'Nothing really. Just that they happened to be there when the sabotage occurred. I'm clutching at straws. We have damn little else to clutch at.' Dermott smiled wryly.

'I think we can do that,' Morrison said. 'And the other?'

'Dr Blake tells me that the two dead engineers were brought back here today. Do you know where they were put?'

Morrison knew and told them, said his goodnights and left.

Brady said: 'I think I shall go and rest lightly in my room. Notify me if the heavens fall in. But not after the first half hour or so. I take it you are about to indulge your morbid curiosity in viewing the departed.'

*   *   *

Dermott and Mackenzie looked down at the two murdered engineers. They had been covered in white sheets. No attempt had been made to clean them up since they last saw them at Pump Station Four. Perhaps it had been impossible. Perhaps no-one had had a strong enough stomach for the task. Mackenzie said: 'I hope they're going to be sewn up in canvas or something before being taken to Anchorage tomorrow, or their relatives are going to have the screaming heebie-jeebies. Whatever you're looking for, George, look for it quick. I'm not enjoying myself.'

Nor was Dermott. Not only was the sight revolting, but the smell was nauseating. He lifted the hand of the man he'd briefly examined before and said: 'How would you say that fore-finger got that way?'

Mackenzie bent, wrinkled his nose and said: 'It sounds crazy, but it could have been broken by a pair of pliers. The trouble is that charring's obliterated any marks that might have been made on the skin.'

Dermott went to a wash-basin, soaked his handkerchief and cleaned up the charred area as best he could. The black carbon came off surprisingly easy. It didn't leave the skin clean—the pitting was too deep for that—but clean enough to permit a closer examination.

'No pliers,' Mackenzie said. 'To break the bone, pliers would have had to close right into the flesh and would have been bound to leave saw-tooth marks. No saw-tooth marks, so no pliers. But I agree with you. I'm sure that bone was deliberately broken.'

Dermott rubbed some carbon off the charred clothing and smeared it on the cleaned area so that it did not look as if it had been wiped. He opened the jacket and slid his hand into the inside pocket: it came out empty. Mackenzie said: 'The papers and cards have taken wing and flown. With assistance, of course.'

'Indeed. Could have been Poulson or one of his pals. Could have been Bronowski when he was out there yesterday. Could have been the kindly healer himself.'

'Blake? He does look like a first cousin of Dracula,' Mackenzie said.

Dermott raised the damp handkerchief again and started to clear the area round the bullet hole in the forehead. He peered closely at the wound and said to Mackenzie: 'Can you see what I imagine I see?'

Mackenzie stooped low and peered closely. Still stooped, he said softly: 'With the hawk eyes of my youth gone forever, I could do with a powerful magnifying glass.' He straightened. 'What I imagine I see is the brown scorch marks of burnt powder.'

As before, Dermott smeared some carbon back on the cleaned area. 'Funny—my imagination runs the same way. This guy was shot at point-blank range. The scenario reads that it was a very close thing indeed. The killer had a gun on this engineer and was probably searching him. What he didn't know was that the engineer not only had a gun of his own, but had it out. However it was, he must have seen it just in time and shot to kill—there could have been no time to indulge in any fancier gun-work. The engineer's gun-hand must have gone into muscular spasm—irreversible contraction; not unknown at the time of violet death. To free the gun, the killer had to wrench it so violently that he snapped the trigger finger. Don't you think that fits in with the peculiar angle at which the finger was broken?'

'I think you have it. It fits, anyway.' Mackenzie frowned. 'There's only one thing I see wrong with your scenario. Why should the killer take the gun in the first place? He had a gun of his own.'

'Sure he had, but he couldn't use it any more,' Dermott said. 'More accurately, he couldn't afford to keep it any more. Having seen no exit holes at the back of the head he knew he had left two bullets in the region of two occiputs, and that the police could match up the bullets with the gun he was carrying. Which meant he would have to get rid of it. Which meant that he would be gunless, at least temporarily. So he took the engineer's gun. My guess is that he will have got rid of both guns by this time, and he's almost certainly got another weapon by now. In these United States—and don't forget Alaska is the United States—getting hold of a hand-gun is extremely simple.'

Mackenzie said slowly: 'It all fits. We may well be up against a professional killer.'

'We may well be up against a psychopath.'

Mackenzie shivered. 'My Scottish Highland ancestry. Some ill-mannered lout has just walked all over my grave. Let's take counsel with the boss. Counsel and something else. If I know our worthy employer, he'll already have had half the contents of the jet's bar brought to his room.'

'And you want his ideas?'

'I want some of those contents.'

*   *   *

Mackenzie had exaggerated somewhat. Ferguson hadn't brought across more than a tenth of the plane's stock, but even that represented a goodly amount; Mackenzie had already had his first Scotch and was on his second. He looked at Brady, propped up in bed in a pair of shocking heliotrope pyjamas, which served only to accentuate his massive girth, and said: 'Well, what do you make of George's theory?'

'I believe in the facts and I also believe in the theory, for the adequate reason that I see no alternative to it.' Brady contemplated his finger-nails. 'I also believe we're up against a trained, ruthless and intelligent killer. I don't doubt that he might be a psychotic on the loose. In fact there may be *two* psychopaths—an even more unpleasant prospect. The trouble is, George, I don't see how this advances us much. We don't know when this nut will hit again. What can we do to prevent it?'

'We can scare him,' Dermott answered, 'that's what we can do. I'll bet he's already worried by the fact that we're raking in fingerprints and records all over the shop. Let's try to worry him a little more. I'll go down to Anchorage tomorrow while you and Mackenzie stay here and do some work.' Dermott sipped his Scotch. 'It should be a change for at least one of you.'

'I could be deeply wounded,' Brady said, 'but slings and arrows from an ungrateful staff are nothing new to me. What, precisely, do you have in mind?'

'Drastically narrowing the range of suspects is what I have in mind. All very simple, really. This is a close-knit community here in Prudhoe Bay. They more or less live out of each other's pockets. Everyone's movements must be known to at least a handful of other people, probably a great deal more. Check on everybody and find out who has a definite alibi for being here on the morning the engineers were being killed out in the mountains. If two or more people, say, can honestly tell you that X was here at the time of the crime, you can strike X off the suspects' list. At the end of the day we'll know how many suspects we have. Not even a handful, I bet. I wouldn't be surprised if there were none at all. Remember that Pump Station Four is a hundred and forty miles away, and the only feasible way of getting there is by helicopter. One would have to have the time and opportunity and the ability to fly a helicopter to get there, and there would be no hope of taking a chopper without someone noticing. I think you'll find it all very straightforward.

'Less straightforward is the next enquiry—who was in Anchorage on the day that the original phone message was sent from there to Sanmobil? There must have been quite a few. Don't forget they go on holiday every three or four weeks and, almost without exception, they go to Fairbanks or Anchorage. It will be more difficult to establish alibis: you won't find many people who have witnesses as to their whereabouts at six a.m. of a black winter morning in Alaska.

'In this case, though, we're more concerned about those who are not in the clear than those who are. I'll bring back a Photostat of the prints they've taken. We should be able to get the doubtfuls' fingerprints without too much trouble, and, with luck, match one set up with the phone booth's set. I don't know how this sounds to you, but it seems quite straightforward to me.'

'And to me,' said Brady. 'I think Don and I can manage that little chore without too much difficulty. Don't forget, though, that there's a fairly large community of people down at Valdez.'

'As you're my boss,' Dermott said, 'I'll refrain from giving you a withering stare. Who in Valdez is going to fly a round trip of 1,300 miles during a winter night, stopping occasionally for fuel and so giving his identity away? And who's going to fly or helicopter the 1,600 miles round trip to clobber Bronowski and very possibly do away with Finlayson, especially as he would be immediately recognised as a stranger the moment he set foot in this area?'

Mackenzie said: 'He has a point, you must admit. In fact, two points.'

Dermott went on: 'And don't tell me they could have come from one of the pumping stations. They don't have helicopters.'

'I didn't say anything of the sort.' Brady sounded aggrieved. 'All right, we'll go along with the assumption that it's Prudhoe Bay or nothing. But what if we turn up zero?'

'Then it will be your turn to come up with the next bright idea.'

'Hard day,' Brady said. 'You for bed?'

'Yes. I had intended to look at those records and prints tonight but the prints aren't going to be of any use to me until I return from Anchorage. Reports can wait, too. I'll just hunt up that Edmonton telex and take it down to the Anchorage police and see if they can help me.' He stood up. 'By the way: has it occurred to you that you yourself may be in danger tonight?'

'Me!' It was as if Dermott had suggested some unthinkable form of *lèse-majesté*. Then a look of vague apprehension crept into Brady's face.

'It may not be just your family who are at risk,' Dermott persisted. 'Why should these people bother about kidnapping when they could achieve their ends by putting a bullet in your back—which is not, if I may say so without offence, a very easy target to miss? How are you to know there isn't a homicidal maniac in the room next door to you?'

'Good God!' Brady drank deeply from his daiquiri. Then he sat back and smiled. 'At last, action! Donald, get the Smith and Wesson from my case.' He took the gun, thrust it deep under his pillow and said, almost hopefully: 'Don't you think you two are at risk also?'

'Sure,' Mackenzie said. 'But not nearly as much as you. No

Jim Brady, no Brady Enterprises. You're the legend. Without either of us, you could still function quite efficiently. This homicidal maniac doesn't strike me as the type who would go for a couple of lieutenants while the captain is around.'

'Goodnight, then,' Dermott said. 'Don't forget to lock your door as soon as we're gone.'

'Don't worry. You're armed, right?'

'Of course. But we don't think we'll be needing any weapons.'

9

When Dermott woke up it was with such a heavy-headed feeling of exhaustion that he could have sworn he hadn't been to sleep at all. In fact, less than an hour had elapsed since he'd switched out the light, closed his eyes and dropped off. He did not wake up of his own volition. The overhead light was on and Morrison, looking as distraught as a senior F.B.I. agent is ever likely to look, was shaking him by the shoulder. Dermott eyed him blearily.

'Sorry about this,' Morrison began. 'But I thought you'd like to come along. In fact, I want you to.'

Dermott peered at his watch and winced. 'For God's sake, where?'

'We've found him.'

Sleep, and all desire for it, dropped from Dermott like a cloak. 'Finlayson?'

'Yes.'

'Dead?'

'Yes.'

'Murdered?'

'We don't know. You'll need warm clothing.'

'Wake Mackenzie, will you?'

'Sure.'

Morrison left. Dermott rose and dressed for the cruel temperatures outside. As he pulled on a quilted anorak his mind went back to his first meeting with Finlayson. He thought of the neatly-parted white hair, the grizzled Yukon beard, the hobo clothes. Had he been too hard on the man? No good worrying now. He pocketed a flashlight and moved into the passageway. Tim Houston was standing there. Dermott said: 'So you know too?'

'I found him.'

'How come?'

'Instinct, I guess.' The bitterness in Houston's voice was unmistakable. 'One of those finely-honed instincts that comes into operation about ten hours too late.'

'Meaning that Finlayson could have been saved if this instinct of yours had been operational ten hours ago?'

'Maybe—but almost certainly not. John was murdered.'

'Shot? Knifed? What?'

'Nothing like that. I didn't examine him. I knew that Mr Morrison and you wouldn't want me to touch him. I didn't have to examine him. He's outside, it's thirty below, and all he's wearing is a linen shirt and jeans. He's not even got shoes on. That makes it murder.'

Dermott said nothing, so Houston continued. 'Apart from the fact that he'd never have crossed the outside doorstep voluntarily without his Arctic clothing, he'd never have been permitted to do so anyway. There are always people in the reception area, besides a person who mans the central telephone fulltime. By the same token, it would have been impossible for anyone to carry him out.'

'Lugging corpses is conspicuous. So?'

'He wouldn't even have had to be a corpse. I think he was silenced in his own bedroom and bundled straight out the window. The cold would have finished him off. Here come your friends. I'll go get some more flashlights.'

Outside, the cold was breathtaking. The temperature, as Houston had said, stood at thirty below. The forty-mile-per-hour gale brought the combination of temperature and chill-factor down to minus seventy. Even double-wrapped as a polar bear, without an exposed inch of flesh, the fact remains that one still has to breathe—and breathing in those conditions, until numbness intervenes, is a form of exquisite and refined agony. In the initial stages it is impossible to tell whether one is inhaling glacial air or super-heated steam: a searing sensation dominates all else. The only way to survive for any length of time is to breathe pure oxygen from a suitably insulated tank—but those are not readily available in the Arctic.

Houston led them round the right-hand corner of the main

building. After about ten yards he stopped, bent down and shone his flashlight between the supporting pilings. Other beams joined his.

A body lay face down, an insignificant heap already half-covered by the drifting snow. Dermott shouted: 'You have sharp eyes, Houston. A lot of people would have missed this. Let's get him inside.'

'Don't you want to examine him here, have a look around?'

'I do not. When this wind drops we'll come back and look for clues. In the meantime, I don't want to join Finlayson here.'

'I agree,' Morrison said. His teeth chattered audibly, and he was shaking with the cold.

Recovering the body from under the building provided the four men with no problem. Even if Finlayson had weighed twice as much, they would have had him out in seconds flat, such was their determination to regain shelter and warmth as soon as possible. As it was, Finlayson was slightly-built, and handling him was like handling a 150-pound log, so solidly frozen had he become. When they were clear of the pilings Dermott looked up at a brightly lit window above and yelled through the wind: 'Whose room is that?'

Houston shouted: 'His.'

'Your theory fits, doesn't it?'

'It does.'

When they brought Finlayson into the reception area, there were perhaps half-a-dozen men sitting or standing around. For a moment nobody said anything. Then one man stepped forward and, with some diffidence, asked: 'Shall I bring Dr Blake?'

Mackenzie shook his head, sadly. 'I'm sure he's an excellent doctor, but no medical school has yet got round to offering a course on raising a man from the dead. Thanks all the same.'

Dermott said: 'Have we got an empty room where we can put him?' Houston looked at him and Dermott shook his head in self-reproach. 'Okay. So my mind's gummed up with cold or lack of sleep or both. His own room, of course. Where can we find a rubber sheet?'

So they took Finlayson to his room and laid him on the

rubber sheet on top of his bed. Dermott said: 'Is there an individual thermostat control in here?'

'Sure,' said Houston. 'It's set on seventy-two.'

'Turn it up.'

'What for?'

'Dr Blake will want to do a post-mortem. You can't examine a person who's frozen solid. We're getting experienced at this sort of thing. Too experienced.' Dermott turned to Mackenzie. 'Houston thinks Finlayson was silenced in this room. Killed, knocked out, we don't know. He also thinks that our friends got rid of him by the simple expedient of opening the window and dumping him on to the snow-bank beneath.'

Mackenzie crossed to the window, opened it, shivered at the icy blast of air that swept into the room, leaned out and peered down. Seconds later he had the window firmly closed again.

'Has to be that. We're directly above the spot where we found him. And it's in deep shadow down there.' He looked at Houston. 'Is there much traffic along there at night?'

'None. Nor during the day. No call for it. Track leads nowhere.'

'So the killers left either by the front door or by this same window. They did the obvious thing—just stuffed him under the building, hoping the snow would have drifted over him before daylight came.' Mackenzie sighed. 'He couldn't by any chance have felt sick, opened the window for some fresh air, fell and crawled under the building?'

Dermott said: 'You believe that's possible?'

'No. John Finlayson wouldn't get a *breath* of fresh air that way. He caught his death of it. Murder.'

'Well, I think the boss should be told.'

'He's sure going to be pleased, isn't he?'

* * *

Brady was furious. His black scowl accorded ill with his heliotrope pyjamas. He said: 'Progress on all fronts. What do you two intend to do?'

Mackenzie said pacifically: 'That's why we're here. We

thought you might be able to give us a lead.'

'A lead? How the hell can I give you a lead? I've been asleep.' He corrected himself. 'Well, for a few minutes, anyway. Sad about Finlayson. Fine man, by all accounts. What do you reckon, George?'

'One thing's for sure. The similarities between what happened here tonight and what occurred at Pump Station Four are too great to be a coincidence. As with the two engineers, so with Finlayson. They all saw or heard too much for their own health. They recognised a person or persons they knew well and who knew them, and those people were engaged in some things that couldn't be explained away. So they had to be silenced in the most final way.'

Brady thought for a moment, and asked: 'Is there a direct connection between Bronowski being clobbered and Finlayson being killed?'

'I wouldn't bet on it,' Dermott said. 'Tie-up looks too obvious. You could argue that Bronowski escaped because he didn't catch his assailants red-handed in whatever they were doing, and that Finlayson died because he did. But that's too easy, too glib.'

'What does Houston think?'

'He doesn't appear to have any more idea about it than we do.'

' "Appear".' Brady seized on the word. 'You mean he may know more than he's telling?'

'At the moment he's not saying or telling anything.'

'But you don't trust him?'

'No. And while we're at it, I don't trust Bronowski.'

'Hell, man, he's been savagely assaulted.'

'Assaulted. Not savagely. I don't trust Dr Blake, either.'

'Because he's unhelpful and unco-operative?'

'A good enough reason.'

Brady became tactful. 'Well, you do tend to ride a bit roughshod over people's feelings.'

'To hell with their delicate sensibilities! We're dealing here with three cases of murder. Come to that, I don't trust Black either.'

'You don't trust Black? General manager, Alaska?'

'He can be the King of Siam for all I care,' Dermott said forcefully. 'Some of the most successful businessmen in history number in their ranks the biggest swindlers ever. I'm not suggesting he *is* a swindler. All I say is that he's crafty, cagey, cold, and unco-operative. In short, I don't trust anyone.'

'Look, friends. We're looking at this from the wrong angle,' Brady suggested. 'We're on the inside trying to look out. Maybe we should be on the outside trying to look in. Think of it this way. Who *wants* to hit the pipeline here and the tar sands of Athabasca? Do you see any significance in the fact that here they receive their instructions from Edmonton while in Alberta they come from Anchorage?'

'None.' Dermott was positive. 'May be just coincidence, at best a crude attempt to confuse us. Surely they can't be so naïve as to try to convey the impression that Canada is trying to interfere with America's oil supplies and vice versa. Idea's ludicrous. In these times of an acute oil shortage, what have two friendly neighbours to gain by cutting each other's throats?'

'Then who *has* to gain?'

Mackenzie spoke quietly.

'O.P.E.C.,' he said.

Mackenzie was just as positive as Dermott had been. 'If they could put a stranglehold on the two countries' supplies from the north, they stand to gain immensely in both profits and power. Both our governments have made it clear that they're prepared to go to any lengths to shake free once and for all from this crucifying dependence on O.P.E.C. oil. This wouldn't suit our foreign friends at all. They have us over a barrel—an oil barrel, if you will—and they want to keep it that way.'

'Why now?' Jim Brady said. 'Although I know as well as you do.'

'They have tremendous leverage at the moment, and the last thing they'd ever want to do is to abdicate this position of almost dictatorial power. Decisions are being made now in both countries. Should North America become anywhere near self-sufficient in oil, our blackmailing friends would lose their power-base. They'd be forced to abandon their pretensions to playing an authoritative role in world affairs, and, perhaps worst of all for them, their profits would be reduced to such a trickle that they'd have to forgo their grandiose schemes for industrial and technological expansion, for hauling their countries into the middle of the late twentieth century, without any of the intermediate struggle or leasing and developmental process. When it comes to national survival, desperate men are prepared to go to desperate lengths.'

Brady paced for some time, then said: 'Do you really think the O.P.E.C. countries would take concerted action against us?'

'Hell, no. Half of them are barely on speaking terms with the other half, and you can't imagine relatively moderate countries like Saudi Arabia participating in any such combined operation. But you know as well as I do that among the O.P.E.C. rulers there are some certifiable loonies who would stop at nothing to achieve their own ends. And you won't have forgotten that some of those countries play host to the most ruthless terrorist trainers in the business.'

Brady said: 'What would you say to that, George?'

'It's a theory, and a perfectly tenable one. On the other hand, since coming here I haven't seen a single person who looks remotely like an Arabian or Middle Eastern terrorist.'

'So what would your guess be?'

'As a *wild* guess, I would suspect our troubles are caused by good old-fashioned capitalistic free enterprise. And if that's the case, the potential sources of our troubles are legion. I'm afraid we won't solve this by looking at it from the outside: we'll have to look out from the inside.'

'And the motive?'

'Blackmail, obviously.'

'Cash?'

'Well, the only other bargaining counter is hostages. Nobody's holding any hostages. So what's left? They're now in the process of softening us up by proving they can carry out their threats when and as they wish.'

'They won't be asking for pennies.'

'I shouldn't think so. To start with, the pipeline and Sanmobil have a combined investment of ten billion. For every day that delivery is held up they'll be losing millions more. Most important of all, our two countries are desperate for oil. Whoever those people are, they have us not over but in a barrel. Naked. The ransom will be high. I should imagine it would be paid.'

'Who'd pay it?' Mackenzie said.

'The oil companies. The governments. They've all got a stake in this.'

Brady said: 'And once the blackmailers have been paid, what's to prevent them repeating the process all over again?'

'Nothing that I can see.'

'God, you're a Job's comforter.'

'Let me comfort you some more, shall I? There could be a link-up between Don's theory and mine. *If* this is blackmail, and *if* the killers do collect, what's to prevent some of the O.P.E.C. countries approaching them and offering to double or triple their money if they destroy the supply lines for keeps—and get out? You've a big responsibility on your shoulders, Mr Brady.'

'You, George, are a rock of strength and compassion in times of trouble and stress.' Brady sounded plaintive. 'Well, if there are no constructive suggestions forthcoming, I suggest we all retire. There is thinking to be done and I must take counsel with myself. On such nights, the best company.'

*   *   *

Dermott still felt unaccountably tired when the alarm clock dragged him up from the depths of a troubled sleep. It was just on eight in the morning. He rose reluctantly, showered, shaved, made his way to Finlayson's room, and was about to knock when the door was opened by Dr Blake. At that time of the morning the doctor's beaked nose, hollow cheeks and sunken eyes lent him a more cadaverous look than ever—not the kind of physician's face, Dermott thought, to inspire hope and confidence.

'Ah, come in, Mr Dermott. I've finished with Finlayson. Was just about to send for his casket. He and the two engineers from Pump Station Four are being flown out at nine-thirty. I understand you're going with them.'

'Yes. You have caskets?'

'Macabre, you think? Well, we do keep a few tucked away. Apart from natural illnesses, this is an accident-prone profession, and we have to be prepared. You can't very well whistle up an undertaker from Fairbanks or Anchorage at a moment's notice.'

'I suppose not.' Dermott nodded at the dead man. 'Any luck in establishing the cause of death?'

'Well, normally it requires a full autopsy to discover whether the victim has been suffering from cerebrovascular disease or cardiac arrest. Fortunately—or unfortunately—it wasn't necessary in this case.' Blake sounded grim. 'What was before only a suspicion is now a certainty. What would be natural causes elsewhere are unnatural here. John Finlayson was murdered.'

'How? Other than by exposure?'

'None of your usual methods. He was rendered unconscious and left to die in the cold. Clad as he was in those abnormally low temperatures, I'd say his heart must have stopped in under a minute.'

'How was he knocked out?'

'Sand-bagged. In the classic spot, at the base of the neck. An expert. You can see the slight contusion and roughness there. A contusion can only be caused by blood still circulating, so he was clearly alive after the blow. The cold killed him.'

'Where could the attacker have got sand in this Godforsaken frozen hole?'

Dr Blake smiled. Dermott wished he hadn't: the long narrow teeth only accentuated the death's-head effect. 'If you aren't too squeamish, you can smell what they used.'

Dermott bent and rose almost immediately. 'Salt.'

Blake nodded. 'Probably slightly dampened. Makes an even more effective cosh than sand.'

'They teach you this in medical school?'

'I was on the forensic side once. If I make out and sign the death certificate, will you be kind enough to hand it in at Anchorage?'

'Of course.'

*　　*　　*

Big, burly, high-coloured and irrepressibly cheerful, John Ffoulkes looked more like a prosperous farmer than a tough, competent senior police officer. He produced a bottle of whisky and two glasses and smiled at Dermott.

'In view of those ridiculous prohibition laws they have up at Prudhoe Bay, maybe we can make up here in Anchorage ...'

'My chief would like your style. We don't do so badly there. Mr Brady claims to have the biggest portable bar north of the Arctic Circle. He has, too.'

'Well, then, to help erase the memory of your flight. I gather you didn't enjoy it much?'

'Extreme turbulence, an absence of pretty stewardesses, and the knowledge that you're carrying three murdered men in the cargo hold doesn't make for a very relaxed flight.'

Ffoulkes stopped smiling. 'Ah, yes, the dead men. Not only a tragic affair but an extremely unpleasant one. I've had reports from my own State troopers and the F.B.I. I wonder if you could have anything to add to what they said?'

'I doubt it. Mr Morrison of the F.B.I. struck me as a highly competent officer.'

'He's all that, and a close friend of mine. But tell me anyway, please.'

Dermott's account was as succinct as it was comprehensive. At the end Ffoulkes said: 'Tallies almost exactly with the other reports. But no hard facts?'

'Suspicions, yes. Hard facts, no.'

'So the only lead you really have are the prints we got from that telephone booth?' Dermott nodded, and Ffoulkes brought out a buff folder from a desk drawer. 'Here they are. Some are pretty smudged but a few are not too bad. Are you an expert?'

'I can read them with a powerful glass and a lot of luck. But an expert—no.'

'I've got a first-class young lad here. Like to borrow him for a day or two?'

Dermott hesitated. 'That's kind. But I don't want to tread on Morrison's toes. He's got his own man up there.'

'Not in the same class as our David Hendry. Mr Morrison won't object.' He pressed an intercom button and gave an order.

David Hendry was fair-haired, smiling and seemed ridiculously young to be a police officer. After introductions, Ffoulkes said: 'Lucky lad. How do you fancy a vacation in a winter wonderland?'

Hendry looked cautious. 'Which wonderland, sir?'

'Prudhoe Bay.'

'Oh, my God!'

'Good, glad you're happy. That's settled then. Pack your equipment and, of course, your clothes. Three parkas should be enough—worn on top of each other. When's your plane out, Mr Dermott?'

'Two hours.'

'Report back in an hour, David.' Hendry opened the door to leave, then stood to one side as a lean man, white-bearded like an Old Testament prophet, bustled into the room.

'Apologies, John, apologies. Couldn't have caught me at a worse time or on a worse day. Two court cases, two suicides—people get more thoughtless every day.'

'You have my sympathies, Charles—as I, one hopes, have yours. Dr Parker—Mr Dermott.'

'Hah' Parker looked at Dermott with an ill-concealed lack of enthusiasm. 'You the fellow who's come to add to my burden of woes?'

'Through no wish of mine, doctor. Three burdens, to be precise.'

'I'm afraid I can't do anything about them today, Mr Dermott. Snowed under, just snowed. Very likely I can't do anything about them tomorrow either. Most unprofessional.'

'What is?'

'My two assistants. Going down with the flu at the busiest time of the year. This modern generation—'

'I daresay they couldn't help it.'

'Namby-pambies. What happened to those three anyway?'

'Two we know for sure. They were in the close vicinity of an explosion. After that an oil fire broke out. Savagely scarred. The fumes alone would have finished them off.'

'But they were already finished off. So. Blasted to death, burnt, asphyxiated. Doesn't leave very much for an old sawbones like me to do, does it?'

'Each of them has also a low-velocity bullet lodged somewhere near the back of his skull,' Dermott said.

'Hah! So you want them out, is that it?'

'Not me, Dr Parker. The State police and the F.B.I. I'm no cop, just an oilfield sabotage investigator.'

Parker looked sour. 'I hope my efforts aren't as thoroughly wasted as usual.'

Ffoulkes smiled. 'What odds would you offer, Mr Dermott?'

'About a million to one that they'll be wasted. That gun has almost certainly been tossed out of a helicopter somewhere over the Brooks Range.'

'I'll still have to ask you, Charles,' said Ffoulkes.

Dr Parker was unimpressed. 'What about this third man?'

'B.P./Sohio's field production manager in Prudhoe Bay, John Finlayson.'

'Good lord! Know the man well. Suppose I should say "knew", now.'

'Yes.' Dermott nodded to Ffoulkes's desk. 'That's his death certificate.'

Parker picked it up, screwed on a pince-nez and read through the report.

'Unusual,' he said testily. 'But it seems a straightforward medical report to me. There's no autopsy required here.' He peered at Dermott. 'From your expression, you appear to disagree.'

'I'm neither agreeing nor disagreeing. I'm just vaguely unhappy.'

'Have you ever practised medicine, Mr Dermott?'

'No.'

'And yet you presume to take issue with a colleague of mine?'

'You know him, then?'

'Never heard of him.' Parker breathed deeply. 'But, dammit, he's a physician.'

'So was Dr Crippen.'

'What the devil are you insinuating?'

'You read into my words what you choose,' Dermott said flatly. 'I'm insinuating nothing. I merely say that his examination was perfunctory and hurried, and that he may have missed something. You wouldn't claim a divine right of infallibility for doctors?'

'I would not.' His voice was still testy, but only a testy mutter now. 'What is it you want?'

'A second opinion.'

'That's a damned unusual request.'

'It's a damned unusual murder.'

Ffoulkes looked quizzically at Dermott and said: 'I'll look in at Prudhoe Bay tomorrow. There's nothing like adding a touch of chaos to an existing state of confusion.'

10

Dermott and David Hendry flew in from Anchorage to Prudhoe Bay in the leaden twilight of late afternoon to find the
weather distinctly improved, with the wind down to ten knots,
the top of the drifting snow-cloud not more than five feet
above ground level, visibility in the plane's headlights almost
back to normal, and the temperature at least twenty degrees
higher than in the morning. In the administration building
lounge the first recognisable face Dermott saw was that of
Morrison of the F.B.I., who was sitting with a young, ginger-
haired man incongruously dressed in grey flannels and blazer.
Morrison looked up and smiled.

'Trust John Ffoulkes,' he said. 'No faith in the F.B.I.' He
gestured towards the ginger-haired young man. 'Nick Turner.
Ignore the way he dresses. He's been to Oxford. *My* fingerprint man. On your right, David Hendry, *your* fingerprint man.'

Dermott said mildly: 'John Ffoulkes just observed that two
pairs of eyes were better than one. No developments?'

'Not one. You?'

'Largely a waste of time. Had a thought on the way up.
Why don't we print John Finlayson's room?'

'No dice. We've done it.'

'Clean as a whistle?'

'Close enough. Lots of unsatisfactory smudges which can
only be Finlayson's, a couple belonging to a plumber who was
there on his rounds, and one—would you believe it, just one—
belonging to the bull cook, who must be a real whiz-kid with
duster and polishing cloth.'

'Bull cook?'

'Kind of house-keeper. Bed-maker and cleaner.'

'Could some other industrious soul have been busy in there
with a duster?'

Morrison produced two keys. 'His room key and the master key. Had them in my pocket since Finlayson was taken out this morning.'

'Here endeth the lesson.' Dermott laid the buff folder on the low table before Morrison. 'Prints from the Anchorage phone booth. Now, I must go and report to the boss.'

Morrison said: 'It should amuse the two young gentlemen here to compare your Anchorage prints with the ones in the office safe.'

'You don't sound very optimistic,' Dermott said.

The F.B.I. agent smiled. 'By nature I've always been an optimist. But that was before I crossed the forty-ninth parallel.'

*　　*　　*

Dermott found Brady and Mackenzie taking their ease in the only two chairs in Brady's room. He looked on them without favour.

'It's very pleasant and reassuring to see you two so comfortable and relaxed.'

Brady said: 'Rough afternoon, huh?' He waved a hand towards the serried row of bottles on the sideboard. 'This'll restore your moral fibre.'

Dermott helped himself and asked: 'Any news from Athabasca? How are the family?'

'Fine, fine.' Brady chuckled. 'Stella passed on a lot more stuff from Norway. Apparently they've got that fire licked. No need to keep in touch any longer.'

'That's good.' Dermott sipped his Scotch. 'What are the girls doing?'

'Right now, I guess, they're touring the Sanmobil plant, courtesy of Bill Reynolds. Very hospitable lot, those Canadians.'

'Who've they got to protect them?'

'Reynolds's own security man, Brinckman—the boss, you remember—and Jorgensen, his number two.'

Dermott was unimpressed. 'I'd rather they had those two young cops.'

Brady snapped: 'Your reason?'

'Three. First, they're a damned sight tougher, more competent than Brinckman's lot. Second, Brinckman, Jorgensen and Napier are prime suspects.'

'Why prime?'

'For having the keys that opened the Sanmobil armoury door, for having given the keys to those who did. Third, they're security men.'

Brady smiled blandly. 'You're bushed, George. You're becoming paranoid about the security men of the great northwest.'

'I hope you don't have reason to regret that remark.'

Brady scowled but said nothing, so Dermott changed the subject. 'How did the day go?'

'No progress. Along with Morrison we interviewed every man on the base. Every one had a cast-iron alibi for the night of the explosion in Pump Station Four. So it's all clear there.'

'Except—' Dermott persisted.

'Who do you mean?'

'Bronowski and Houston.'

Brady glowered at his chief operative and shook his head. 'You're paranoid, George, I say it again. Shit, we *know* they were both out there. Bronowski's been hurt, and Houston didn't *have* to find Finlayson. If he *had* been crooked, it would have suited him far better to let the drifting snow obliterate every last trace of Finlayson. What do you say to that?'

'Three things. The fact that we know they were out at the pump station makes them *more* suspect, not less.'

'Second guessing,' growled Brady. 'Hate second guessing.'

'No doubt. But we've agreed that the bombers must be people working on the pipeline. We've eliminated everyone else, so it has to be them—does it not?'

Brady did not answer. Dermott went on: 'The third thing is this: there must be some reason, albeit devious, why Bronowski was clobbered and Houston made the discovery. Look at it this way. What evidence do we have that Bronowski *was* assaulted? The only certain thing we know about him is that he's lying in the sick bay with an impressive bandage round his head. I don't think there's a damn thing wrong with

Bronowski. I don't think anybody hit him. I suggest that if the bandage were removed, his temple would be un-blemished, except, perhaps, for an artistic touch of gentian blue.'

Brady assumed the expression of a man praying for inner strength. 'So, besides not trusting security men, you don't trust doctors, either?'

'Some I do. Some I don't. I've already told you that I'm leery of Blake.'

'Got one single hard fact to back up your suspicions?'

'No.'

'Okay, then.' Brady didn't enlarge on this brief statement.

'We also rounded up the Prudhoe Bay members who were in Anchorage on the night of that telephone call,' Mackenzie said. 'Fourteen in all. They seemed a pretty harmless bunch to me. However, Morrison of the F.B.I. did call up the law in Anchorage, gave names and addresses and asked them to see if they could turn up anything.'

'You printed those fourteen, right?'

'Yes. One of Morrison's assistants did. Some Ivy League kid.'

'No objections offered?'

'None. They seemed eager to co-operate.'

'Proves nothing. Anyway, I brought along the prints found on the phone booth. They're being checked now against the prints of the fourteen.'

'That won't take long,' Mackenzie said. 'Give them a call, shall I?' He called, listened briefly, hung up and said to Dermott: 'Cassandra.'

'So.' Brady looked positively lugubrious, no easy feat for a man without a line in his face. 'Houston's finest have run into a brick wall.'

'Let's not reproach ourselves too much,' Dermott said. He looked less downcast than the other two. 'Our business is investigating oil sabotage, not murder, which is the province of the F.B.I. and the Alaskan State police. They appear to have run into the same brick wall. Besides, we may have the lead into another line of investigation—John Finlayson's autopsy.'

'Huh!' Brady gave a contemptuous lift of his hands. 'That's over. It turned up nothing.'

'The first one didn't. But the second one might.'

Mackenzie said: 'What! *Another* autopsy?'

'The first one was pretty superficial and perfunctory.'

'Unprecedented.' Brady shook his head. 'Who the hell authorised this?'

'Nobody really. I did *ask* for it, but politely.'

Brady cursed, whether because of Dermott's words or because he had spilled a goodly portion of a daiquiri over his immaculately trousered knee. He refilled his glass, breathed deeply and said: 'Took your own goddamned good time in getting round to telling us, didn't you?'

'Everything in its own good time, Jim: just a matter of getting priorities right. It'll be a couple of days before we get the results of this autopsy. I really can't see why you are getting so steamed up.'

'I can damn well tell you. Who the hell gave you the authorisation to make such a request without first getting permission from me?'

'Nobody did.'

'You had time before you left here this morning to discuss the matter with me.'

'Sure I had time, but I hadn't had the idea by then. I was half-way down to Anchorage before it occurred to me that there could be something far wrong. Do you imagine I'd talk to you in Prudhoe Bay over an open line?'

'You talk as if this place is an international hotbed of espionage,' Brady came back to him sarcastically.

'It only requires one disaffected ear, and we might as well pack our bags and return to Houston. We already know how good those people are at covering their tracks.'

'George.' It was Mackenzie. 'You've made your point. What triggered your suspicions?'

'Dr Blake. You know that as far as the murdered engineers at Pump Station Four and Bronowski's alleged accident were concerned, I already had reservations about Blake. I began to wonder if there was anything that could tie Blake in with Finlayson's death. I was the only person who saw the body between the completion of Blake's autopsy and the time the lid was screwed down on the coffin.' Dermott stopped to sip.

'During that period Blake showed me marks on the back of the neck where, he said, Finlayson had been sand-bagged into unconsciousness. On the plane it occurred to me that I had never seen a bruise or contusion of that nature. There was no sign of discoloration, or of swelling. It seemed to me more than likely that the skin had been roughed up after death. Blake said Finlayson had been struck by a bag of damp salt. His neck smelled of salt all right, but it could have been rubbed on during the night, after the body had been brought back up to the room. If he *had* been coshed, the vertebrae would have been depressed or broken.'

Mackenzie said: 'Obvious question—were they?'

'I don't know. They looked okay to me. But Dr Parker will know.'

'Dr Parker?'

'Works with the Anchorage police in a forensic capacity. Struck me as a very bright old boy. My request wasn't too well received at first. Like yourselves, he regarded the concept of a second autopsy as unprecedented or unconstitutional or whatever. He read Blake's death certificate and seemed to think it perfectly in order.'

'But you persuaded him to the contrary?'

'Not exactly. He promised nothing. But he seemed interested enough to do something.'

Brady said: 'You *are* a persuasive cuss, George.'

Dermott paused reflectively. 'It may be nothing, or it may be another straw in the wind—but Dr Parker has never heard of Dr Blake.'

Brady resumed his favourite steeple-fingered pontificating attitude. 'You're aware that Alaska is more than half the size of Western Europe?'

'I'm also aware that in Western Europe there must be the odd hundred million people. In Alaska, a few hundred thousand. I'd be surprised, if, outside the few hospitals, there are more than sixty or seventy doctors, and a veteran like Parker would be bound to know or know of them all.'

Brady unsteepled his fingertips and said: 'There is hope for you. An immediate investigation into Doctor Blake's antecedants would appear to be in order.'

'Immediate,' Mackenzie agreed. 'Morrison's the man for that. Wouldn't it be interesting, too, to have a run-down on the man who appointed or recommended Blake to this post?'

'It would,' Dermott said. 'And it would certainly narrow the field a bit. I wonder. You remember just after we arrived here asking whether there were any ideas about the type of weapon used on Bronowski, and Morrison said—I think I quote him accurately—"Dr Blake says he's no specialist in criminal acts of violence"?'

Brady nodded.

'So. This morning, when I was with him in Finlayson's room discussing the reasons for the man's death, he mentioned in an off-hand way that he used to be an expert in the forensic field. Obviously he said it to lend credence to his diagnosis. But it was a slip, all the same. One time or the other, he was lying.'

Dermott looked at Brady and asked: 'Your agents in New York who are investigating Bronowski's security firm there ... they aren't, shall we say, exactly burning up the track. Give them a nudge?'

'Negative. You said yourself that an open line ...'

'Who's talking about an open line? We do it through Houston, in your code.'

'Huh! That damn code. You encode any message you like and authorise it in my name.'

Mackenzie winked unobtrusively, but Dermott ignored him and began to spell out a message to the telephone operator. It said much for his mastery of a code which its inventor found insupportably burdensome that he encoded the words straight out of his head, without having to make a prior transcript.

He had barely finished when a knock on the door announced the arrival of Hamish Black. The pencil moustache on the Alaskan general manager was as immaculately trimmed as ever, the central parting of the hair still apparently drawn by ruler, the eyeglass so securely anchored that it looked as if it could have ridden out a hurricane. He still dressed in pure City accountant, first class. At that moment, however, there was a difference in his general demeanour: he looked like a first-class accountant who had just stumbled across proof of unmistakable and gross embezzlement in the books of his favourite client. Yet he maintained his cool—or cold.

'Good evening, gentlemen.' He was a specialist in wintry smiles. 'I hope I do not intrude, Mr Brady?'

'Come in, come in.' Brady was affability itself, a sure sign that he didn't care too much for his visitor. 'Make yourself at home.' He glanced around the cramped confines of his room and at the only three already occupied chairs. 'Well—'

'Thank you, I'll stand. I shall not detain you for long.'

'A drink? One of my incomparable rum drinks? How about a cigar?'

'Thank you. I neither smoke nor drink.' The minuscule twitch of the left-hand corner of his upper lip clearly indicated his opinion of those who did. 'I have come here because in my capacity of general manager of Sohio/B.P. I felt it my duty to ask how much progress you have made in your investigations to date.'

Dermott said: 'What have we found out so far? Well—'

'Will you please be quiet, sir. I was addressing—'

'George!' Brady made a downward placatory movement of the hand towards a Dermott who was already half-way out of his seat. He looked coldly at Black. 'We are not employees of yours, Mr Black. We are not even retained by you, but directly by your head office in London. I suggest that if you want to leave this room the way you entered it, you watch your language.'

Black's lips had disappeared somewhere. 'Sir! I am not accustomed—'

'Okay, okay. We all know that. You're obviously in a hostile mood. Our progress so far? Not much. Would there be anything else?'

Black was clearly taken aback. It is difficult for an old-time man-of-war to attack when the wind has been taken out of its sails.

'So you admit—'

'No admission. We're just making a statement. Can we be of further help?'

'Indeed you can. You can explain to me the justification for your staying on here. The firm can scarcely afford the fees you seem likely to charge, if it gets no advantage. You have achieved nothing, and seem unlikely to achieve anything. You investigate industrial sabotage, specifically oil-flow interruption. There is, I suggest, a considerable difference between the spilling of oil and the spilling of blood. One cannot but suspect but that you are out of your depth and that events are beyond your control. One further suspects that the investigation should be left to those qualified to investigate criminal matters—the F.B.I. and the Alaskan State police.'

'We'd be interested to know what they've found out. Or don't you feel free to tell us?'

Black compressed his lips still tighter. Mackenzie said: 'May I have a word, Mr Brady?'

'Certainly, Donald.'

'Mr Black: Your attitude here is singularly reminiscent of the one you adopted when first we met you. Have you the power to make us leave?'

'Yes.'

'Permanently?'

'No.'

'Why not?'

'You know very well why not. London head office would reinstate you.'

'Possibly with the qualification that if any such situation arose again it would be the general manager, Alaska, who would be required to leave.'

'I couldn't really say.'

'I can. Or didn't you know that Mr Brady is a close personal friend of the chairman of your company?'

From the way that Black touched his collar, it was clear that this was news to him. From the way Jim Brady experienced a sudden difficulty in swallowing a mouthful of daiquiri, it was clear that it was news to him also.

'To return to your earlier attitude, Mr Black,' Mackenzie persisted. 'On that occasion Mr Dermott said he thought you might have something to hide. Mr Brady suggested you were being unduly secretive and had—what was it again?—some undisclosed and possibly discreditable reason for choosing to obstruct the best interests of your company. Reasonable requests you regarded as being preposterous. Finally, as I recall,

Mr Dermott said that you were either standing on your high horse as general manager, Alaska, and were above such petty annoyances, or that you were concealing something you didn't want us to know about.'

Black was possibly a shade or two paler, but his pallor could well have been caused by anger. He reached for the door handle.

'This is intolerable! I refuse to be the subject of character assassination.'

As he pulled open the door, Mackenzie said, reproachingly, 'I think it's impolite to interrupt a man's speech.'

Black's eyes matched well the icy conditions outside. 'What does that mean?'

'Just that I would like to finish what I've been saying.'

Black looked at his watch. 'Make it short.'

'I know you have a great deal to do, Mr Black.' Two tiny spots of pink appeared on the pale cheekbones, for Mackenzie's tone had made it abundantly clear he didn't believe Black had anything to do. 'So I'll keep it short. Your intransigence interests us. You have made it abundantly clear that you would be happy to be rid of us. By your own admission you've acknowledged that we would be back very soon afterwards, perhaps even in a matter of days. The conclusion is that you want us out of the way even if for only a brief period. One wonders what you intend to do or have done during that short time?'

'I see. You leave me with no alternative other than to report your gross incompetence and insolence to my board of directors in London.'

When the door had closed Dermott said: 'Not a bad exit line. He'll do nothing of the kind, of course—not when he's had time to reflect on Mr Brady's close personal relationship with his board chairman.' Dermott looked at Brady. 'I didn't know—'

'Neither did I.' Brady was positively jovial. He smacked one fat fist into the other podgy palm. 'Tell me, Donald, how much of what you said did you mean?'

'Who's to know? Not me. I just don't like the bastard.'

'Hardly the basis for a dispassionate judgment,' Dermott

said. 'But a splendid demolition job, Donald. There are times when a man rises above himself.' He paused for a moment, then looked at Brady. 'Remember the last time we had a run-in with our friend, you said that it was a pity that he acted so suspiciously, otherwise he would have made a splendid suspect? Maybe we're outsmarting ourselves. It's barely possible that he should be a suspect. Maybe, in addition, he's outsmarting us. This won't have escaped you?'

Brady stopped being jovial. 'Double-guessing again. How often do I have to tell you, George, I hate this goddamn double-guessing. General manager, Alaska. Jesus, George, *somebody*, by definition, has to be beyond suspicion.'

* * *

In Dermott's cabin Mackenzie said: 'Took you a long time to transmit that coded message to Houston. Your brief was merely to ask them to expedite the boss's earlier instructions. What the hell else did you say?'

'I asked them to find out if anybody had left Bronowski's security firm within six months before or after Bronowski's leaving.'

'Maybe Brady's right. Maybe this security bit is getting to you. And even if Bronowski has hauled some of his old associates along with him, they may have changed their names.'

'Hardly matters. Descriptions will be enough. And as for my being bitten by the bug, it's high time you and Jim were too. How would you try to account for the fact that the bastards in Alberta know the Alaskan company's code, while the villains in Alaska know the Albertan code, the private Sanmobil code?'

'Ever since the first identical messages were received at Prudhoe Bay and Sanmobil, we've known our Alaskan and Athabascan friends were in cahoots, nicely co-ordinating their efforts to keep us wrong-footed and ensuring that we were in A while we should have been in B, and vice versa. There's no doubt in my mind that both security corps have been infiltrated. Our only suspects on both sides are security people.'

'So you think the overall co-ordinator must be a security man?'

'Not necessarily. But what I'm sure of is that pretty soon we're going to hear of some fresh calamity that has struck in Athabasca. The master puppeteer must be thinking it's time the puppets were dancing again.'

'Co-ordination,' Mackenzie said darkly.

'In this instance?'

'You heard what I said to Black. That he wants us out for a few days for some purpose. If he can't get rid of us in one way—by asking us to leave—then he'll do it in another by arranging a fresh Athabascan calamity.'

Dermott sighed, drew a line under a list of names he had printed, and handed it over. 'Names for investigation—let's hope—by our friend Morrison of the F.B.I. What d'you think of it?'

Mackenzie took the list and studied it. His eyebrows went up. 'Make Morrison jump, for sure,' he said.

'I don't care if he jumps over the moon, as long as he gets on with it when he comes down,' said Dermott heavily. 'We've got to get action somewhere.' He was about to say something else when the telephone rang. He picked up the receiver to listen, and gradually his face went chalk white. He seemed not to notice when the glass in his left hand shattered, crushed by the pressure he had put on it, and a little rivulet of blood ran down his palm.

'What a *place*!' exclaimed Stella as she came back into Corinne's office. 'Heavens—I had no idea it was so big. We seem to have driven about fifty miles.'

'Well, it's quite a size, that's for sure.' Corinne grinned, pleased that her guests had enjoyed themselves. 'I hope *you* found it interesting too, Mrs Brady?'

'Incredible!' Jean eased off the hood of her parka and shook her hair loose. 'Those draglines—I never saw anything like them. They're—they're sort of prehistoric monsters, burrowing into the bowels of the earth.'

'That's right!' Stella's imagination had been fired no less. 'Brontosauruses. Absolutely. Sure was kind of Mr Reynolds to fix our tour. *And* to ask us to supper.'

'Don't mention it.' Corinne tried out the deprecating smile she had been cultivating. 'We all like having visitors—makes a change. You'll enjoy meeting Mary Reynolds, too. Now, let's see if the boss is ready to leave.'

She buzzed the intercom and announced that the ladies were back. Over the loudspeaker they heard him say: 'Fine—I'll be through in a minute.'

'Be right with you,' she said. 'All set?' She tidied her desk. locked the drawers, put the keys in her handbag and pulled on a fetching, roly-poly combination suit of powder-blue quilted nylon, as well as a pair of blue fur-topped boots. A moment later Reynolds himself came through the connecting door, similarly muffled in navy blue and white.

'Evening, ladies,' he said pleasantly. 'Had a good tour, I hope. Not too dull?'

'Not at all!' Jean had no trouble sounding enthusiastic. 'It was wonderful. Fascinating.'

'Good.' He turned to Corinne. 'Where are our strong-arm boys, then?'

'Waiting for us in the lobby.'

'Great. We'd better not leave them behind, or your father'll give us hell.' He winked at Stella and ushered her through the door.

Terry Brinckman, Sanmobil's security chief, and his deputy Jorgensen were hovering in the entrance hall. As the party approached the two men opened the outside door and let in a blast of the Arctic evening. Out on the tarmac one of the firm's yellow-and-black chequered minibuses stood ready, with its engine running. Reynolds opened the passenger door, helped Jean and Stella into the front seat, nipped round to the driver's side and slammed the door, cursing the knifelike wind. Corinne hopped into the back seat between the two security men.

As they cruised down towards the main gates Reynolds called up the guard on his two-way radio and identified the vehicle, to save the man coming out into the cold. At the bus's approach the high weldmesh gates began to roll open, driven by electric motors. A few snowflakes drifted fast through the blaze of the arc-lamps that illuminated the perimeter fence. Reynolds gave a couple of toots on the horn to signal his thanks, and a moment later they were out in the open, with the headlight beams boring into the frozen darkness ahead.

The bus was warm and comfortable. The journey would take only twenty minutes. Yet Corinne somehow felt uneasy. Her boss had been on edge all day, and although she had maintained a sunny enough exterior, she wasn't looking forward to the evening: it could be sticky. Maybe they could get a bit of a concert or sing-song going—that would help. She leaned forward and asked Stella if she could play the guitar.

'Why, sure—if no-one else is listening.'

'Ah, come on! I thought we could maybe have a sing-song.'

'Course she can play,' Jean said firmly. 'Pick up any tune you care to sing.'

'That's great.' Corinne's settled back between her two solid escorts. The bus had left the inhabited outskirts of the site and was winding through the low hills that separated the tar sands from Fort McMurray. Reynolds drove smoothly, without violent acceleration or braking, for the surface of the road was dusted with the ever-travelling snow, which flashed and glittered in the headlamp beams.

They had just passed a sharp corner which Brinckman said was known as Hangman's Turn when Reynolds *did* jam on his brakes. He cursed as the bus slewed to the left, then corrected the skid. Ahead, the road was blocked by a black truck which had also skidded sideways-on.

'Look out!' Corinne shouted. 'There's someone on the road!'

The bus juddered to a halt a few yards short of the huddled figure lying face-down. The flying snow cleared for a few seconds to reveal another body, also on its front, but moving.

'Oh my God!' Jean cried from up front. 'There's been an accident!'

'You ladies, sit tight,' Reynolds ordered sharply. 'Terry, go and see what's happened.'

Brinckman opened his door and got out. Corinne felt the blast of air hit her from the right. Then she saw another figure running, or rather staggering, towards them from the stranded vehicle. The man had his hands up, as if to shield his eyes from the minibus's lights. He was limping and lurching; she thought: he's been badly hurt.

Corinne felt Brinckman yank the first-aid box out from under the back seat. Next thing she knew, he was flat on his side, his feet having gone from under him on the ice. He got up at once and advanced more cautiously, with his feet apart, apparently to the aid of the injured man.

What happened next was so fast that Corinne afterwards wondered a hundred times whether or not she had remembered it right. Everything seemed to go into a blur. One moment Brinckman was advancing to meet the crippled figure. Next second the cripple seemed suddenly to shake off his injuries: he stood upright and let fly an expertly-timed blow that felled Brinckman like a tree. The instant the man lowered his shielding hand, Corinne saw he was wearing a stocking mask.

Stella screamed: 'Back up—quick!' Corinne also shouted

something. But before any of them could move the attacker was at Reynolds's window. In a second he had wrenched it open and thrown in something that hissed.

Instinctively Corinne threw herself down flat on the floor in the back. From the front she heard stifled screams and ghastly tearing noises as people struggled for breath. Then the gas got her too, and she found herself fighting and choking as if for her life.

In spite of her distress she became aware the people in front were being dragged out into the snow. She crouched flat on the floor, struggling to control her stinging throat and eyes. Then she heard a man shout: 'Where's the other chick? We've only got two.' In the next second she felt someone seize the hood of her combination suit and drag her bodily out onto the road.

Without knowing why, she pretended to be unconscious. Somehow it seemed safer. She felt herself sliding easily along the icy surface, being dragged like a sack of potatoes. Her backside skidded smoothly over the snow. As she was pulled round the front of the minibus, into the headlights, she noticed that the supposedly injured men had vanished. The bus's engine was still running, but the vehicle blocking the road had started up as well. Suddenly she was hoisted and dumped in the open back of the truck.

For the first time she felt afraid—not of being kidnapped, but of freezing to death. In spite of her thick suit she was shivering already, and if they were going to be driven miles in an open truck, the cold would soon kill them all ...

Her fears on that score proved groundless. After a rough, bumpy drive of only a few seconds the truck crunched to a halt. The noise of its motor was suddenly swamped by a far louder, heavier roar that burst out all round and over them. Corinne opened her eyes in terror and saw that they had pulled up beside a grey-white helicopter. Even as she looked up one of the rotor blades moved past her line of sight.

She felt she should scream or run—but would it do any good? Even a second's hesitation was too long. She felt herself grabbed by shoulders and ankles and swung aboard, again like an inert sack.

The noise was terrific. The engine-roar increased to a furious pitch, but through it she could hear a woman screaming and men yelling. She saw a bundle she recognised as Stella struggling frantically with one of the men in stocking masks, rolling across the bare steel. Another of the men slid the door in the side of the fuselage nearly shut, but he kept his head stuck out through the gap, bellowing at someone still on the ground.

The engine-note rose and fell, rose and fell, as though the pilot was having mechanical difficulty. Then it went up and stayed up—but only for a few seconds. Again it dropped. Corinne had never been in a helicopter before and did not know what to expect. She didn't know whether the pilot was going through his normal take-off routine, or whether he had some problem. What she did notice, however, was that the man who'd been shouting to his colleague on the ground had failed to close the door properly: it still stood a few inches ajar. A desperate idea flashed into her head: at the moment of take-off, whenever it came, she would dart to the door, drag it open, and fling herself out.

Before she'd had time to evaluate the risks, she felt the floor tilt—they were off already. Then came a heavy bump. Down again, she thought. Next time they did lift. It was then or never.

She rolled over, flung herself at the door and hauled it back. She was hit by a stunningly cold wash of wind. Too late she realised that they were already off the ground. She was caught by the slipstream, whirled round and sucked out. She clutched wildly at the door-frame but her gloves slipped uselessly over the bare metal. At the edge of her consciousness she heard a man screaming: 'You're crazy! You'll be killed!' Then she was falling through the snow-laden wind. She tumbled over in mid air and glimpsed a pair of headlights snaking through the night way below. That was the last thing she saw. The next couple of seconds would bring her nightmares for the rest of her life. Time stopped. She fell endlessly through the freezing sky, convinced that her body would be smashed to pieces any instant. She tried to scream, but could not. She tried to breathe, but could not. She tried to turn over, but could not alter her attitude in the slightest. She dropped help-lessly, rigid with terror.

The impact was unbelievably gentle. Instead of smashing into iron-hard tundra, she landed in something soft and yielding. She hit it back-first, and went right on down through several feet of blessed cushioning. She was winded by the impact, but that was all. She lay on her back gasping and groaning for breath, but once she had got it back, she began to shake with relief. To her own amazement she found she was laughing as well as crying. She had landed on her backside in a great big drift of snow.

*   *   *

Jay Shore was just about to leave his office at the Sanmobil plant when the telephone rang. He picked up the receiver and said 'Yes?'

'Switchboard operator here,' said a voice high with stress. 'Got an emergency. Driver Pete Johnson is on the radio. Wants to talk to you immediately.'

'I'll take it. Patch him through.' Shore waited.

'Hullo? Hullo?' Johnson's voice crackled through, even more excited than the operator's. 'Mr Shore, sir?'

'Speaking. Take it easy. What's the problem?'

'I'm on my way down to Fort McMurray, sir. Driving bus MB 3. Just come round a corner and found Bus MB 5 aban-doned in the middle of the road.'

'*Abandoned?*'

'That's right. Doors open, motor running, lights on. Point is, it's the bus Mr Reynolds took to go home in.'

'Jesus! Where are you?'

'About a mile past Hangman's Turn. Mile towards Fort McMurray.'

'Okay. I'll get someone right out there.'

'Mr Shore?'

'What is it?'

'I just saw a chopper take off from near the road, and *somebody fell out of it.* And two of our security guys—Mr Brinckman and Mr Jorgensen—are lying in the road, like

147

they've been hurt real bad.'

'Damn!'

'Yeah, and there's a truck stuck in the snow by where the plane took off. It's trying to get back on the road, facing towards Fort McMurray.'

'Keep away from it,' Shore ordered. 'Stay in your own vehicle. Back off a bit. But don't go near the truck. I'll get someone right down.'

'Okay, Mr Shore, sir.'

Shore banged down the receiver and snatched up another, an outside line. He dialled and waited. He knew that Carmody and Jones, the two R.C.M.P. men assigned to protect the Brady family, were also due at the Reynolds's for supper, so he called directly there. Someone answered—Mrs Reynolds.

'Mary? Jay Shore speaking. Look—I'm afraid there's been some sort of a ... mix-up. Bill and the ladies have got delayed. What's that? No—I hope not. Nothing to worry about. Have you the two constables there already? Great. Yet please. Either will do.'

John Carmody came on the line.

'Emergency,' said Shore quietly. 'I think your party's been hijacked. Yes—I do.' He explained all he knew in a couple of sentences. 'What I want *you* to do is come right up the road to Hangman's Turn. You see anybody coming to meet you, stop him: it could be the grey truck we're after. O.K?'

'O.K. We're on our way.'

'That's fine. Get moving.'

*   *   *

Carmody drove. Jones rode shotgun, his .38 revolver ready in his hand. The Cherokee Jeep station wagon, in four-wheel drive, held the road better than a regular sedan, but even so they had to go carefully.

Carmody swore steadily as he nursed the wheel. 'Goddam it to hell!' he kept muttering. 'The first time we leave them, *this* happens. What in hell were the Sanmobil security guys doing, for Christ's sake?'

They drove on, snow whirling through the headlight-beams.

148

Suddenly they saw lights coming the other way.

'Block the road!' Jones ordered. 'Get sideways on.'

'Better to keep head on—dazzle him. He can't get past, anyway.'

Carmody stopped in the middle of the road and switched on the station wagon's flashers. The oncoming driver rounded a bend, saw them, braked and slewed violently from side to side before sliding to a halt.

Jones got out and moved towards the vehicle. He'd only gone three or four yards when a spurt of fire flashed from the driver's window, followed instantly by the crack of a gun. Jones spun sideways, clutching his left shoulder. The other driver slammed into gear and let out the clutch. For a second his tyres raced griplessly on the snow. Then he shot forward, cannoned into the Jeep, shunted it sideways enough for him to scrape past, and accelerated away in the direction of Fort McMurray.

Carmody tried to open his door but found it jammed: the bodywork was buckled all down that side. He bunked across to the other side and ran to the aid of his wounded colleague. Jones was conscious but bleeding badly from a wound in the top corner of his chest: a large, dark stain had spread out across the snow beneath his body.

Carmody thought fast. It was too cold to administer first aid to the wound. If he took off any of Jones's clothes, the man would die of exposure and shock. First priority was to get him somewhere warm, then to hospital. He ought to call up an ambulance.

'Come on, Bill,' he said gently. 'You gotta get up.'

'O.K.,' Jones muttered. 'I'm O.K.'

'On your feet, then.' Carmody got him round the waist, avoiding his chest and shoulders, in case he made anything worse there, and hoisted him upright. Then he propelled him gently towards the Jeep and opened one of the back doors.

'In there,' he said. 'Front door's jammed.'

He got the wounded man safely in, closed the door, climbed aboard himself and turned up the heater to maximum. Then he addressed himself to the radio. To his chagrin, he could get nothing out of it. The set was live, but no signal came through. Something had been broken by the impact of the truck.

For a moment Carmody considered turning and giving chase. Then he realised the other driver had too much start on him: even with his four-wheel drive, he would never overtake him in the short distance between there and Fort McMurray. He was closer to the Sanmobil plant, in any case. Better get on and make contact with the bus driver who had first raised the alarm.

He set off as fast as he dared. Jones was ominously silent, not answering questions about how he felt. Carmody set his jaw and drove through the snow.

Five minutes later he came on the stranded minibus. Immediately he recognised the black-and-yellow chequered MB 5, which he had seen and ridden in many times before. Beyond it a line of vehicles had piled up, the drivers being kept at bay by Johnson, who had told them that the police were about to arrive, and that no-one must touch the bus until the cops had checked it out. The beaten-up security men were hunched in the seats of Johnson's bus, apparently comatose.

Carmody sized up the position in a moment. 'Get it out the way,' he ordered. 'Let everybody else through.'

They pushed the Reynolds bus to one side and waved the other vehicles past. Three back in the line was a Sanmobil truck with two storehands aboard—the only men Shore had been able to conscript immediately at that late hour. Over Johnson's bus radio Carmody called for police reinforcements and alerted the Sanmobil sick bay, warning them that three injured men were being brought in. Then he detailed one of the Sanmobil men to drive his own Jeep right on to the plant, with Jones still in it. Brinckman and Jorgensen, unsteady on their feet, also climbed aboard.

'Get back in the warm,' Carmody told them. 'I'll talk to you guys later.' As they drove off he turned to Johnson. 'O.K., so what happened?'

'I just came on the bus in the middle of the road, like you saw it. The two security guys were lying in front of it, trying to get up. I got out to see what the matter was, and heard the racket of a helicopter engine, right close.'

'Where was it?'

'Just over there. I'll show you.'

He switched on a big flashlight and led the way over the frozen tundra. 'Sounded like he had a problem with the motor—kept running it up and letting it die again. Then he *did* go: lifted off and headed thataway—north. Here—you can see the ski-marks.'

In the torch-beam the imprint of long, heavy skis was still visible, though dusted over with the snow blown about by the rotor's down-draught.

'Any markings on the chopper, identification?' Carmody asked.

'Nothing—it was just like a big black shadow against the sky. Couldn't even tell the colour exactly but it looked off-white. Pair of small fins near the tail too.'

'And then what happened? Where did the person fall?'

'A woman, it was: she screamed. Someplace over there.' Johnson pointed. 'Not too far.'

'How high did she fall from?'

'Maybe a hundred feet. Maybe more.'

'Must be dead. We'd better look, all the same. Oh my God! One of the Bradys killed.'

They went up an incline into the teeth of the wind. On top of the slope the ground was rounded into smooth, gentle humps. The torch-beam, sweeping the snow, revealed nothing.

'Must have been around here,' said Johnson doubtfully. 'Can't have been much further, or I'd never have seen the body at all. Try over there a bit.'

They cast a little to their left. Suddenly Carmody, who had been walking on hard frozen tundra, sunk to his waist in snow. As he exclaimed and struggled to extricate himself from the drift, Johnson called: 'Listen, I thought I heard something.'

They waited, catching only the whine of the wind. Then Johnson heard the sound again—a cry that sounded faint yet close at hand.

'There it is!' he shouted. 'Sure as hell, someone calling. This way!'

They tried to move eastwards, but both lunged into the

deep snow again and realised that a rift in the ground ran in that direction.

They regained the hard edge of the invisible miniature valley and followed it another twenty steps. Then they heard the cry again, almost beneath them. This time they shouted back and got an answer. A few more steps brought them to the lip of a hole about a yard across that had been punched vertically downwards into the drift. Shining the light down it, they saw a bundle of powder-blue snowsuit.

'Hey! You! Mrs Brady? Stella?' Carmody called. 'Are you hurt?'

'No,' came the muffled answer. 'I'm not Mrs Brady or Stella, and I'm not hurt. Just stuck.'

'Who are you, then?'

'Corinne Delorme.'

'Corinne! Heaven's sakes! John Carmody here. Hold on, and we'll get you right out of there.' He sent Johnson running to the truck for a shovel and a rope, and in five minutes they had dug and hoisted the girl out. Considering she had been outdoors for more than half an hour, she was in remarkably good shape, mainly because the snow had insulated her and given her complete protection from the wind. But as soon as they got her into the warmth of the truck-cab, reaction set in and she began to shudder uncontrollably.

Carmody's first impulse was to drive her to hospital, but then he changed his mind. Something—he could not quite tell what—made him favour a more devious approach. The guys in the helicopter must reckon she was dead: they must think they had another murder on their hands. It was a million-to-one that she had fallen into the drifted-up ravine rather than onto the ground: five yards to either side, and every bone in her body would have been broken. Something might be gained, Carmody thought, if the kidnappers did not realise anyone had survived; therefore he decided to move her away into safe-keeping, at any rate until Brady and his team returned.

'Know what I want you to do?' Carmody said to Johnson. 'Drive Miss Delorme to the isolation unit on the plant. The *isolation* unit. When you reach the main gates, have her keep down out of sight, on the floor. I don't want anyone to know where she is. Any bother, say you're on a special run for Mr Shore, O.K.?'

Johnson nodded.

'You hear that, Corinne?' Carmody lifted up her chin. 'He'll take you to a good place at Athabasca. Nice and warm and comfortable. Out of the way, too. I'll see you back there as soon as I can make it.'

Shock and reaction had knocked the girl to pieces for the moment, and she could not answer.

'Go on, then,' Carmody told Johnson. 'Drive.'

It was past midnight and still snowing heavily when Brady arrived back in Fort McMurray, but the lobby of the Peter Pond Hotel was as crowded and bustling with activity as if it had been just after noon. Brady sank wearily into a chair. The flight from Prudhoe Bay had been a grim one: between them Brady, Dermott and Mackenzie had uttered hardly a word.

A tall, lean man, dark-moustached and heavily tanned, approached. 'Mr Brady? My name's Willoughby. Glad to make your acquaintance, sir, though not in these damnable circumstances.'

Ah—the police chief.' Brady smiled without humour. 'And rough for you, Mr Willoughby, to have this happen in your territory. I was sorry to hear that one of your men had been killed.'

'I'm glad to say that report was premature. There was a great deal of confusion around here when we made that phone call to you. The man was shot through the left lung and certainly looked bad, but now the doctor says he has a more than even chance.'

'That's something.' Brady smiled wanly again.

Willoughby turned to two other men. 'D'you know ... ?'

'Those two gentlemen I've met,' said Brady. 'Mr Brinckman, Sanmobil security chief, and his deputy, Mr Jorgensen. Odd—for a couple of reportedly injured men, you look remarkably fit to me.'

Brinckman said: 'We don't exactly feel it. Like Mr Willoughby said, things got exaggerated in the heat of the moment. No broken bones, no knife or gun injuries, but they did knock us about a bit.'

'Pete Johnson—the guy who raised the alarm—will vouch for that,' said Willoughby. 'When he got there, Jorgensen was lying on the road, out cold, and Brinckman was wandering round in a daze. He didn't know if it was last night or last month.'

Brady turned to another man who had appeared at his side. 'Evening, Mr Shore. Morning, rather. The Brady family seem to have disturbed a lot of people's sleep, I'm afraid.'

'To hell with that.' Shore was visibly upset. 'I helped show Mrs Brady and your daughter round the plant yesterday. That this should happen to her. Just as bad, that this should happen to you when you and your family were virtually our guests and you were trying to help us. A black day and a black eye for Sanmobil.'

'Maybe not all that black,' said Dermott. 'God knows, it must be a traumatic experience to be kidnapped, but I don't believe any of the four is in immediate danger. We're not dealing with political fanatics such as you get in Europe or the Mid East. We're up against hard-headed business men with no personal animosity against their victims: they almost certainly regard them as bargaining counters.' He clasped and unclasped his big hands. 'They're going to make demands, probably outrageous, for the return of the women, and if those demands are met, they'll honour the bargain. Professional kidnappers usually do. In their own twisted terms, it's sound business practice and plain commonsense.'

Brady turned to Willoughby. 'We haven't really heard what happened. I assume you haven't had time to make wide-ranging enquiries?'

'Afraid not.'

'They've just vanished into thin air?'

'Thin air is right. Helicopter, as you heard. They could be a few hundred miles away in any direction by this time.'

'Any chance of airfield radars having picked up their flight-path?'

'No, sir. It's a million to one that they were flying below radar level. Besides, there are more palm trees in Northern Alberta than there are radar stations. Down south, it's different. We've alerted the stations there to keep a watch, but nothing's been reported so far.'

'Well—' Brady steepled his fingers, sinking back in his

chair. 'It might help if we could have a brief chronological account of what happened.'

'That won't take long. Jay?'

Shore said: 'Yes. I was the last person to see them, apart from these two'—he pointed at Brinckman and Jorgensen. 'They left in one of Sanmobil's minibuses, with Bill Reynolds driving.'

Mackenzie cut in: 'Were there any phone calls before they left?'

'I wouldn't know. Why?'

'Let me ask another question.' Mackenzie looked at Brinckman. 'How did the kidnappers stop your bus?'

'They had a truck slewed across the road. Blocked it completely.'

'It couldn't have been there long. There's a fair bit of traffic on that road, and drivers wouldn't take kindly to being held up. Was there, in fact, any other traffic at the time?'

'I don't think so. No.'

Willoughby said: 'Your point, Mr Mackenzie?'

'Plain as a pikestaff. The kidnappers were tipped off. They knew the precise time when Reynolds's bus left and when it could be expected at the interception point. Phone or short-wave radio—even a CB would have been enough. Two things are for sure: there was a tip-off, and it came from Sanmobil.'

'Impossible!' Shore sounded shocked.

'Nothing else makes sense,' said Brady. 'Mackenzie's right.'

'Good God!' Shore sounded outraged. 'You make Sanmobil sound like a den of thieves.'

'It's not a Sunday School,' said Brady heavily.

Dermott turned back to Brinckman. 'So Reynolds pulled up when he saw this truck across the road? Then?'

'It was all so quick. There were two men lying in the road. One was face-down and very still, as if he were hurt real bad. The other was moving—he'd both hands clutching at the small of his back and was rolling from side to side. He seemed to be in agony. Two other men came running towards us—well, hardly running, more staggering. One was limping badly, and he had an arm stuck inside his mackinaw jacket as if he was trying to support it. Both of them had a hand up in front of

156

their faces, covering their eyes.'

Dermott said: 'Didn't that strike you as odd?'

'Not at all. It was dark, and we had our headlights on. It seemed natural they should shield their eyes from the glare.'

There was a pause. Then Brinckman went on: 'Well—this guy with the damaged arm—as I thought—came weaving up to my side of the bus. I grabbed the first-aid box and jumped out. I slipped on the ice, and by the time I had my balance I saw the man had dropped his hand and was wearing a stocking mask. Then I saw his left arm coming up. It was almost a blur, but I could see he had some kind of sap in his hand. I had no time to react.' He fingered his forehead gingerly. 'That's all, I guess.'

Dermott crossed to him and examined the contusion on the side of his forehead. 'Nasty. Could have been worse, though. An inch or so further back and you'd likely have had a fractured temple. Looks as if your friend was using lead shot. A leather cosh wouldn't have done that.'

Brinckman stared at him in an odd fashion. 'Lead, you reckon?'

'I should think so.' Dermott turned to Jorgensen. 'I take it you hadn't much better luck?'

'At least I wasn't blackjacked. I just thought my jaw had been broken. The other guy was either a heavyweight champion, or he was clutching something heavy in his fist. I couldn't see. He jerked open Mr Reynolds's door, flung in some kind of smoke-bomb, then banged the door shut again.'

'Tear gas,' said Willoughby. 'You can see his eyes are still inflamed.'

'I got out,' Jorgensen went on. 'I waved my gun around, but it might have been a water pistol, the use it was. I was blind. Next thing I remember, Pete Johnson was trying to shake some sense into us.'

'So, of course, you don't know how Reynolds and his passengers made out.' Brady looked round. He was taking over. 'Where's Carmody?'

'Down at the station,' said Shore. 'Still making his report. Pete Johnson's with him. They'll be here presently.'

'Good.' Brady turned back to Brinckman. 'The man who

attacked you—was he wearing gloves?'

'I'm not sure.' Brinckman thought and then said: 'Once he'd passed out of the beam of the headlights, he was in pretty deep shadow, and, as I said, it all happened so damn quickly. But I don't think so.'

'Your man, Mr Jorgensen?'

'I could see his hand pretty clearly as he threw the tear-gas canister. No—no glove.'

'Thank you, gentlemen. Mr Willoughby, a few questions if I may.'

'Go ahead.' Willoughby cleared his throat.

'This truck the kidnappers used—you say it was stolen?'

'That's right.'

'It's been identified?'

'Belongs to a local garage proprietor. It was known he was off on a couple of days' hunting trip.'

'At this time of year?'

'Your true enthusiast goes hunting any time. At all events, it was seen passing through the streets yesterday afternoon, and we assumed the owner was taking it along for his trip.'

'Which argues a fairly intimate local knowledge?'

'Sure, but no help to us.' Willoughby smoothed his dark moustache. 'Fort McMurray's no longer a village.'

'Have you fingerprinted the truck, inside and out?'

'Being done now. It's a long job—there are hundreds of prints.'

'May we see them?'

'Of course. I'll have them Photostatted. But, with respect, Mr Brady, what do you hope to achieve that we, the police, can't?'

'You never know.' Brady smiled enigmatically. 'Mr Dermott here is an international expert in fingerprinting.'

'I didn't know!' Willoughby smiled at Dermott, who smiled back. He hadn't known either.

Brady changed his tack. 'Any chance of identifying the helicopter from the measurements of the ski-marks that Carmody took?'

Willoughby shook his head. 'It was a good idea to record them, but no—the chances of identifying any one machine

158

from its ski-prints are extremely remote, because there will almost certainly be dozens of its particular type around. This is helicopter country, Mr Brady, like Alaska. Here in Northern Alberta our communications are still very primitive. We have no divided highways—freeways—in this part of the world. In fact, north of Edmonton there only two paved roads that reach up north. Between them—nothing. Apart from ourselves, and Peace River and Fort Chipewyan, there are no commercial airports in an area of 200,000 square miles.'

'So,' Brady nodded. 'You use choppers.'

'The preferred form of transport at all times. In winter, the only form.'

'It's a good bet that an intensive air search wouldn't have a hope in hell of locating the getaway machine?'

'None. I've made a bit of a study of kidnapping, and I can answer you best by a comparison. The world's most kidnap-happy place is Sardinia. It's a kind of national pastime there. Whenever a millionaire is snatched, all the resources of the law and the Italian armed forces are brought into play. The Navy blockades harbours and virtually every fishing village on the coast. The Army sets up road-blocks, and specially-trained troops sweep the hills. The Air Force carries out exhaustive reconnaissance by plane and helicopter. In all the years these searches have been carried out, they've never yet located a single kidnapper's hideout. Alberta is twenty-seven times larger than Sardinia. Our resources are a fraction of theirs. Answer your question?'

'One begins to feel the first faint twinges of despair. But tell me, Mr Willoughby: if you had four kidnapped people on your hands, where would you hide them?'

'Edmonton or Calgary.'

'But those are towns. Surely ...'

'Cities, yes—and the population of each must be crowding half a million. The captives wouldn't be hidden—they'd be lost.'

'Well.' Brady pulled himself up in his chair. He looked weary. 'Okay. I suppose we have to wait word from the kidnappers before we make a move. You two gentlemen—' he turned to Brinckman and Jorgensen—'I don't think we need keep you any longer. Thank you for your co-operation.'

The two security men said their goodnights and left. Brady hoisted himself to his feet. 'No sign of Carmody yet? Let's go and make ourselves more comfortable while we wait for him. The desk will no doubt inform us when he arrives. This way, gentlemen.'

*   *   *

Once in the privacy of his own room, armed with a fresh drink, Brady seemed suddenly to shake off his exhaustion.

'O.K., George,' he said briskly. 'You've been holding out on us. Why?'

'In what way?'

'Don't pussy-foot. You said you were more concerned about the demands the crooks are going to make than about my family. You love my family. Now what did you mean?'

'The first demand will be that you, Don and I take off for Houston. They must be convinced we're on the verge of a breakthrough.

'The second demand will be a ransom message. To keep things within reasonable bounds they can hardly ask for more than a couple of million dollars. But that would be peanuts compared with the stakes our friends are playing for.

'Third, the greater stakes. Obviously, they'll demand a fortune to cease their harassment of both Prudhoe Bay's and Sanmobil oil supplies, and the increasing destruction of their equipment. That's where they hold all the aces: as we've seen, both systems are embarrassingly vulnerable to attack. For as long as the criminals' identity remains undiscovered, they can keep on destroying both systems piecemeal.

'Their price will be high. I imagine they'll base it on the development cost of the two systems—that's ten billion for starters—plus the daily revenue, which is the cost of over two million barrels a day. Five per cent of the total? Ten? Depends what the market will bear. One thing's for sure: if they demand too much and price themselves out of the market, the oil companies are going to cut their losses and run, leaving the insurance companies to hold the baby—and it will surely be the most expensive baby in insurance history.'

Brady said querulously: 'Why didn't you bring this up downstairs?'

'I have an aversion to talking too much in crowded hotel foyers.' Dermott leant towards Jay Shore. 'Did your Edmonton office send the fingerprints we asked for?'

'I have them in the safe at home.'

'Good.' Dermott nodded approval; but Willoughby was curious: 'What prints?'

Shore hesitated until he received an all-but-imperceptible nod from Dermott, and said: 'Mr Brady and his men seem pretty well convinced that we have at Sanmobil one or more subversives actively aiding and abetting the men trying to destroy us. Mr Dermott particularly suspects our security staff and all those who have access to our safe.'

Willoughby shot Dermott a cool, quizzical look. It was clear that he considered the matter one for the Canadian police and not for foreign amateurs. 'Would you mind explaining why?' he asked coldly.

'They're the only suspects we have—especially the men in charge of the security shifts. Not only do they have access to the key of the armoury from which the explosives were stolen, they actually carry the damn thing around with them on duty. More, I have good reason to suspect the security staff on the Alaskan pipeline. Further, it appears more than likely that both security staffs are working hand-in-glove under the same boss or bosses. How else can you explain how some villains here know the Sohio/B.P. code, while the villains there know Sanmobil's?'

Willoughby said: 'This is just conjecture ...'

'Sure. But it's conjecture shading into probability. Isn't it a basic police philosophy to set up a theory and examine it from all sides before discarding it? Well, we've set up our theory, examined it from all sides, and don't feel like discarding it.'

Willoughby frowned, then said: 'You don't trust the security men?'

'Let me amplify that. The majority are straight, no doubt, but until I know for sure, they're all under suspicion.'

'Including Brinckman and Jorgensen?'

' "Including" is not the word. "Especially".'

'Jesus! You're talking crazy, Dermott. After what they went through?'

'Tell me what they went through.'

'They told you already.' Willoughby had become incredulous.

Dermott was unmoved. 'I've only got their word for that—and I'm pretty sure in both cases that word's worthless.'

'Carmody corroborated their story—or rather, Johnson did. Maybe you don't trust him either?'

'I'll decide that when I meet him. But the point is, Johnson *didn't* corroborate the story. All he said—correct me if I'm wrong—was that when he arrived on the scene he found Brinckman unconscious and Jorgensen staggering around. That's all he said. He had no more idea what went on before that than you or I do.'

'Then how d'you account for their injuries?'

'Injuries?' Dermott smiled sarcastically. 'Jorgensen didn't have a mark on him. Brinckman did, but if you'd been watching him, you'd have seen him jump when I told him he'd been struck by a lead-filled cosh. That didn't fit. There was something wrong with the scenario.

'I suggest both men were in perfectly good health until they saw the lights of Johnson's minibus approaching, whereupon Jorgensen, acting on instructions, tapped Brinckman on the head just hard enough to lay him out briefly.'

'What do you mean, "under instructions"?' Willoughby demanded doggedly. 'Whose?'

'That remains to be discovered. But you might like to know that these aren't the first peculiar injuries we've come across. A doctor in Prudhoe Bay, for one, has discovered that we have highly suspicious minds on this subject. Donald and I had to examine a murdered engineer whose finger had sustained a curious fracture. The good doctor explained it away to his own apparent satisfaction, but not to ours. He probably gave orders that if any other such—ah—marginal incidents happened, any security agents in the vicinity were to display proof of injuries sustained in the loyal execution of their duties—

such as, in this case, their attempts to protect those whom they were supposed to be protecting.'

Willoughby stared at him and muttered: 'You have to be fantasising.'

Dermott answered: 'We'll see.' But his reply was cut short by the sudden arrival of Carmody and Johnson. Both men looked pale and exhausted—a condition Brady sought to remedy by providing them with very large Scotches.

After a suitable pause for congratulation on his night's work, Carmody was taken through his account, step by step. The exercise proved disappointing until, when he came to describe the scene of the helicopter ski-marks, he suddenly became tongue-tied. He broke off in mid-sentence and stammered: 'Say, Mr Brady, could I—er—could I talk with you *privately*?'

'Well!' Brady was somewhat taken aback. 'By all means— but what purpose would it serve? These gentlemen enjoy my fullest confidence. Say what you want in their hearing.'

'O.K., then. It's about the girl—Corinne ...' Whereupon he told them the story of the rescue. Amazement swiftly and thoroughly woke up his audience. They crowded forward, listening intently.

'Maybe I was wrong,' Carmody ended up, 'but I just figured that if news of her survival didn't get out, it might be a card up our sleeve.'

'You figured correctly,' Brady said.

'Where is she, then?' asked Dermott sharply.

'Right now she's in the isolation unit at the plant. She went a bit hysterical, with the reaction, but she's all right.'

Dermott let out a whoosh of air and said, 'My, oh my!'

'A very original observation, George,' Brady remarked wryly. 'Do I detect a certain ... pleasure on your part that the young lady is alive and well and in safe hands?'

'You do,' said Dermott. Then he added quickly, as if feeling he had been over-enthusiastic: 'And why not?'

'Point is, I took a statement from her,' Carmody went on. 'Want to hear it?'

'Certainly,' Brady said. 'Fire away.'

The statement still existed only in Carmody's notebook,

and so took some time to read. The beginning of it merely confirmed what had been established already—but then came a revelation. After the hold-up, the girl reported, 'one man came staggering towards us along the road'.

'*One* man?' snapped Dermott, half-rising out of his chair. 'Did she say *one* man?'

'That's what she said.' Carmody resumed his recitation, back-tracking a sentence to emphasise her account. ' "I saw two men lying in the road, like they were hurt. One was dead still. The other could move a bit. Then one other man came limping back towards us. He had a hand up in front of his eyes. Mr Brinckman was sitting on my right. He jumped out and grabbed the first-aid box from under the seat. I think he slipped and fell over. Then he got up again. Then I saw the other man straighten up and hit him. He went down—Mr Brinckman, that is. The other man had a stocking mask on—I could see that by now. He opened the door where Mr Reynolds was sitting and threw something into the bus ..." '

'That's it!' cried Dermott, smiting his fist on the coffee-table. 'We got them!'

Brady glowered at him. 'Would you favour us slower brethren with an explanation?'

'The whole thing was a frame-up. They told us a load of garbage. They said *two* men came at them, to make it seem more realistic that they hadn't put up any resistance. Now it's obvious they didn't *try* to resist. They were part of the act. Jorgensen just sat there watching his partner get slugged.'

'How come he wasn't much affected by the tear gas?' Brady asked.

'He was prepared for it, of course,' Dermott replied instantly. 'If you screw your eyes shut and hold your breath, tear gas has very little effect on you. Jorgensen only had to hold out for a couple of seconds before opening his own door and getting into the fresh air. Listen to what the girl said: there were no bodies left on the road when she was dragged away. Every damn one of them had got up, right as rain, to help get the captives aboard the chopper. It was only when they saw Johnson's headlights coming that Brinckman and

Jorgensen resumed their artistic poses on the road.'

Willoughby muttered a curse. 'I believe you're right,' he said slowly. 'I really do. And we haven't a shred of hard evidence against them.'

'No way you could dream up a charge and haul them in for preventive detention?' asked Dermott hopefully.

'None.'

'I wish you could,' said Dermott. 'I'd sleep happier for the rest of the night. As it is, I don't intend to sleep at all. I've got a slight aversion to being murdered in bed.'

Brady nearly choked on his drink. 'And what the hell does that mean, mister?'

'Just that I think an attempt will soon be made to murder me. And Donald. And you.'

Brady looked as though he might explode, but remained speechless. Dermott addressed him with some acerbity.

'Whenever you spoke down there in the foyer just now, you were tightening another screw in your own coffin-lid.' He turned to Willoughby. 'Could you spare a guard for Mr Shore's house tonight?'

'Of course; but why?'

'Simple. Mr Brady unfortunately made it clear that he wanted copies of fingerprints found on the stolen truck. Brinckman and Jorgensen know that we've asked your people for what could be damning prints from your Edmonton H.Q. They'll discover, if they haven't already, that the copies of their own prints which we took earlier are in the safe in Mr Shore's house.'

'What good would it do them to get the copies?' Brady asked edgily. 'The originals are at police H.Q. in Edmonton.'

'How far d'you think this rot has spread?' said Dermott. 'The originals may still be there, but they won't be much help once they've been through a shredding machine.'

'Where's the problem?' asked Willoughby. 'We just print 'em out again.'

'On what grounds? Suspicion? Just one moderately competent lawyer, and the town would be looking for a new police chief. They'd refuse point-blank. What could you do then?'

'Point out to them—which is the case—that it's a condition of employment at Sanmobil.'

'So you'd have mass resignations on your hands. Then what?'

Willoughby didn't answer. Mackenzie broke in: 'You said I was the other grave-digger?'

'Yes. You said the kidnappers must have been tipped off from Sanmobil as to when to expect Reynolds's bus. You were right, of course. But Brinckman and Jorgensen must have thought you meant it was they who gave the tip. They may even think we can trace the call to them, even though outgoing calls from the plant aren't normally tapped.'

'Well, I'm sorry.' Mackenzie shifted uneasily.

'Too bad. The damage has been done. And it wouldn't have helped to reproach you and Mr Brady in public.'

The phone rang. Dermott, the nearest, picked it up, listened briefly and said: 'One moment. I think the person you should talk to is Mr Shore. He's right here with us.'

He handed the phone over and listened impassively to Shore's half of the conversation, which consisted almost entirely of muttered expletives. The phone rest rattled as he replaced the receiver, so badly was his hand shaking. His face had gone white.

'They've shot Grigson,' he gasped.

'Who's Grigson?' snapped Brady.

'Sanmobil's president. That's all.'

13

The police doctor, a young man named Saunders, straightened and looked down at the unconscious man on the pile of blankets. 'He'll be all right, eventually, but that's all I can do for him now. He needs the services of an orthopaedic surgeon.'

'How long will it be before I can question him?' Brady asked.

'With the sedative I've given him, it'll be several hours before he comes round.'

'Couldn't that damned sedative have waited a little?'

Dr Saunders looked at Brady with a marked lack of enthusiasm. 'I hope, for your sake, you never have your shoulder and upper arm shattered, the bone structure completely fragmented. Mr Grigson was in agony. And even had he been conscious, I wouldn't have let you question him.'

Brady muttered something about medical dictators, then looked at Shore and said testily: 'What the hell was Grigson doing here anyway?'

'Dammit, Brady, he's more right to be here than you and I and the rest of us put together.' Shore sounded shocked and angry. 'Sanmobil is the dream-come-true of one man and one only, and he's lying there before you. Took him nine years to turn his dream into reality, and he had to fight all the way. He's the president. Do you understand that—the president?'

Mackenzie said pacifically: 'When did he arrive?'

'Yesterday afternoon. Flew in from Europe.'

Mackenzie nodded and looked round Reynolds's office. It wasn't a small room, but it was fairly crowded. Apart from himself, Brady, Shore, Dr Saunders and the unconscious Grigson, there were Willoughby and two young men who had clearly been in the wars during the recent past. One had a bandaged forehead, the other an arm strapped from wrist to elbow. It was to this last person, Steve Dawson, that Mackenzie addressed himself.

'You were in charge of the night-shift?'

'Nominally. Tonight there *was* no night-shift. The plant's closed down.'

'I know. So how many of you were here tonight—yourself apart?'

'Just six people.' He glanced down at the wounded man. 'Mr Grigson was asleep in his private room along the corridor there. Then there was Hazlitt—charge-hand of the night security shift—and four security guards deployed around the plant.'

'Tell us what happened.'

'Well—I was patrolling, reinforcing the security team, as I had nothing else to do. I saw a light come on here in Mr Reynolds's room. First I thought it must be Mr Grigson—he's a very active, restless person, and an erratic sleeper. Then I got to wondering what he could be doing, because he'd already spent a couple of hours with Mr Reynolds yesterday. So, quiet as I could, I came along the passage to Grigson's room.

'The door was closed, but not locked. I went in, and there he was asleep. I woke him, told him there were intruders in the plant, and asked to borrow a gun. I knew he had one, because he used to practise on a little private target range he'd set up here.

'He'd have none of it. He produced his automatic, but kept it himself. He said he'd had it for years and knew how to use it. I couldn't argue with him—after all, I'm only twenty-eight, and he's crowding seventy.

'Anyway, in here we found a man with the door of that safe open. He'd smashed Corinne's desk open with a fire-axe to get at the keys. He was wearing a stocking mask and examining a bunch of keys he had in his hand.

'Mr Grigson told him to turn around, real slow, and not to try anything, or he'd kill him. Then suddenly came two pistol shots, right close together, from behind, and Mr Grigson pitched headlong to the floor. He was wearing a white shirt, and blood from his right shoulder and arm was pumping

168

through it. I could see he was hurt real bad.

'I dropped to my knees to help him. The man who'd fired the shots probably figured I was going for Mr Grigson's gun. Anyway, he fired at me too.'

Dawson was breathing quickly, his distress evident. Brady poured him a Scotch and handed the glass over. 'Take this.'

Dawson's smile was wan. 'I've never had a drink in my life, sir.'

'Maybe you'll never have another,' said Brady agreeably. 'But you need this one, and we need your story.'

Dawson drank, spluttered and coughed. He screwed up his eyes and drank some more. He clearly detested the stuff, but his system didn't, for almost immediately some colour began to return to his cheeks. He touched his bandaged forearm.

'Looks worse than it is. The bullet just grazed me, wrist all the way to elbow, but very superficial. Stung, more than anything. One of the masked men forced me to help lug Mr Grigson to the armoury. On the way out I picked up two first-aid kits—they didn't object. They pushed us into the armoury, locked the door and left.

'Then I took off Mr Grigson's shirt and staunched the wound as best I could. It took a lot of bandages—there was so much blood coming. I thought he was going to bleed to death.'

'He could have,' Saunders said with certainty. 'No question, your quick action saved his life.'

'Glad I was some use.' Dawson shuddered, looked at the doctor and went on; 'Then I bandaged my own arm and had a go at the door, but there was no way I could get it open. I looked around and found a box full of detonators, each with a fuse attached. I struck one and dropped it out through one of the ventilation grilles. It went off with quite a bang. I must have let seven or eight of them off before Hazlitt came hammering on the door and asked what the hell was going on. I told him, and he ran off to fetch a duplicate key.'

Dawson drank some more, spluttered, but less than before, and put his glass down. 'I guess that's about all.'

'And more than enough,' said Brady with unaccustomed warmth. 'A splendid job, son.' He looked round the assembled group, then asked sharply; 'Where's George?'

Until then no-one had noticed that Dermott was missing. Then Mackenzie said: 'He slipped out with Carmody some time back. You want me to go find him?'

'Leave him be,' said Brady. 'I have little doubt our faithful bloodhound is pursuing some spoor of his own.'

*   *   *

In fact the bloodhound was pursuing a fancy, not a line. He had taken Carmody aside and whispered in his ear that he urgently wanted to question the girl, Corinne. Where was she?

'In the isolation ward, like I said,' Carmody replied. 'But I doubt you'll find it on your own. It's way out by itself, near Dragline One. Want me to come with you?'

'Sure. That'd be real kind.' Dermott swallowed his disappointment. He wanted to go alone. The instincts at work inside him made him feel uncomfortable: nothing like this had happened to him in years. But he had better be realistic and accept the offer of guidance.

By then the wind had increased, as it often did late in the night, and was whistling across the flat, open site with a deadly chill. The noise made it almost impossible to talk in the open—not that anyone in his senses would remain in the open for more than the minimum time.

Carmody had been reunited with his damaged Cherokee. Shouting an excuse into the wind, he got in first at the passenger door and slid across behind the wheel. Dermott heaved his massive frame in close behind him and slammed the door.

Carmody drove steadily across an apparently unmarked plain. The film of drifting snow had obscured the road, and the flat ground all looked the same.

'How the hell do you know which way to go?' Dermott asked.

'Markers—there.' Carmody pointed as a small stumpy, black-and-white post went past, with the number 323 stencilled on it in bold figures. 'We're on Highway Three. In a minute we'll turn onto Highway Nine.'

Altogether they drove for nearly ten minutes before lights showed up out of the darkness ahead. Dermott was amazed once again at the sheer size of the site: by then they were four or five miles from the administration buildings.

The lights grew to a blaze of several windows, and they pulled up outside a single long hut. As they went through the door the heat hit them like a hammer as did a smell of disinfectant. Dermott at once began to wrestle his way out of his outdoor clothes: he felt he would stifle if he kept them on for one more second.

They found Corinne propped up on a pile of pillows, looking pale but (to Dermott's eye) very sweet in a pair of pea-green pyjamas. Contrary to Carmody's predictions, she was wide awake. She'd been asleep, she said, and had woken up thinking it was already morning.

'What time is it, anyway?' she asked.

'Four o'clock, near enough,' Dermott answered. 'How d'you feel?'

'Fantastic. Not even a bruise, as far as I can tell.'

'That's wonderful. But my, were you lucky!' Dermott began asking routine questions, to which he didn't really want the answers. He wished to hell Carmody would go away someplace and leave him alone with the girl. What he would say to her if that happened, he didn't quite know: all the same it was what he wanted.

'You've given us a real good lead, you know,' he said enthusiastically. 'Can't say just what it was, but it may be the breakthrough we needed. Mr Brady's delighted ...'

His voice tailed off as a heavy rumble suddenly shook the building. 'Jesus!' he looked up sharply. 'What was that?'

Carmody was gone already, out of the room and down the short passage. Dermott caught up with him at the outside door.

'Helicopter!' Carmody snapped. 'Made a low pass right over the building. There he is, turning now.' Way out in the blackness a red and a green light converged and then separated again as the aircraft swung round. As the two men stood watching a pair of car headlamps snapped on from a point about a hundred yards in front of them. The vehicle moved forward, turned and stopped, with its headlights steady on a patch of snow.

'It's a marker!' Carmody cried. 'He's gonna land. Quick, get the girl out of here. They must have come for her.'

'How in hell do they know she's here?' said Dermott.

'Don't worry about that. Let's get her away.' Moving like a sprinter, Carmody slipped back into the building, bundled Corinne up in a cocoon of blankets and carried her out to the Jeep, where he dumped her in the back seat. Dermott lumbered behind him, envying his speed, and hauled himself into the front.

Without putting on any lights Carmody started the engine and moved off into the inky night, heading out into the open behind the parked marker-vehicle. A couple of hundred yards beyond it he swung round and faced in the same direction as the lights, so that he and Dermott could watch what happened through the windshield.

They sat there with the heater going full blast.

'Warm enough?' asked Carmody over his shoulder.

'Plenty, thanks.' Corinne sounded as though she was enjoying herself. 'I've got enough blankets to keep an elephant warm.'

Dermott wondered uneasily whether that was any sort of a joke at his expense, but his speculation was cut short by the arrival of the helicopter. Suddenly it was there, large and grey-white, riding down on a storm of snow into the headlight pool. The rotor flashed brilliantly in the silvery beams, and the snow flew outwards from the downdraught.

'That's the one!' said Carmody in a voice charged with excitement. 'The getaway chopper. Description tallies perfectly with Johnson's: grey-white, no markings, small fins by the tail. That's our baby. Damn!'

As soon as the machine had landed, the car's headlights cut. The watchers sat blinded by the sudden darkness. They saw a flashlight bobbing about in the blackness, but nothing else.

'Boy, will they be mad when they find you've gone!' Carmody said happily.

'D'you think they're still in it?' Corinne asked. 'The others, I mean?'

'Could be—easily. Depends where the chopper's been these past few hours. Must have been waiting on the ground someplace.'

'Come on!' snapped Dermott. 'Let's get out of here.'

'Wait a minute,' Carmody said easily. 'I wanna see what they do. Any moment now they'll be at the building. There— I can see them now.'

Two figures moved swiftly past the lighted windows. More light showed as the door opened and shut.

'Can't we ram the helicopter or something?' Corinne suggested. 'Stop it taking off?'

'Too big,' said Carmody immediately. 'You notice the legs and skis? Higher than our roof. All we'd do would be to damage the landing gear, which wouldn't stop them getting off. Besides, if I know them, there's a couple of guys with guns guarding the thing, at least. Hey—what was that?'

'What?' Dermott looked at him.

'I heard something. Machinery. Sure I did.' Carmody looked out past Dermott into the darkness. 'Open your window a minute.'

Dermott obeyed, and instantly the noise was far louder: a huge squealing and clanking, as of some giant engine.

'Jesus Christ!' Carmody shouted. 'The dragline. It's right here beside us.'

Dermott opened his door and got out. His eyes, accustomed to the dark, could just make out the gigantic outline towering above them. Suddenly the noise seemed terrific. 'Good God!' Dermott yelled into the wind. 'It's alive. It's *moving*!'

Instinctively he began to run towards the machine, or rather, round it, for already he was alongside. Beside him he could hear the whine of electric motors, the squeal of metal and the crunch of frosted dirt as the mighty shoe ground forward. The coldness of the wind seared his lungs and made his eyes stream briefly before they froze. In spite of the discomfort, he felt fired by excitement and by rage, for here was a final and outrageous act of sabotage taking place right on top of him. In a flash of intuition he saw what they intended: to drive the monster machine over the edge of the pit which it had been excavating.

173

The facts and figures that had been flung at him came crowding into his head. Six and a half thousand tons. It could move at some 250 yards an hour. The pit was 150 feet deep. Although he was no engineer, he knew instinctively that if the monster went over the edge, it would never come out again.

He came round the front of it and got another shock. The edge of the pit, showing as a limitless black hole, was less than thirty yards away. Perhaps only twenty-five. That meant he had a tenth of an hour—six minutes—to get the damn thing stopped. He looked up desperately. The boom disappeared into the night, like an Eiffel Tower tilted over. Somehow he had to get into the cab and throw the right switches.

He ran back right under the thing, between the shoes. Somewhere there must be a ladder. At last he found it. But as he looked up towards the cab, far above him, he saw someone moving there in a faint glow of light. He hesitated, one foot on the steel ladder, wishing he had a gun and wondering whether he should go back for Carmody. That was the last thought that entered his head for a couple of minutes, for the blow caught him squarely on the back of the neck, and brilliant points of light seemed to shoot outwards through his head as he slumped to the ground.

*　　*　　*

He came round shaking from the cold and stuck in an awkward position. His hands were jammed, somehow—jammed behind him. He needed to straighten his arms and get them back into action. He strained to sort himself out and realised with a shock that his wrists were manacled together, *and manacled to something.*

He gave a grunt and heaved, whereupon a man spoke out of the dark behind him.

'Ah, Mr Dermott,' said a voice he half-recognised but could not place. 'Struggling will not help. You are anchored to a steel ring let into concrete. The ring is directly in the path of Dragline One, which, as you can see and hear, is now only a few feet from you. The controls have been preset and locked in position so that the middle of the right shoe will pass over you. Goodbye, Mr Dermott. You have less than two minutes to live.'

Fear cleared Dermott's head. 'Bastards!' he cried. 'Sadistic bastards! Come back!' But even as he shouted, he knew it was useless. In the whistle of the wind and the monstrous grinding of the dragline, his voice was nothing and carried nowhere. He twisted round and discovered that he was tethered almost on the lip of the pit: the edge of the black abyss was no more than a yard away. In the opposite direction, the front of the dragline's shoe had ground remorselessly to within fifteen feet of him. The front of it was coming on like a tank. Above him, the steel tracery of the boom seemed to fill the sky with an angry black pattern.

Dermott stopped shouting and began to fight the manacles. At least there was some movement: he could feel that a length of chain had been passed through the shackle on the ground. He jerked it furiously back and forth in the faint hope that the chain would break, but all he achieved was to chafe his wrists viciously and expose them to the cold. He could feel the icy steel biting into his bare skin. Frostbite, he thought dully. But what did frostbite matter if he was going to be crushed like a beetle?

'Carmody!' he yelled desperately. 'Help!' Where the hell had Carmody gone? Why didn't he come looking?

Dermott fought the chain again and flopped flat, gasping. The shoe was only twelve feet off, scrunching on inch by inch. The whine of the electric motors seemed to fill the night, as if hell had claimed him.

He threw his body feverishly to left and right, experimenting to see if he could get clear of the shoe's line of advance. Nothing he tried was the slightest good: the shoe was ten feet wide, and he was tethered right in the middle of its track. The monster had been set marching with hideous precision.

He lay still again, panting, beaten. Suddenly images began flashing through his mind, conjured up uninvoked by the extremity of his desperation. Once again he witnessed the final terrifying seconds of the car-crash that had killed his wife, the time when an explosion had blown him clean off a rig in the Gulf of Mexico, into the shark-infested sea ...

All at once he became aware of a light flashing over him. Then someone was crouching, pulling at his arms. Then he heard a high, feminine cry.

'Corinne!'

'My God!' she cried. 'What's happened? Oh, Jesus!' She leapt to her feet and began to run. '*Wait*!' she screamed over her shoulder.

Dermott saw her fall, get up again, and go like a greyhound, round the the corner of the shoe, the flashlight swinging wildly in the blackness. He shouted something after her, but she was gone. *Wait*, she'd said. Wait! What a hell of a thing to say! How could he wait? The shoe was scarcely ten feet from him: one minute, give or take a few seconds.

He found his eyes were full of tears, though whether they were of fear or relief or gratitude or what, he couldn't tell. He was crying like a baby.

Seconds were passing. He began to count. He got to ten and couldn't go on. He had been overtaken by a horrific vision of the exact physical process of destruction that was about to annihilate him. He would feed his feet and legs to the monster first. Or could he? Could he listen and watch while his ankles, shins and knees were crunched and flattened on the tundra? No—he would have to get the end over quickly and give it his head. But what would *that* be like, for God's sake? To hear his skull crack and feel that unthinkable weight! Impossible! Never!

He roared again: 'CARMODY!' As if by a miracle, his shout was answered. Headlights came boring up out of the night and swept across him as the vehicle turned. Dermott stared incredulously as the lights came on at speed, heading right for him and the front of the shoe. At the last moment the vehicle slowed, but not enough to stop. The driver deliberately slid it into the front of the shoe, using it as a last-ditch barrier to stop the monster's progress. There was a sharp crash and the tinkle of falling glass. Then the door of the Jeep opened and Corinne leapt out.

There was so little space left that Dermott had all but been run over. The Jeep's left-hand wheels were almost on him. The next thing he saw was the tyres being forced bodily sideways towards him by the irresistible pressure of the dragline's advance.

Corinne had the tail-gate of the Jeep open. She dragged out a steel box—the emergency equipment—and dumped it behind Dermott with a crash.

'Keep still!' she shouted above the noise. 'No—come back a bit. There. Keep there! I've got the bolt shears.'

Dermott leant backwards in the attitude she ordered, speechless with tension. He saw the wheels of the Jeep come sideways at him again. The back wheel was touching his feet already. The Jeep was being pushed like a toy. At that rate it was going to do more harm than good: it was merely acting as an extension of the shoe, and would crush him before the dragline itself reached him.

He felt Corinne struggling behind him. Suddeny she gave a desperate cry. 'Oh my God! I can't do it. I'm not strong enough.'

Dermott's voice returned. 'What's happening?' he shouted.

'The cutters!' she sobbed. 'The bolt shears are biting into the chain, but I can't get enough pressure on them. It's too bloody hard!'

'Put one end on the ground,' he ordered calmly. 'One handle on the ground. Then get your weight on the other.'

He felt her try, but she slipped and went down with a crash. 'Try again!' he yelled.

By then the noise of the dragline was overwhelming: its roaring and grinding filled the night. But suddenly a new sound: a sharp crack told him that the great steel treads of the shoe had hooked into some part of the Jeep's bodywork. Instead of being pushed back, the vehicle had been gripped and held down. Dermott stared incredulously as the Cherokee began collapsing like an eggshell. The remaining headlight was snuffed out. Cracking, snapping noises accompanied the collapse of the hood and front wheels.

Behind him Corinne gave a despairing scream. 'I just can't do it. I've got half-way through, but that's all.'

'Look for a hacksaw!' Dermott shouted. 'In the emergency pack.'

'Got one!' She began working again frantically.

177

For Dermott time seemed to have stopped. He saw that the Cherokee's engine block had at last offered the dragline a spot of serious resistance: only a spot, it was true, but a definite token. Ponderous as a dinosaur, the machine lifted one foot slowly into the air as it ground the little human vehicle beneath its steel sole. As if in a trance, Dermott saw the windshield shatter, the front of the roof crumple down, the passenger compartment flatten. Right in front of him a back wheel snapped off and was squashed flat onto the ground. If his arms had been free, he could have reached out and touched the front of the shoe—it was that close.

But his arms were *not* free.

'I can't!' Corinne screamed in desperation.

Dermott's head cleared, and he shouted: 'Is there an axe?'

'A what?'

'An axe.'

'Yes—here.'

'Smash the chain with that. Aim for the link you've been working on.'

'I might hit you.'

'To hell with that. Belt it.'

He felt the thump as she let drive. The chain snatched sharply at his wrists and nearly jerked his arms from their sockets. Suddenly he smelt the stink of gasoline: the tank had been crushed.

Clank! She brought the axe down, then again. When Dermott twisted to see how she was doing, the clawing thread of the shoe scraped down past his shoulder. The thing was touching him. He shrank away from the monstrous beast, and brought out his last, terrible idea.

'Chop my hands off!' he ordered, quite calmly.

'I can't!'

'Go on. It's them or me.'

'*No!*' She gave a piercing shriek and swung the axe down with every ounce of her behind it. Next second she was on her knees sobbing: 'Oh my God, it's gone! It's gone!'

Dermott fought his instinct to leap up. He held himself down as she struggled with the severed link. The tread was bumping and bruising him now. In a few moments it would hook him under, as it had the car.

'For Christ's sake!' he shouted. 'Hurry!'

Miraculously, his hands came free. He got his arms back to their normal position and twisted sideways. 'Look out for the pit!' he yelled. He himself was on the very lip. Hardly had he rolled clear of the dragline when there was a huge *whumph* and a roar of dark-red flame shot sideways at ground level. A chance spark had ignited the car's gasoline. By a fluke he had rolled into the wind, so that the fiery blast went the other way and left him unscathed. Corinne was there behind him, also intact.

The blaze made no difference to the monster's advance. The flames roared for a few seconds, then went out, and the dragline continued without faltering towards the brink.

Dermott felt weak with reaction—but not as weak as the girl. One moment she was standing behind him; the next, as Dermott struggled to find the words to express his gratitude to her, she had collapsed in a heap on the ground. He picked her up as tenderly as he knew how, laid her gingerly over his shoulder in a fireman's lift, and began carrying her towards the still-lighted windows of the isolation quarters. His eyes seemed to have gone blurred with the strain. Or was it just ice? He scrubbed them with his free hand and saw better. Out in the patch of white light ahead of him, the helicopter was preparing to take off, lights flashing, rotor spinning. Even as he watched, it lifted off and slanted away into the sky.

At once the car whose lights had provided the marker moved off and accelerated. Once again, Dermott realised, the villains had melted into the night. He knew he ought to feel disappointed: as it was, he could concentrate on nothing except getting back into the warmth of the hut and lying down.

He was very close to the building, going slow, when he saw someone pass across the lighted windows in front of him. Fear seized him. Maybe it was one of them. Was he going to be shot after making such an effort? Before he had time to put down his burden or alter course, a flashlight came on, searched briefly and found his face.

'Good God! Dermott!'

'Carmody! Where in hell have you been?'

'Trying to ditch the chopper. What about you?'

'Had a ... had a bit of bother.' Suddenly Dermott found he could hardly talk. He was about to break down. 'Take her, will you?' he croaked. 'I've had it.'

With an exclamation Carmody relieved him of his inert burden. 'Quick,' said the policeman. 'Inside.'

They laid Corinne on one bed and Dermott collapsed on to another with the manacles still dangling from his wrists. 'Ring Shore!' he gasped. 'Tell him for Christ's sake to switch off the power to Dragline One. Tell him and Brady to get up here like they never drove before.'

*   *   *

They had turned on the floodlamps to illuminate the 150-foot depths of the pit below. They had also hammered in spikes ten yards back from the lip, and to these they had attached ropes so that the vertiginously-inclined or the less-than-sure-footed could cling to them as they peered over the edge.

Dragline One had ended up on its nose, tilted backwards towards the near-vertical face at an angle of thirty degrees. The massive casing appeared undamaged, as did the triangular arm over which the control cables passed. Even the boom, its enormous length stretched out horizontally across the uneven valley floor, seemed undamaged, at least from above.

Brady had prudently wrapped his belaying rope three times round his mighty girth. 'Surprisingly little damage,' he said. 'Or so it looks. I suppose some of the electric motors were wrenched free from their beds.'

'That'll be the least of our troubles.' Jay Shore looked stricken, ashen-faced in the floodlights. The sight of the crippled monster had far more effect on him than on any of the others. 'It's getting the damn thing out of there.'

'Wouldn't it be easier to get a replacement?' asked Brady.

'Jesus! Do you know what a replacement would cost at today's prices? Forty million dollars. Probably more. And you don't order one up, just like that. If we could have one on our doorstep tomorrow, I'm sure Sanmobil would order it. But it can't be done that way. You can't transport a thing that size overland. Electric motors apart, the whole caboodle comes crated in tens of thousands of pieces, and it takes a team of skilled engineers months to assemble it.'

'Cranes?' Brady suggested. He seemed fascinated by the sheer size of the problem. Or he was trying to be diverted, trying not to think of his missing wife and daughter.

Shore made a dismissive gesture with his gloved hands. 'The biggest cranes in the world—a whole battery of them—couldn't lift the dragline an inch off the floor. We'll either have to dismantle it piece by piece and raise the bits up here for reassembly, or build a road from down there back up to the surface level and have it towed up on bogies—or, perhaps, under its own steam. The road would have to be a very gentle gradient, which would mean a length of over a mile, heavily metalled on massive foundations. Whatever we do, it'll cost millions.' He swore at some considerable length. 'And all this in just seven minutes' work!'

'Why in hell couldn't you *stop* it, when we phoned you?' asked Carmody.

'The bastards knew what they were doing,' said Shore savagely. 'They'd gone into the generator room, thrown the breaker that fed power to Dragline One, locked the door from the outside, left the key in the lock and smashed it so thoroughly that it'll need an oxy-acetylene torch to open it again. We just couldn't get in to shut down the power.'

'They sure knew how to cause the maximum damage and disruption with the minimum of effort,' said Brady. 'I suggest, Mr Shore, there's no point in our remaining here a moment longer: all you're doing is twisting the knife deeper into your wound. Let's all get back inside and ask George what happened.'

'O.K. Let's go.' Shore, who had supervised the construction of the dragline, working along with the contractors Bucyrus-Erie, seemed strangely reluctant to leave the fallen giant. It was as if he were abandoning an old friend. Brady could appreciate how he felt. But he could also appreciate how he felt himself: he had become acutely conscious of the cold.

Shore took one last look at the dragline and turned back towards the heated haven of the minibus. 'O.K.,' he repeated automatically. 'Let's go hear Dermott's story.'

They drove the short distance back to the isolation block, where they found Dermott lying on a bed, already being questioned by Willoughby. Corinne was sitting on a chair in the corner of the small room, looking in better shape than the man she'd rescued.

'How is he?' Brady whispered to the nurse out in the corridor.

'His wrists look pretty bad: they got chewed up by the manacles, and frost-bitten as well. They're going to be real painful for the next few days. They'll mend, though.'

'What about his general condition—exposure?'

'What are you *talking* about? He's got the constitution of an ox.'

By the time Brady, Mackenzie and Carmody had filed into the room, the place was crammed full. Brady seemed much moved by the sight of his senior operative brought low, with hands and forearms heavily bandaged.

'Well, George,' he began, clearing his throat heavily. 'I am informed that you plan to survive.'

'Sure do.' Dermott grinned up at them. 'But boy—I wouldn't want to go through *that* again.'

'I got the story,' Willoughby cut in, brisk and businesslike. He gave a quick précis of what had happened, including the arrival and departure of the helicopter. 'I'm sorry to say it, Mr Shore, but it seems the plant is riddled with corruption. Number one, somebody sabotaged the generator room, so that you couldn't turn the power off. Number two, somebody else set the controls of the dragline to take it over the edge. Number three, somebody else hit Dermott and manacled him to the steel ring. Number four, somebody else again informed the kidnappers that the girl had survived her fall out of the helicopter and was back in the isolation unit. That makes quite a lot of villains for one plant.'

'Too right, it does,' Shore said bitterly. 'You don't think the chopper came back to do the dragline job—that somebody on board got out and set the controls?'

'Impossible. The dragline was moving before the chopper landed. Isn't that right, Mr Dermott?'

'Right. At least—no—not quite. But we saw men from the chopper go straight to the building here—and then we heard the dragline moving, right near us. The guys from the helicopter didn't have time to reach the dragline and set up the controls.'

'What I'd like to know is whether your family, Mr Brady, were still on board the helicopter,' Willoughby said.

'Yes, they were.' Carmody startled them all with his sudden pronouncement. 'And Mr Reynolds. He was with them.'

'How d'you know?' Jim Brady asked. Dermott sat up abruptly.

'I *saw* them. That's what I was doing all the time you were involved with the dragline. I made a wide circle on foot and approached the helicopter from the back. There was a man armed with a machine pistol guarding the ladder, but I climbed up onto the skid-struts from the opposite side and got a look in through the cabin windows. They were all there —Mrs Brady, Stella, Mr Reynolds.'

'How ...' Brady faltered. 'How did they look?'

'Fine—just fine. Quite calm, all of them. But they weren't quite as passive as they looked.'

'What d'you mean?' Dermott asked quickly.

'One of them managed to drop this out of the door, or out of a window.' From his breast pocket Carmody drew a brown leather bill-fold, which he handed to Brady. 'Looks like one of yours—J.A.B., nicely embossed in gold.'

'My God!' Brady took it. 'That's Jean's. Her middle name's Anneliese. This was a birthday present. Anything in it?'

'Sure is. Take a look.'

With his fingers trembling a little, Brady opened the bill-fold, unbuttoned a flap and drew out a small scrap of paper. '*Crowfoot Lake Met. Station,*' he read out loud. 'Well I'm damned.'

Dermott was elated. 'I knew it! I knew it!' he kept saying. 'I knew the bastards would over-reach themselves. Didn't I say they'd make a major mistake through over-confidence or desperation? Well, they've made it. Somebody couldn't resist the temptation to talk. Jean heard the name and wrote it down. Great, Jean!'

'Sheer luck I found it,' said Carmody. 'When the chopper took off it blew hell out of the snow and all-but buried the bill-fold. I was just having a quick look-round when I saw the corner sticking up out of a drift.'

'We got it, anyway,' said Dermott. 'What are we waiting for?'

'Not so fast,' Brady countered. 'For one thing we don't know where Crowfoot Lake is.'

'Oh yes we do,' said Willoughby. 'It's up beyond the Birch Mountains, seventy, eighty miles north. I know it well.'

'How do we get there?' Dermott asked.

Willoughby looked at him reproachfully. 'Helicopter. No other way.'

'It's four o'clock in the morning, gentlemen,' Brady said heavily. 'An error to pursue further tonight. For one thing, we are all exhausted.'

'And for another we don't have a helicopter,' said Dermott.

'Precisely, George. I must say, your ordeal doesn't seem to have blunted your wits any.'

'Thank you.' Dermott lay back happily. 'Maybe Mr Willoughby can help us in the morning—I mean, later this morning.'

'Sure, sure.' Willoughby stood up. 'But everyone please be careful. We're up against professionals. Their performance has been pretty impressive to date. Nothing would please them better than to catch one of your gentlemen on your own, Mr Brady. Or you, for that matter.' He turned to Corinne, only to find she had fallen asleep, sitting upright, in the corner. 'O.K.,' he said gently to Mackenzie. 'Look after her. But whatever you do, all keep together.'

'Like now,' said Brady. 'We'll all get in that bus together and drive back to town. Mr Carmody—it doesn't sound as though your vehicle's too serviceable. May I offer you a ride?'

'Flat as a pancake,' said Carmody wryly. 'Never saw anything to match it. Thank you.'

They all piled in, with Shore driving. But before they even

reached the administration block a radio message caught them.

'Mr Shore—urgent.' It was Steve Dawson, charge-hand of the night-shift. 'We got another emergency.'

'Oh *no*!' Shore groaned. 'I'm coming. Be right there.'

Dawson met them and led them straight into a room off the main corridor which held six beds and was obviously a dormitory. On one of the beds lay the body of a fair-haired young man whose sightless eyes gazed at the ceiling.

'Oh my God!' said Shore.

'Who is it?' Dermott snapped.

'David Crawford. The security man we were talking about.'

'The one we suspected?'

'That's him. What happened?'

'Stabbed through the heart, from behind,' said Saunders, the doctor, who was standing by the bed. 'He's been dead some hours. We only just found him.'

'How come?' Dermott demanded. 'Isn't this the security men's dormitory?'

'One of two,' said Saunders. 'The other's larger. Normally both are occupied by off-duty shifts. But since the shut-down, the men have been living at home. Nobody had any cause to come in here tonight.'

'Ruthless bastards,' said Brady, very low. 'Four dead and two critically injured so far. Well, Mr Willoughby. You've got a murder investigation on your hands.'

14

At 11.30 that same morning Brady and his team were the sole occupants of the hotel's dining-room. Outside, the wind had gone, the snow had been reduced to the occasional flurry, and the sun was making a valiant effort to shine through the drifting grey cloud. Inside, the mood was one of expectancy and suppressed excitement.

'One thing's for sure,' said Brady firmly. '*You*'re not coming on this little jaunt.'

'Oh yes I am,' Dermott countered. 'I most certainly am. You try leaving me behind.'

'What can you *do*?' Brady was half-scornful, half-sympathetic. 'You can't use a gun, knock anybody down, tie anybody up.'

'All the same, I've got to be there.' Dermott was grey from lack of sleep and the pain in his savaged wrists. He could use his hands for gentle tasks, but his fingers were stiff, and to ease the discomfort he kept both elbows propped on the table with his forearms sticking straight up. 'I really need two slings,' he muttered. 'One for each arm.'

'Why not stay here and look after your gallant saviour?' Mackenzie suggested slyly.

Dermott coloured perceptibly and grunted: 'She's O.K., I guess.'

'She's being guarded, sure,' Mackenzie agreed. 'But she might be even safer if she came with us. With the rot spreading as far as it has ...' He broke off and went back to eating as he saw Willoughby, the police chief, approaching across the room.

'Good morning, Chief,' Brady beamed at him. 'Get any sleep?'

'One hour.' Willoughby tried to smile, but his heart wasn't in it. 'Call of duty. Can't complain.'

'News,' Brady announced abruptly. 'Take a seat.' He handed

a letter across the table. 'Communication from our friends. Mailed yesterday in the local post office.'

Willoughby read the first paragraph without alteration of expression. Then he looked slowly round the watching faces and said matter-of-factly: 'One billion dollars.' Suddenly his calm gave way. 'One billion dollars!' he cried. 'Jesus!' He qualified the word 'dollars' several times. 'The sonsabitches are crazy. Who's going to pay attention to this kind of drivel?'

'You think it's drivel?' Dermott asked. 'I don't. Probably a rather optimistic estimate of what the market will stand, but not very, I would think.'

'I can't believe it.' Willoughby threw the letter down on the table. 'A billion dollars! Even if they mean it, how could the money be transferred without being traced to the recipient?'

'Nothing simpler,' said Mackenzie, forking a pancake. 'You could lose Fork Knox in the labyrinth of Eurodollars and off-shore funds.'

Willoughby glared at him over the breakfast table. 'You'd actually pay this blackmailing monster?'

'Not me,' Mackenzie answered. 'I couldn't. But somebody sure enough will.'

'Who'd be so crazy?'

'There's no craziness involved,' said Dermott patiently. 'Just calculating, common business sense. The people who stand to lose most—our two governments, and the major oil companies who've invested in Alaska and Alberta. I don't know what the position is in Canada, but this is going to pose an intriguing problem in the States, because any governmental operation in tandem with the oil companies requires Congressional approval —and as every schoolkid knows, Congress would cheerfully immolate the oil companies. Looks like it'll make a highly diverting spectacle.'

Willoughby looked baffled.

'Read some more,' Brady prompted. 'The next paragraph is only a minor shock to the nervous system.'

The policeman picked up the letter and started again. 'So they want you out of Alaska and Alberta—specifically, south of the forty-ninth parallel.'

'As predicted,' said Brady.

'But no mention of any ransom?'

'Again, as predicted.' Brady sounded smug.

'You're not getting out, I take it?'

'Oh no? I'm going to contact my pilot in a moment and have him file a flight plan for Los Angeles.'

Willoughby stared at him. 'I thought you wanted to go to Crowfoot Lake?'

'We do. But we don't want to advertise our destination to any ill-natured persons who may be listening-in. Therefore, we file a flight plan for L.A.'

'O.K., I get it.' Willoughby grinned. 'What do you want *me* to do?'

'Well ...' Brady became evasive. 'First, we need a guarantee from you.'

'You can't make deals with the police.' Willoughby's tone suddenly hardened.

'Rubbish!' said Brady comfortably. 'It's done all the time. Felons even make deals with judges in court.'

'O.K. So what do you want?'

'What we *don't* want is a company of paratroopers. Sure, they could mop this lot up with their hands tied behind their backs, but they might mop up a few wrong people too. Softly, softly on this one. Finesse. Stealth. Secrecy. Our way or not at all.'

'You making a point or something?'

'Tell me about Crowfoot Lake,' said Brady.

'It's an ideal place for this sort of thing. Tucked right away in the hills. Big, covered helicopter shelter right by the station. A chopper would never be spotted from the air. I was up there a year back, investigating a reported murder which turned out to be death by misadventure. Couple of young city boys newly arrived at the weather station. Happens at the beginning of the hunting season every year, without fail: all the Dan'l Boones and Buffalo Bills dropping like flies all over the place.'

'How big's the lake?' Dermott asked. 'Can a plane land on it?'

'Well, you *can* land on it.' Willoughby paused. 'But I don't think it would do you much good. See here: the lake's only two miles long, so wherever you came down on it, the people in the Met. Station would be bound to hear you. I've got a better idea.'

'We need one.'

'Now, Mr Brady. I've got a request. I'm in a delicate position. I am the law around these parts, and I'm supposed to know what's going on. I'm also a blackmailer. In return for guaranteeing that I can get you to the Met. Station undetected, I'd like some degree of participation in your expedition. You can't operate without police authority, and I'm the authority. All cards very close to the chest, O.K. But I'd like an official watching brief—a presence.'

'I know whose presence I'd like,' Mackenzie said. Up till then he had been chewing steadily throughout the conversation, but a delicate patting of his big face with the napkin indicated that his meal was over. 'I'd like Carmody.' Willoughby said: 'That's not a bad idea. I'll get him right away.'

He went off to telephone, came back and said: 'A couple of minutes.'

'Fine.' Brady turned to Mackenzie. 'Don, tell Ferguson to go out to the airport and file a flight plan for Los Angeles. Tell him to expect people with provisions out there in just over an hour. Ask the kitchen to give us provisions for two or three days.'

'Just food, Mr Brady?'

Brady loftily ignored the insinuation. 'Ferguson is in charge of the commissariat. He'll know of any shortfalls. George, we'll need some hand compasses and, I guess, ammunition. Be generous with the ammunition.'

Willoughby said: 'Hand compasses we have in abundance. What guns?'

'Colt .38's.'

'No problem.'

Dermott said: 'Well, thank you. Tell me, Mr Willoughby, you have a deputy chief?'

'Indeed. And a good one.'

'Good enough to be left in sole charge here?'

'Sure. Why?'

'Why don't you come with us? Giving us the directions is all very well, but it's not the same as having you on the spot.'

'Don't, Mr Dermott. You tempt me. You tempt me sorely.' From the momentary gleam of anticipation in his eyes, it was clear that he spoke the truth. 'Duty, alas, before pleasure. I have a murder investigation on my hands.'

'You've just reported zero progress. There are short-cuts, Mr Willoughby. You wouldn't want us foreign amateurs to do the job for you, would you now?'

'I'm afraid I'm not quite at my best.'

'You would be when we introduced you to Crawford's murderer. Where else would he be but at Crowfoot Lake?'

'Mr Dermott, forget my last remark. I'm back at my very best. Ah, here he is.'

Carmody looked as large and formidable as ever.

Dermott said: 'With Mr Willoughby's consent, a request to make on behalf of Mr Brady, Mr Mackenzie and myself. As alien civilians we can only request. Those kidnappers—you're aware they are multiple killers, desperate men. They'll shoot on sight and shoot to kill.'

Carmody looked round in slight puzzlement but politely said nothing.

Dermott went on: 'Mrs Brady, her daughter and Mr Reynolds: we know where they're being held.'

Carmody, almost like a man in prayer, clasped his two hands lightly together and said, in a suitably churchlike whisper. 'Boy, oh boy. Let's go get them.'

Brady said: 'Thank you. We appreciate it. One hour from now, O.K.?'

Willoughby said: 'I'll just nip back to the office and put in a call to Edmonton.'

'Aha! I thought secrecy was the watchword?'

'It still is.'

'Then may I ask?'

'You may not. A surprise. To be revealed at Crowfoot Lake. Or in the very close vicinity. You wouldn't rob me of my surprises?'

*　　*　　*

As the jet lifted off Brady looked across the aisle to where Carmody had just withdrawn a peculiar metallic device from its chamois-lined leather casing. It appeared to consist of a small telescope attached to a curving, semi-circular arm which in turn was bolted to a rectangular metal box. Brady said: 'What do you have there, Mr Carmody?'

'John, please Mr Brady. Makes me feel less self-conscious. We cops are used to being called many things, but not "Mister". This? This is an infra-red telescopic night sight. These are the securing clamps. Fits on a rifle.'

'You can see in the dark with that?'

'A little light helps. But total darkness is rare.'

'You can see the enemy but he can't see you?'

'That's the idea behind it. Unsporting and unfair. Never give the bastards a break—especially, Mr Brady, if they're pointing guns at wives and daughters.'

Brady turned to Willoughby who was in the window seat. 'And what lethal armaments are *you* carrying?'

'Apart from the regulation revolver? Just this little number here.' He reached down and picked up a zipped leather bag some eighteen inches by ten.

'Funny shape for a gun,' Brady said, intrigued.

'Two pieces that screw together.'

'It wouldn't be a sub-machine gun?'

'It would.'

There was a short silence and then Brady said: 'No chance you'll be carrying a few hand grenades on you?'

Carmody gave a deprecating shrug. 'Only a few.'

'Infra-red sights, sub-machine guns, grenades—aren't those illegal?'

'Could be.' Carmody sounded vague. 'I'm not sure they are at Crowfoot Lake. You'd have to ask Mr Willoughby about that.'

The angle of climb had levelled off, and Brady nodded his thanks as Mackenzie brought him a daiquiri.

'Cruising altitude, Donald? No way could we possibly have reached that yet.'

'Maybe this is high enough. You'd have to ask our police chief there.' He nodded forward. Willoughby had gone up to the co-pilot's seat and was bent over a map with Ferguson. 'Doing his navigator's bit, I see.'

Some five minutes more passed before Willoughby rose and headed back to sit by Brady.

'How long, Mr Willoughby?'

'Seventy minutes.'

'Seventy minutes! But I thought Crowfoot was only seventy miles away?'

'We filed a flight plan for Los Angeles, remember. Our first leg takes us through the radar control at Calgary. So, we're flying south. We're also flying low to lose the radar control at Fort McMurray. When we do, we'll circle to the west and then north. After ten minutes, north-east. We'll keep low. No danger of bumping into anything; it's pretty flat all the way.' He spread out a chart. 'Even the Birch Mountains here are really nothing of the sort. The highest peak is less than twenty-seven hundred feet. Really, it's just a low divide, a watershed: the streams on the west side flow west and north-west into the Peace and Birch rivers: the streams to the east flow east and south-east into the Athabasca river.'

'Where's Crowfoot Lake?'

'Here, just on the west side of the divide.'

'It doesn't have a name printed.'

'Too small. Neither does Deerhorn—here—on the east side of the divide. That's where we're going. It's a lake, too, but it's always called just Deerhorn.'

'How far from Deerhorn to Crowfoot?'

'Six miles. Maybe seven. Far enough, I hope. We go into Deerhorn low and we go into Deerhorn slow—as near stalling speed as possible. The chances of our being heard at that distance are remote. The only time we'll make any real noise is when we land. The only way a fast-landing jet like this can stop on a relatively short stretch of ice is to use reverse thrust on the engines. That makes quite a racket. But I'm pretty sure that the divide between the two lakes will act as a suitable baffle. I'm a little more concerned about the helicopter.'

'Helicopter?' Brady said carefully.

'Yes. Left Edmonton about half an hour ago. Due in about an hour after us.'

'You promised me—'

'And I keep my promise. No troops, no police, not even a peashooter. Just some Arctic gear I want. It's due to arrive just after dark.'

'And without radar transmission or airfield landing lights, how's he going to find his way here?'

'A signal from us by radio beacon. He's only to follow his nose. What worries me slightly is the noise the helicopter will make in landing. It's the biggest you've ever seen, and the racket is corresponding.'

'Of course.' Brady showed his disquiet. 'Our friends at Crowfoot Lake have their own helicopter. Won't they hop in and come over to investigate?'

'I hope not. I want them,' Willoughby said grimly, 'to stand trial, and they won't be able to if they're dead. If they come across, I'll have no option but to shoot them down.'

'Fair enough.' Brady seemed unperturbed at the thought. Then he added: 'You can do that?'

'We came here equipped with weapons for the express purpose of doing just that.'

'Ah! I was asking Carmody about some of his equipment and he mentioned this infra-red night sight. But I thought that was for shooting people.'

'It can do that, too. Did he mention the fact that he's also got a rifle than can switch from single-shot to automatic at the touch of a switch? The combination of that, the night-spot and a squirrel-hunter's eye makes for a fairly lethal outcome. You know I have a sub-machine gun? He did? Did I also mention that it has a special large capacity magazine—the old circular drum type—and that every sixth shell is a tracer so that I can see how I'm doing?'

'No.'

Willoughby smiled. 'And of course we didn't mention my own modest contribution—the jumping jacks. For use when we're not seeing too well what's going on up above. Just like fireworks, really—except that you get no fancy explosion of colour, just a blinding magnesium flare that drifts down slowly on a parachute. Lasts only ninety seconds, but if you can't accomplish what you want to in ninety seconds, you should have stayed at home in the first place.'

'If I were a devout Christian I could almost weep for my adversaries.'

'Don't.'

'Who said I was a devout Christian?' Brady nodded to Carmody. 'He really goes about killing people?'

'He *leans* on people.'

'What, with sub-machine and high-powered rifles?'

'We'll use them if we have to.'

Brady said dryly: 'You surprise me. Those weapons are illegal, of course—for police use. Right?'

'That's the trouble with being in a remote northern town —you don't keep up as much as you might with all the notes, minutes and regulations that Edmonton issues every other day.'

'Of course not.'

Some time later, Brady winced as the jet engines went into reverse thrust. Even though reason told him that the decibel level was no higher than normal, his apprehensive frame of mind made him feel he was listening to a continuous thunderclap of sound. When they had landed, he said to Willoughby: 'You could have heard that racket clear back in Fort McMurray.'

'Wasn't all that bad.' Willoughby seemed unconcerned. 'Well, stretch the legs, a little fresh air. Coming?'

'What? Out in that mess?'

'What mess? It's not even snowing. And it's seven miles to Crowfoot Lake. A little exercise, a little acclimatisation. Remember what you told me back in Sanmobil? Inside the human frame there's no room for both cold and daiquiris. Let's put it to the test, shall we?'

'Hoist on your own petard,' Dermott said behind him. Brady scowled, hauled himself upright and followed Willoughby to the fore end of the cabin. He looked at Ferguson and stopped.

'You look worried, boy. That was a perfect touchdown.'

'Thank you. But I am, as you say, a little concerned. Aileron controls got a bit stiff as I came in to land. Nothing much, I daresay. Soon locate the trouble. First landing on ice, and maybe I was being a little oversensitive.'

Brady followed Willoughby out and looked around. Deer-horn was a singularly bleak and unprepossessing place. Snow-dusted ice beneath their feet, flat, barren land, devoid of any form of vegetation, stretching away in featureless anonymity on three sides. To the north-east lay a range of low hills, sparsely covered with a scattering of stunted, snow-laden trees.

'Those are the Birch Mountains?'

'I told you. I don't think the person who named them knew much about mountains.'

'And those are *birch* trees?'

Willoughby said: 'He wasn't much of a botanist either. These are alders.'

'And seven miles beyond—'

'Look out! Stand back!' Both men whirled round to see Ferguson racing down the boarding steps clutching in one hand a cylindrically-shaped object about ten inches long and three in diameter.

'Keep clear, keep clear!' He sprinted by them, covered another fifteen yards, arched his back while still running and, like a cricket bowler, over-armed the cylinder with a convulsive jerk of his body. The cylinder had travelled not more than three yards when it exploded.

The blast was powerful enough to knock both Brady and Willoughby, even at a distance of almost twenty yards, off their feet. For several seconds they lay where they had fallen, then made their way unsteadily towards the prone figure of Ferguson. Even as they reached him they were joined by Dermott, Mackenzie and Carmody, who had been inside the plane.

Ferguson had fallen face-down on the ice. Gently, they turned him over. His face and body appeared unmarked. It was diffi-cult to tell whether or not he was breathing.

'Into the plane with him,' Brady said. 'Warm blankets and heating pads from the Red Cross chest. His heart may have stopped. Anyone here know anything about heart mas-sage?'

'We do,' Carmody said. He picked up Ferguson and headed for the plane. 'First-aid certificates.'

Three minutes later Carmody, still kneeling in the aisle, sank back on his heels and smiled.

'Ticker's going like a watch,' he said. 'Bloody fast watch, mind you, but it's going.'

'Good work,' Brady said. 'We leave him there?'

'Yes,' Dermott said. 'Even when he regains consciousness—no reason why he shouldn't, there no sign of any head injury—he's still going to be in shock. Heat pads we have in plenty. That's all we can give him, and probably all he requires. Can someone tell us what the hell happened? He came running up the aisle shouting "Stay where you are!" and clutching this damned thing in his hand. He was out through the door like a greyhound clearing his trap.'

'I know what happened,' Brady said. 'He complained that the controls were a bit stiff when he came in to land. That was because whoever placed this charge made a sloppy job of it. The thing stayed in place while we were climbing or cruising at a steady altitude but slid forward and wedged itself against the ailerons when we started to descend. As we left the plane he told me he was going to look for the cause of the stiffness.' Brady pursed his lips. 'He found it all right.'

'He was lucky,' said Dermott. 'Had it been a metal-cased bomb, the casing would have turned into shrapnel when it exploded and the back-lash would have caught him. Not a mark on him. So, a plastic bomb. For plastic bombs, plastic fuses—chemicals, really. You have two acids separated by some synthetic plastic barrier. One of them eats through the barrier, and when the two different acids meet they detonate. When an acid eats its way through the plastic barrier it generates considerable heat. I'm sure Ferguson not only felt this heat but he knew right away what it meant.'

Brady looked sombre. 'If we weren't such a devious bunch, we'd have been flying at 30,000 feet on the way up. Our last trip, gentlemen.'

'Right,' said Dermott. 'Even flying low, like we did, we had the luck of the devil. The drawback of a chemical detonator is that it's almost impossible to get timing accuracy within ten or fifteen per cent. The timing could have gone off ten minutes earlier—and that would have been curtains for us. Our friends didn't want us out of this country: they wanted us out of this world. What better way to do it, neatly, cleanly and efficiently, than have your plane's tail fall off six miles up?'

*   *   *

The Sikorsky Sky-Crane landed in darkness just after three-thirty in the afternoon. It was, as Willoughby had promised, the biggest helicopter they had ever seen. The engines cut, the huge rotors idled to a standstill, and there was left only the sound of a generator whining somewhere inside the massive hull. Telescopic steps snaked down from an opened door and two men climbed nimbly down to the ice and approached the waiting group.

'Brown,' the leading figure said. 'Lieutenant Brown, Air Force, alleged skipper of this craft. This is Lieutenant Vos, co-pilot, also alleged. Which of you gentlemen are Mr Willoughby and Mr Brady?'

They shook hands and Brown turned to introduce a third person who had joined them. 'Doctor Kenmore.'

'How long can you stay?' Willoughby asked.

'As long as you wish.'

'Very kind. You have some cargo for me?'

'We have. O.K. to unload now?'

'Please.'

Brown shouted instructions. Brady said: 'Two requests, Lieutenant?'

'You have but to ask.'

'I wish we had some more of this civility in the United States Air Force,' Brady said. He addressed Dr Kenmore. 'My pilot's been hurt. Would you look at him?'

'Of course.'

'Donald?' The two men left for the aircraft. 'We have an excellent transmitter on our plane, Lieutenant, but unfortunately the pilot, who operates it, is out of action ...'

'We've got an excellent transmitter and a first-class radio operator who's ready for action. James!'

A young man appeared at the head of the steps. 'Take this gentleman to Bernie, will you?'

Bernie was a bespectacled young man seated by a huge RCA transceiver. Dermott introduced himself and said: 'Could you get me some numbers do you think?'

'Local, sir? Albertan, I mean.'

'Afraid not, Anchorage and New York.'

'No problem. We can patch in through a radio link via our Edmonton H.Q.' Bernie's professional confidence was reassuring in the extreme. 'Numbers and names, sir?'

'I have them here.' Dermott handed over a notebook. 'I can actually speak to those people?'

'If they're home, sure.'

'I may be gone for a few hours. If I am, and you get through, will you ask them to hold themselves available or let me know where I can reach them?'

'Of course.'

Dermott rejoined the group outside. Two low-profiled vehicles were already on the ice. A third was being lowered. 'What are those?' Dermott asked.

Willoughby said: 'My surprise for Mr Brady. Snowmobiles.'

'They're not snowmobiles,' a black-haired slender youth said.

'Sorry.' Willoughby turned to Dermott. 'John Lowry, an expert on those machines. The Edmonton people sent him up to show us how to operate them.'

'They're everything-mobiles,' Lowry said. 'Snow, roads, rough terrain, marshes, sand—you name it. Comparatively, the American and Canadian snowmobiles belong to the age of steam radio. Made by the firm of V.P.L.O.—initials only, the full name is unpronounceable—in Oulu, Finland. Called, naturally, the Finncat. Made of fibre-glass. Unlike the ordinary snowmobile, it has no skis up front. That motor-driven traction belt you see extends under the full length of the body.'

'Where did they come from?'

'We got three to put through extended tests—you know, the old test-to-destruction bit. Those are the three.'

Dermott said to Willoughby: 'Nice to have friends.'

'Not quite standard models,' Lowry went on. 'The front compartments are usually for stowage of gear. We've converted them into jump seats.'

Brady said: 'You mean I can ride in one of those right now?'

Dermott said, *sotto voce* to Willoughby: 'Test to destruction is right.'

Lowry said: 'I should think so, sir.'

'That's great, just great.' Brady's tone was hushed and reverent. The prospect of trudging a fourteen-mile return journey through Albertan snows had held singularly little appeal for him.

'Driving is simple,' Lowry said. 'Changing the inclination of the traction belt changes the direction of travel: done by the handlebars. You have forward and reverse gears and, a very sophisticated touch, hydraulic disc brakes. It can also do forty miles an hour.'

'Forty?' Dermott said. 'It looks as if it would be hard pushed to touch five.'

Lowry smiled. 'Forty. Not on rough terrain, of course. Incidentally, these don't come cheap—four thousand dollars—but then the unique never does. I understand that you gentlemen are in a hurry. First three drivers up, please.'

Dr Kenmore returned from the plane with Mackenzie while Willoughby and his two men were learning the controls of the Finncats. Kenmore said: 'Concussion. Nothing very serious, not the blast, he must have hit his head on the ice—there's a beauty of a bruise just above his right ear. I'll have him brought across here—we have a heating and lighting generator running all the time when the motors are switched off.'

Brady said: 'Thank you, doctor. We appreciate it.'

'Nothing. May one ask where you're off to in those toys?'

'Don't let young Lowry hear you. He'd have a fit,' Dermott said.

Brady said: 'Please understand we don't mean to be churlish. We'll tell you when we come back. How's your expertise on shotgun wounds and bones shattered by high-velocity bullets?'

'Not very extensive, I'm afraid.' Kenmore's expression hadn't altered. 'You plan to remedy that before the night is out?'

'I hope not.' Brady's face was suddenly serious. 'But it may come to that.'

The six men left at four-thirty, exactly one hour after the Sikorsky had touched down. The helicopter's crew were there to see them go. Lieutenant Brown said: 'Air Force personnel are not as stupid as they look. We know where you're going, naturally. Good fortune.' He looked at the arsenal of weapons they carried, ready for action, shoulder-slung or in holsters. 'Dr Kenmore may be in for a sleepless night.'

The Finncats were everything that Lowry had promised, nimble, manoeuvrable, and possessed of remarkable traction. Two carried small but efficient headlamps which picked out a path through the straggling alders. It said much for the dogged willingness of the little two-cylinder engines that a heroically suffering Brady had only to get out twice—the Finncat on those occasions had refused to budge another inch—and walk a total of two hundred yards on the way to the gently-rounded convexity which marked the watershed of the Birch Mountains. Shortly before the little army reached this point they had switched off their headlights.

The descent was simple but just as slow as the ascent because, in the absence of lights, the half-seen alders had to be negotiated with care. The engines, no more than idling, were gratifyingly quiet. Willoughby called softly and the three Finncats came to a halt.

'Far enough,' he said. 'We can't be more than three hundred yards from the shore.'

'O.K.,' Dermott agreed. 'How many crew at the Met. Station, Willoughby?'

'Just two. I shouldn't imagine that any harm has come to them. They have to keep sending their regular radio reports: any breakdown in those would have brought an official helicopter out here very quickly. So the reports must have continued to go out—under duress.'

They made their way down to the lake's edge, keeping their voices low—sound travels as well over ice as it does over water. Tall reeds grew by the frozen shore. Carmody parted these, unshipped his infra-red night-sight, pressed his face against the rubber eye-piece and switched on.

The Crowfoot Lake meteorological station consisted of only two huts, one about three times the size of the other. The smaller one had a variety of poles, boxes and what appeared from that distance to be uncovered recording instruments on its roof. This smaller hut was dark; the larger, presumably the living quarters, showed two brightly-lit windows. Beyond this hut was parked a large, white-painted helicopter.

Jones passed the night-sight to Brady, who studied the station briefly, then handed the instrument on. The last man to use it, Dermott, took the sight from his eye and said: 'As a target for tonight, I've seen worse. We go now?'

'We go now,' Brady said. 'And we don't treat them like human beings. No warnings. No fair play. No sportsmanship. Shoot first, questions afterwards. People who plant bombs in aircraft—or steal my Jean and Stella—know nothing of finer feelings—or the rules of civilised warfare.'

Willoughby said: 'Fair enough. But shoot to cripple, not to kill. I want those men to stand trial.'

Brady said: 'Of course, the conduct and termination of the trial would be greatly speeded if we had their confessions in advance.'

'And how do you figure on getting those?' Dermott asked.

'Simple, George. It all depends upon how intrepid you're feeling this afternoon.'

15

The wicked wind hissed through the clump of alders some twenty yards behind the meteorological station. The trees offered little in the way of cover, but it was the best and closest that the men could find. Luckily, the night was moonless: the buildings showed as black lumps in the snowy landscape.

Bulky as bears in their Arctic gear, the raiders silently watched another figure, flattened to the snow, inch his way up towards them, propelled only by elbows and toes. Arrived in the shelter of the trees, John Carmody rose to a kneeling position.

'They're there,' he whispered. 'Reynolds and the ladies. The ladies are handcuffed together, but they seem all right. Don't look as though they've been maltreated. There are five other men in there, smoking and drinking, but not drinking too much. A little room leads off the big one. Could be there's someone asleep in there, but I don't think so. The door's ajar and the light's on. Any person who wanted to sleep would have switched the light off.'

'Well done, boy,' said Brady.

'Three other things, sir. At least three of the men are armed, although none actually had a gun in his hand. The whole group is sitting round the table listening to a radio. They're listening pretty hard, too—trying to catch something. That made me think there wouldn't be another of them in the small room: he'd have been out there listening too.'

'Could be the two station operators are in there,' said Dermott. 'Tied up, I mean.'

'I thought that too,' said Carmody.

'I know what they're listening for,' Brady whispered. 'News of a certain jet having crashed in Alberta this afternoon. What was the third thing you saw?'

'All five men are wearing stocking masks.'

Dermott said: 'Which they wouldn't bother with if they intended to dispose of the hostages.' His husky murmur dropped to a whisper. 'Keep low. Keep quiet.'

A rectangle of light had appeared at the side of the cabin. A figure walked through the opened doorway and headed towards the smaller building. Moments later lights came on there.

'One of them,' Brady said. 'Hardly likely to let one of the operators stroll across there and send off an S.O.S. Perfect. Come, George, this is where you earn your Congressional Medal of Honour or whatever.'

Brady moved out, travelling quickly and silently, no trace of the comfort-loving fat man left. Arriving at the main cabin door, he looked over his shoulder to check the smaller cabin. The light was still on, the door still closed. Brady turned back to the cabin door, gripped the handle, opened the door and walked inside, .38 in hand, Dermott and Mackenzie at either elbow, with their guns levelled. Brady advanced on the four stocking-masked men sitting round the table. Several started up.

'Keep your hands on that table,' he said. 'If you're not entirely mad. We're just looking for an excuse to shoot you through the head. One of you turn that radio off—the good news you're waiting for has just arrived.'

'Jim! Jim!' Jean Brady was on her feet. 'You've come!'

'Of course.' Brady's voice held a curious mixture of irritation and smug self-satisfaction. 'You thought I wouldn't? Brady Enterprises always delivers.' As his wife made to approach him, he raised his left hand. 'Just a minute. Don't come too close. These are desperate men. Mr Reynolds, Stella. Sorry we took so long about this but—'

'Dad!' Stella was on her feet, a desperate urgency in her voice. 'Dad, a man—'

'Drop your guns.' The deep voice came from the doorway. 'Don't turn round or you're dead.'

'Do what the man says.' Brady set the example. Within a second the other two guns had clattered to the floor.

'Stay where you are,' the same voice ordered. 'Billy.'

Billy didn't have to be told what to do. His search was quick but thorough. He stepped back and said: 'Clean, boss.'

'So.' The door closed and a burly man appeared before them. Like the others, he was masked. 'Sit on that bench there.' He waited until they had done so, seated himself by the table and said: 'Watch them.' Three of his men produced pistols and covered the three seated men. He put away his gun.

'The ladies, I must say, seem very disappointed. They shouldn't, really.'

Brady looked at them. 'What he means is that things could be worse. If his plan had worked, we three would be dead. As it is, Ferguson is critically ill and two others seriously injured.' He looked at the leader. 'You placed that bomb in the plane?'

'I can't take all the credit. One of my men did.' He lit a cigarette and struck it through a hole on the stocking mask which had been cut out for that purpose. 'So now I have Mr Jim Brady and his two invaluable associates. A full hand, one might say.'

Brady said: 'Designed to blow our tail off at 30,000 feet?'

'What else? It would be interesting to know how you're alive.'

'*We're* alive. But one man's probably dying, and two are seriously injured. God, man, what are you—a psychopathic killer?'

'Not psychopathic. Just a businessman. How come *you* didn't die?'

'Because we landed before the bomb went off.' Brady sounded very tired. 'We got a report from a forest ranger saying that an off-white helicopter had been seen in these parts. Nobody paid attention except us—we knew you had a white helicopter.'

'How did you know that?'

'A lot of people saw it around the plant at Athabasca.'

'No harm done.' He waved a hand. 'All the aces in the pack.'

'Whoever placed that explosive charge in my plane made a lousy job of securing it,' said Brady sarcastically.

'I can vouch for that. He was interrupted.'

'The package moved forward and jammed the controls—the tail ailerons. The pilot had to land—it was on the way down that we caught a glimpse of your helicopter. We crash-landed on another lake. Pilot told us to get out. He tried to remove the charge, and the two others stayed with him. I guess they felt they had to—they were cops.'

'We know that, too.'

'So they were expendable. You had no compunction about murdering them, too?'

'Compunction is not a word in my vocabulary. Why did you come here?'

'For your helicopter, of course. We have to get those injured men to hospital.'

'Why hold us up?'

'Don't be so stupid. We can't fly the damn thing.'

The leader turned to one of the masked men. 'Sorry about that, Lucky. A pleasure spared.'

'And of course, you people killed Crawford.'

'Crawford?' He turned to another of his men. 'Fred, that lad you attended to—'

'Yeah. That was him.'

'And you critically wounded Sanmobil's president, and a policeman?'

'Seems to have been an awful lot you didn't know.'

'And it was you who blew up the plant and destroyed the dragline. A pity you had to kill and wound so many in the process.'

'Look friend, we don't play kiddies' games. Too bad if someone gets in our way. This is a man's world, and we play for keeps.'

Brady bowed his head in apparent acceptance, raised his hands to cross them behind his neck. His fingers touched.

What should have been the tinkling of shattered glass was lost in the crash of three shots that sounded almost as one. The masked men with the guns yelled out in agony and stared in shocked disbelief at their shattered shoulders. The door was kicked violently open and Carmody jumped in, machine pistol steady in his big hands. He moved a couple of steps forward. Willoughby ran into the cabin carrying a revolver.

Dermott said: 'Your words. This is a man's world, and we play for keeps.'

Carmody advanced on the masked leader and thrust the barrel of his machine pistol hard against the man's teeth. 'Your gun. By the barrel. Do you know what is my one ambition in life right now?' The man, apparently, did. Carmody pocketed the pistol and turned to the remaining and unwounded member of the quintet, who had his gun on the table before Carmody could even speak to him.

Brady said: 'Satisfactory, Mr Willoughby? The floor is yours.'

'An Oscar, Mr Brady. They sang beautifully.' He advanced to the table. 'I think you all know who I am?'

Nobody spoke.

'You.' He indicated the person who had so hastily placed his gun on the table. 'Towels, cotton wool, bandages. Nobody's going to mind very much if your three friends bleed to death, but personally I would sooner see them die legally. After they've been tried, of course. Let's see your faces.' He walked round ripping off masks. The first three faces apparently meant nothing to him. The fourth, belonging to the man he'd just appointed to first-aid duty, clearly did.

'Lucky Lorrigan,' Willoughby said. 'Erstwhile helicopter pilot, more recently a murderer on the run from Calgary. Severely wounded a couple of officers in your breakout, Lucky, didn't you? My, aren't they going to be pleased to see you again!'

He tore the mask from the leader's face. 'Well, well, would you believe it? No less than Frederick Napier himself, second senior charge-hand in Sanmobil security. You've strayed a bit from home, haven't you, Freddie?

'All five of you are hereby taken into arrest and charged with murder, attempted murder, kidnapping and industrial sabotage. I don't have to remind you about your legal rights, silence, access to lawyers. You've heard it all before. Not that it will do any of you the slightest good. Not after the beautiful way Napier sang.'

Brady said: 'Would you say he was the best singer of the lot, Mr Willoughby?'

Willoughby stroked his chin. 'A moot point, Mr Brady.' He had no idea what Brady was talking about, but had learned to listen when he suggested something.

Brady said: 'You really are extraordinarily naïve, Napier.

I told you that Mr Willoughby and his officer were severely injured when our plane crash-landed, yet you seemed hardly surprised to see them here. Perhaps you're just stupid. Perhaps events have moved too fast for your limited intellect. Our plane, of course, did not crash-land. No forest ranger pilot spotted you. We never saw your helicopter on the way to our alleged crash-landing.

'Deerhorn, the lake just over the hill there, was our destination from the time we left Fort McMurray, because we knew exactly where you were. You sing like a lark, Napier. But Brinckman and Jorgensen sing like angels. They're going to turn State's evidence. Should get off with five years.'

'Brinckman and Jorgensen!' Napier jumped to his feet then collapsed back in his chair with a whoosh of expelled air as the barrel of Carmody's machine pistol caught him in the solar plexus. He sat there gasping for breath. 'Brinckman and Jorgensen,' he wheezed, and had just started in on a résumé of their antecedents when Carmody's gun caught him lightly on the side of the head.

'Ladies present,' Carmody said pleasantly.

'State's evidence!' Napier said huskily. 'Five years! Good God, man, Brinckman's my boss. Jorgensen's his lieutenant. I'm only number three on the totem pole. Brinckman is the one who fixes everything, arranges everything, gives all the orders. I just do what I'm told. State's evidence! Five years! Brinckman!'

Willoughby said: 'Would you swear to that in court?'

'Too damn right, I would! Treacherous bastard!' Napier stared into space, his mouth no more than a compressed white line.

Willoughby said: 'And before all these witnesses, too.'

Napier shifted his gaze from faraway places to Willoughby. His expression was one of total incomprehension.

'Mr Brady was quite right, Napier. You really are a rather simple person, but as a singer you just got raised to the rank of angel. Until this moment we didn't have a single solitary thing we could pin on either of them. Thanks to you, they'll join you behind bars tonight. It should be a fascinating get-together.'

*　　*　　*

The big white helicopter touched down on Deerhorn at five forty-five in the afternoon. Lucky Lorrigan, with the muzzle of Carmody's pistol screwing into his ear, had flown the seven-minute hop in impeccable style. The two meteorological station operators had been freed and, when told why, had willingly sworn themselves to secrecy for the next twenty-four hours.

Brady was first off the plane, followed by Dermott and the wounded men. A curious reception committee from the Sikorsky, headed by Lieutenant Brown, was there to greet them.

Brown said: 'That was fast work. Congratulations! No problems?'

'Routine exercise.' Brady was a master of the throwaway phrase. 'Some for Dr Kenmore, though. Three silly people got in the way of flying bullets.'

Kenmore said: 'I'll fix them up, Mr Brady.'

'Thanks. But you look mighty young to me to be an orthopaedic surgeon.'

'So it's like that?'

'Patch them up as best you can. Nobody's going to take your licence away from you if they peg out during the night.'

'I understand.' The young doctor's eyes widened as the women descended the steps. 'Well, well.'

'Brady Enterprises,' Brady said with a smirk in his voice, 'associate only with the best and the most beautiful. Well, Mr Lowry, we'll have to see about getting back those splendid machines of yours. And now, Lieutenant, if you will excuse me—a matter of some urgency.'

He had taken some few steps towards his aircraft, when the lieutenant overtook him. 'It got pretty cold in your plane, Mr Brady, so I took the liberty of transferring some essential supplies to our nice warm Sikorsky.'

Brady turned ninety degrees without breaking stride and headed purposefully towards the Sky-Crane. He patted Lieutenant Brown on the arm. 'A very promising future lies ahead of you.'

Dermott said to Bernie, the Sikorsky radio operator: 'Any luck?'

'Got through to all three, sir. Your New York number and one of your Anchorage numbers—a Mr Morrison—said they had no information for you yet and probably wouldn't have for the next twenty-four hours. Your other Anchorage number —a Dr Parker—asked if you would be kind enough to call him back now.'

'Would you get him, please?'

'No bother.' Bernie smiled. 'And then you'd like some privacy?'

Brady had been reduced to the discomfort of sitting on a packing box—admittedly a large one—in the fore part of the Sikorsky's cavernous hold. He appeared not to be suffering too much. He was speaking to a fully conscious Ferguson.

'You've made it, son. You're damned lucky but not nearly as lucky as we are, thanks entirely to you. We'll discuss this— ah—later, in private. Sorry your eyes are still troubling you.'

'Just a damned nuisance, Mr Brady. Otherwise, I could fly the plane with no trouble.'

'You're not flying anything, anywhere,' Kenmore said. 'It may be two or three days before we can be sure that your eyesight is stabilised. I know a specialist in Edmonton.'

'Thank you. How are our wounded heroes, by the way?'

'They'll live.'

'Ah, well. We can't have everything.'

*   *   *

Two and a half hours later Brady was again presiding over a cheerful company, but this time rather more comfortably ensconced in the best armchair in the Peter Pond Hotel. Doubtless inspired by the thought of the enormous fees he would extort, he was positively Maecenas-like in his hospitality. Reynolds had been joined by his wife. The atmosphere was festive; but Dermott and Mackenzie didn't seem very jovial. Dermott approached the beaming Brady—he wasn't beaming at anything in particular but was just sitting there, his wife's hand in his left, daiquiri in his right—and said: 'Donald and I would like to slip away for a bit, sir. Do you mind?'

'Of course not. Do you need me?'

'Minor matters, only.'

'Go right ahead, George.' The beam, which had faded

slightly, lit up again. Brady would now have the field to himself, and it was possible that his retailing of recent events might vary slightly from the one he would have given if his two lieutenants had been present. He glanced at his watch. 'Eight-thirty. Half an hour or so?'

'About that.'

On their way out they stopped by Willoughby's chair. Dermott smiled at a rather misty-eyed Mrs Reynolds, then said to Willoughby: 'Brinckman and Jorgensen?'

Willoughby smiled happily. 'Are the guests of the Canadian government. Heard fifteen minutes ago. Look, gentlemen, I don't know how to—'

'Wait.' Mackenzie smiled. 'We aren't through with you yet.'

'Some more matters to be attended to?'

'Not in Alberta. But we have to cast a net again. Can we see you in the morning?'

'When?'

'Late. May we call you?'

Dermott and Mackenzie spent not half an hour but an hour and a half in Dermott's room, talking, planning, and mostly, telephoning. When they returned to the lounge Brady greeted them effusively. He was totally unaware of how much time had elapsed. The number of the company had increased. Dermott and Mackenzie were introduced to a couple who turned out to be the mayor and his wife. Jay Shore had returned from the plant and they were introduced to *his* wife, too. They were introduced to a charming lady who turned out to be Mrs Willoughby. After that they were introduced to two other couples whose names they failed to catch. Jim Brady was spreading his wings that night.

Willoughby came up and spoke to them quietly. 'Another item, although it's just another unnecessary nail in the coffin. We retrieved the prints from Shore's house and compared them to the ones in the kidnap truck. Two matching sets were found: Napier's and Lucky Lorrigan's.'

At eleven o'clock, Dermott and Mackenzie approached Brady again. He was still in sparkling form: his tolerance for rum passed mortal understanding. Dermott said: 'Mr Brady. We're bushed. We're off.'

'Off? Bed? I'll be damned.' He glanced at his watch. 'The night's young.' He made a grandiloquent gesture with his arm. 'Look at *them*. Are *they* thinking of bed?' Jean gave Dermott a rueful smile which indicated that she was thinking of just that herself. 'They're happy. They're enjoying themselves. Just look!'

Wearily they looked. No question, Brady had the right of it. They were enjoying themselves, not least young Carmody, who had discreetly withdrawn from the main body of the group to sit in a corner with Stella.

'We wish you luck. You want us to collapse dramatically in front of all your guests?'

'That's the trouble with you young people of today. No get-up-and-go.' When the occasion arose Brady could conveniently forget that his associates and himself were of the same generation. 'No stamina. Not fit.' He seemed totally unaware of how preposterous he sounded, but they knew he wasn't.

'We'd like to talk to you in the morning.'

'You would?' He eyed them both suspiciously. 'When?'

'When you're fit, unlimited stamina, the lark singing.'

'Damn it all, *when*?'

'Noon.'

Brady relaxed. 'In that case, why don't you stay?'

Dermott went and kissed Jean goodnight, Mackenzie did the same; they made the rounds with punctilious goodnights and left.

They got to bed just after one in the morning. The previous two hours had been spent on the telephone.

*   *   *

Dermott woke at seven-thirty. By eight, he was showered, shaved, eating off his breakfast tray and busy on the telephone. At nine he was joined by Mackenzie. At ten they were both closeted with Willoughby. At noon, they joined Brady at his breakfast table and explained what they had in mind. Brady chewed through the last of his ham omelette, which had originally been the size of a soup-plate, then shook his head in a decisive fashion.

'It's out of the question. It's all over. O.K., there are a few stray threads in Alaska, but who am I to devote my time to that sort of small potatoes?'

'So it is in order if Donald and I resign?'

Fortunately for Brady he was neither eating nor drinking at the moment, so he had nothing to choke over. 'Resign? What the hell do you mean?'

'It's Donald's fault, really. Half Scots, you know. He hates to see good money being thrown away.'

'Money being thrown away?' Momentarily, Brady looked almost appalled, but his recovery was swift. 'What's this nonsense?'

'How much are you charging Sanmobil for our services?'

'Well, I'm not one to prey on the misfortunes of others. A half million I guess. Plus expenses, of course.'

'In that case, I reckon Donald and I would rate a quarter of a million for picking up stray threads and small potatoes.' Brady was silent, his eyes fixed on something beyond infinity. 'With your name,' Dermott persisted, 'one can see no reason why the Prudhoe Bay oil companies shouldn't also come up with a half million. Plus, of course, expenses.'

Brady brought his gaze back from outer space to the dining-room table. 'It's not, as you may think, that I'm not at my best in the morning. It's just that I have so much on my mind. What time is this meeting tonight?'

16

The meeting was held that evening in the Sanmobil canteen, which was drably lit and decorated in dingy cream and pea-green. Nevertheless, the room had much to recommend it for such a gathering, not least the fact that it was large and warm and a place from which the public could easily be excluded.

The tables and chairs had been rearranged so that the men conducting the proceedings sat in a line—on stage, as it were —facing down the long room. The rest of the seats had been set out in two blocks, divided by a gangway.

In the middle of the top table sat Willoughby, acting as host in his own parish. On the right was Hamish Black, general manager of B.P./Sohio, Alaska, who had flown down from Prudhoe Bay to be present. On Willoughby's left sat Brady, overflowing a rickety wooden chair, and beside him were his two trusty henchmen.

Down on the floor, the home team was represented by Bill Reynolds, Jay Shore and a handful of others. On the Alaskan side there were eight men, among them Dr Blake, gaunt and cadaverous as ever; Ffoulkes, the Anchorage police chief; and Parker, the police forensic surgeon. Morrison of the F.B.I. had come on the same plane, and behind him sat four of his agents. At the back of the room were nearly thirty other men from Sanmobil brought in so that they could hear the full report of what had been happening. Finally, in an unobtrusive position at one side, John Carmody and a couple of fellow-police-men occupied a flat bench, with their backs against the wall; and sandwiched between them was Corinne Delorme, looking small and wan and rather scared.

Willoughby stood up to open the proceedings.

'Good evening, ladies and gentlemen. As the senior representative of the law here in Alberta, and as your nominal host, I would like to thank all you people who've been good enough to come from places as far afield as Prudhoe Bay, Anchorage and even New York.'

A murmur went round the room.

'That's right,' Willoughby confirmed. 'Two gentlemen at least have come all the way from New York. Now: the purpose of this meeting is to explain to the senior employees of Sanmobil and BP/Sohio just what's been going on these past few days, and, if possible, to clear up the few final questions to which we don't yet have the answers. I call on Mr Hamish Black, general manager of BP/Sohio, Alaska, to put you in the picture.'

Black rose to his feet, all disapproval and severity. Yet when he began to speak, he seemed to acquire a stature and authority that thoroughly surprised Brady and his associates.

'I hardly need tell you,' he began, 'that both the Alaskan pipeline and the Sanmobil tar sands complex here at Athabasca have recently been subjected to deadly and intensive industrial sabotage. The action effectively closed down the flow of oil from both centres, and in the process of the sabotage at least four innocent people have been murdered, while several others have been gravely injured.

'We devoutly hope that the savage and brutal attacks are at an end. They certainly seem to be so in Alberta—and for this the sole credit goes to the investigation team of Brady Enterprises, headed by Mr Jim Brady himself and his two senior assistants, Mr Dermott and Mr Mackenzie.'

With the ghost of a smile softening the line of his pencil moustache, Black indicated the Brady team. To his acute discomfort, Brady found himself blushing for the first time in years. He ground his teeth and contrived to look sideways at Dermott without moving his head. The guy they'd treated like dirt was praising them!

'Unfortunately,' Black went on, 'no such happy conclusion has been reached in Alaska. Up there, we have no positive guarantee that the sabotage is at an end, for the simple reason that the individuals responsible for the criminal activity have not yet been brought to justice.

'Brady Enterprises have been as deeply involved in making

enquiries in Alaska as they have here, and since they are the only people with an overall view of the present position, I should like to call upon Mr Brady himself to give us a report.'

Brady heaved himself upright and cleared his throat.

'Thank you, Mr Black. Ladies and gentlemen, I promise to be as brief as possible, and to waste none of your time. First I will ask for a word from Mr John Young, who is director of City Services, a Federally-backed investigative agency in New York. One of its functions is to oversee and regulate the conduct of private detective and investigative agencies in the State of New York. Mr Young?'

In the front row of the Sanmobil team seats a lean, bald-headed man with thick-rimmed glasses rose to his feet. He looked at the papers in his hand and smiled at Brady, and turning to face the body of the hall, he began.

'City Services was asked by Brady Enterprises—this was with governmental consent—to investigate the background of a private security agency owned and run by one Samuel Bronowski, who later became head of security on the Alaskan pipeline.

'Apart from the fact that an unusually large percentage of valuables entrusted to the firm's safekeeping had been missing —for readily explainable reasons—we found no evidence of any outright misconduct. But I was further asked to find out the names and identities of any of Bronowski's associates who left the firm at about the same time as he did—that is to say, within six months either side of his departure date. We came up with ten names—not a particularly high wastage rate in such an agency—but Brady Enterprises were particularly interested in four of them.' Here Young consulted the notes in his right hand. 'Their names are Houston, Brinckman, Jorgensen, and Napier.'

Young sat down and Brady rose again to thank him. 'Well,' he continued, 'for those of you who do not already know, three of the four just mentioned are already in gaol, charged with various crimes from murder downwards. The other man, and Bronowski, you can now see for yourselves.'

He made a small sign to Willoughby, who nodded to one of his uniformed men at the door. Next moment the door opened, to admit Bronowski and Houston, manacled together. They were hustled to seats in the front row of the Alaska-side stalls. Bronowski still sported his impressive head-bandage, and beneath it, his broad, strong face was sullen.

'So.' Brady purred. 'I promised we would not waste time. We have established that at least two security agents from the pipeline and three from Sanmobil were old acquaintances, that they were acting in concert, organised widespread sabotage, exchanged codes and were responsible for murder. We have also established that Bronowski was the undisputed leader. These facts have been put on record by many witnesses, who will testify in court. But let us move on. I would like to call on Dr Parker.'

'Yes, well.' Parker paused reflectively. 'I act in a forensic capacity for the police at Anchorage. Mr Dermott brought down three corpses from Prudhoe Bay. I examined one of them—an engineer who had been murdered in Pump Station No. 4. He had sustained a most unusual injury to his right index finger. I understand that Dr Blake here attributed this to the force of the explosion which destroyed the pump station. I have to disagree. The finger was deliberately broken—there is no other way it could have happened. Mr Dermott?'

Dermott stood up. 'Mr Mackenzie and I have a theory. It's our belief that this dead engineer was carrying a pistol when he was held up by the people who had planted the explosives. We further believe that he recognised his assailants, and they, knowing this, killed him before he could use his gun in self-defence. We also believe that his dead finger locked over the trigger-grip. That would be possible, doctor?'

'Indeed—quite possible.'

'We surmise the criminals had to break the man's forefinger to get the gun away. A dead man found with a gun in his hand would have raised serious doubts as to whether the explosion had been a genuine accident.

'Further, papers seen in his coat pocket were later missing. Neither my colleagues nor I know what those papers were. We can only assume that he had accumulated incriminating evidence against someone—which would account for the fact that he was carrying a gun.'

Dermott paused. Then he said: 'I would like to ask Mr Brady to discuss the vital question of who is ultimately responsible for this spate of crime.'

Brady hoisted himself upright again. 'Mr Carmody—would you be so kind as to stand by Bronowski? I am aware that he is handcuffed, but I'm also convinced he's a man of violence. Dr Parker?'

Dr Parker rose leisurely and walked across to Bronowski. Carmody was already there. The doctor said to him: 'Get behind him and hold his arms.'

Carmody did so. Bronowski yelped with pain as Parker reached forward and ripped away the bandage that covered his forehead and temple. The doctor peered closely at the temple, touched it, then straightened.

'This is a delicate area of the head,' he said. 'A blow such as he is alleged to have received would have left a bruise for at least a fortnight. Probably longer. As you can see, there is no such bruise, no sign of any contusion. In other words,' he said, pausing for effect, 'he was never struck.'

Brady said: 'Things look rather black for you, Dr Blake.'

'They're going to look a damn sight blacker,' Parker said. He had resumed his place. 'Mr Dermott, in Anchorage, made what I then regarded as an extremely strange request. I no longer regard it as such. Despite the fact that you, Dr Blake, had carried out an autopsy on John Finlayson, Mr Dermott asked me to carry out another. Unheard of. But, as it turns out, justified.

'Your certificate said that Finlayson had been struck on the occiput with some form of loaded salt-bag. As in the case of Bronowski, there was no sign of any contusion. The skin had been somewhat abraded, which could have occurred before or after death. What is important is that one of my younger associates discovered traces of ethyl oxide in the blood. It is difficult to conceal such trace elements. On closer examination, we discovered a tiny blue puncture just under the rib cage. Further investigation proved beyond any doubt that a needle or probe had been inserted through this puncture and pierced the heart. Death would have been pretty well instantaneous. In other words, Finlayson had been anaesthetised, then murdered.

I do not think there is one medical authority in either of our countries who would dispute my findings.'

Brady said: 'Comment, Dr Blake?'

He appeared to have none.

The F.B.I.'s Morrison said: 'I have. He's not a doctor. He was trained in an English university and flung out in his fourth year for reasons as yet undisclosed but which I'm sure we can readily ascertain. No doubt he learnt enough in that time to use a needle or probe.'

Brady said: 'Comment, Blake?'

Again he had none.

'I do not know, but I'm pretty sure that this is what happened,' Dermott said. 'Finlayson came across Bronowski and Houston tampering with the fingerprint card index. I suggest that Bronowski was removing his own prints from the file. I suggest he was substituting some other prints for his own. Whose, I do not know, but that again we can ascertain. The next suggestion is straightforward and obvious. The prints on that Anchorage telephone box were Bronowski's. We have only to take his prints to confirm.'

Brady said: 'Comment, Bronowski?'

Silence.

'Well.' Brady looked round the room. 'Guilty as hell. That almost wraps it up.' He stood up, as if to end the meeting. 'But not quite. None of the accused has the intelligence or knowledge to master-mind an operation of this nature. This required a highly specialised degree of knowledge. Someone who had the inside track.'

Willoughby asked: 'We have an idea of this person's identity?'

'I know who he is. But I think I'll let Mr Morrison and the F.B.I. take over here. My colleagues and I had our suspicions as to the identity of the mastermind behind the killings and sabotage both here and in Alaska, but it was Mr Morrison who got the proof.'

'I got the proof,' Morrison said, 'but that was only because my nose was pointed in the right direction. Bronowski claimed to have owned—and maintains he still owns—an investigative agency in New York. This is untrue. As Mr Young discovered in the course of his investigations, Bronowski only acted in the capacity of a front man, a figure-head. The real source of power, the owner, was someone else. Right, Bronowski?'

Bronowski scowled, clamped his lips, and kept his counsel.

'No matter. At least you don't deny it. Mr Young, accompanied by New York detectives and armed with a search warrant, examined the firm's private correspondence. The firm had been so naïve as to file away, instead of destroying, fatally damaging and incriminating evidence. This evidence not only revealed the identity of the true owner: it also revealed the astonishing fact that this same individual owned no fewer than four other protection or investigative agencies in the city of New York.' Morrison glanced to one side. 'Mr Willoughby?'

Willoughby nodded and looked aside. Carmody nodded, rose and walked leisurely to the back of the room.

'This owner,' Morrison went on, 'was an absentee landlord, but only during the past couple of years. Before that he was on the New York stock exchange and an investment counsellor on Wall Street. He wasn't too successful: not really a financial man at all, though he liked money. More like a bull in a china shop: too extroverted.

'The landlord's most recent absence was caused by the fact that he had become busy elsewhere. He was busy in Athabasca, at an inconvenient distance from Wall Street. He was, in fact, working for Sanmobil. He was busy being Sanmobil's operations manager.'

'Don't move. Keep quite still.' Carmody leant over Reynolds's shoulder and relieved him of a silenced automatic which he had begun to slide out of a shoulder-holster. 'You could cause yourself an injury. What's a law-abiding citizen like you doing carrying a hand-gun?'

Gasps of surprise broke out all round the room. Almost everybody stood up to get a better view. Reynolds's face, normally so rubicund, had gone grey. He sat as if paralysed while Carmody slipped manacles on him.

'This is in no way a trial,' Brady announced. 'So I do not propose to question him. Nor will I adumbrate the factors that made him turn the way he did—save to say that his main grievance appears to have been that he had been passed over for promotion. He found his way ahead blocked: he conceived the idea that outsiders were always brought into the firm to occupy senior positions. You may think his reaction a little excessive.'

Brady stopped. He had, at this point, intended to have a dig at Black, by mentioning the oil companies' practice of installing accountants in senior management positions. As things had turned out, however, he decided against it, and merely asked Black to sum up.

This Black did, in a surprisingly warm and human manner. Again he praised Brady Enterprises effusively, and he ended by reassuring everyone present that the campaign of terror and destruction was over. The meeting was closed. Police officers escorted Reynolds, Blake, Bronowski and Houston away to the cells, and in small groups and very slowly everyone else began to leave the hall.

Brady, feeling unwontedly nervous, sidled up to Black.

'My apologies,' he muttered. 'Must offer you my sincere apologies. My associates were infernally rude to you that time in the course of their ... ah ... investigations ... no cause for it.'

'My dear fellow—not at all,' said Black magnanimously. 'I daresay it was my fault anyway. I hardly realised what deep trouble we were in. I thought your investigations were superfluous. Now I know different.'

'I'd like to apologise, too, sir,' muttered Dermott, stiff with embarrassment. 'Trouble was—if I may say so—you seemed so unco-operative.'

'It was the *cost* that frightened me. Don't forget, I'm an accountant by training.' To the amazement of the Brady team, Black actually laughed. They laughed too, from sheer release of tension—and the next second, Black caught them neatly on the rebound.

'Well now, Mr Brady,' he said briskly. 'As to the question of your fee ...'

'Oh ... now!' Brady spluttered, caught right off-balance. 'I assumed all along I would negotiate that with your London office.'

'No need, I'm glad to say.' Black was all breezy sunshine.

'London has empowered me to deal directly with you. Our chairman felt that despite your close friendship, or perhaps because of it—I should settle this up.'

'That's ... well ... NO! I mean, I ... I never discuss fees myself.' Brady sounded lame, and knew it. But he pulled himself together fast. 'I have to consult *my* accountant, even if you don't.'

'Forty love, and Black to serve,' muttered Dermott as they moved away. He was about to go for his coat when, down one side of the room, he spotted Corinne Delorme still sitting on a bench, as if in a trance.

'Come on, honey,' he said gently. 'Time to go.'

'I just can't believe it,' she said. 'It's not possible.'

'Well—it happened. Are you upset?'

'Not really—no. I didn't care that much about him. It's just that I kind of got used to believing what he said.'

'I know, one does. But you saw how devious he was. Anyone who has himself kidnapped to add verisimilitude to the proceedings—anyone who does that is hardly straightforward.'

'I guess that's right. Those murders, too. Oh God, it's awful.'

'It *was* awful. But it's over. Coming?'

'I suppose so.' She stood up, and Dermott helped her into her coat.

'You and I were the two luckiest people in the whole damn business,' he said. 'We both ought to be dead. Without you I would be.'

Suddenly her blank eyes lit up and she smiled.

Dermott smiled back. 'What are you going to do now you've got no boss to work for?'

'I don't know. Find another job first.'

'Not many good jobs in Fort McMurray. Why not come south and work for me?'

'For *you*?' Her eyes widened. 'I hadn't thought of that.'

'Think of it now. Shall we go?'

'O.K.'

'I'd offer you my arm, if it wasn't still so damned sore.'

'And I might even take it.' She looked upward and snuggled close against him as they went out through the door.

The sight seemed to occasion the most immense merriment

221

in Brady and his one remaining associate. They rolled in their seats like clowns, giving vent to noisy explosions.

'Stay me with flagons, Donald,' cried Brady, as he recovered. 'I am seriously in need of liquid refreshment. For unless my investigative powers are dwindling, we have a romance on our hands.'